BETRAYAL AT THE BUFFALO RANCH

BETRAYAL AT THE BUFFALO RANCH

Sara Sue Hoklotubbe

THE UNIVERSITY OF
ARIZONA PRESS

TUCSON

The University of Arizona Press
www.uapress.arizona.edu

ISBN-13: 978-0-8165-3727-3 (paper)

Cover design by Leigh McDonald
Cover photo: *The American Bison* by Adam Cocke

This is a work of fiction. The characters, incidents, and locations portrayed and the names herein are fiction, and any similarity to or identifications with location, names, character, or history of any person, product, or entity is entirely coincidental and unintentional.

Publication of this book is made possible in part by the proceeds of a permanent endowment created with the assistance of a Challenge Grant from the National Endowment for the Humanities, a federal agency.

Library of Congress Cataloging-in-Publication Data
Names: Hoklotubbe, Sara Sue, 1952– author. | Hoklotubbe, Sara Sue, 1952– Sadie Walela mystery.
Title: Betrayal at the Buffalo Ranch / Sara Sue Hoklotubbe.
Description: Tucson : The University of Arizona Press, 2018. | Series: A Sadie Walela mystery | Includes bibliographical references and index.
Identifiers: LCCN 2017042839 | ISBN 9780816537273 (pbk. : alk. paper)
Subjects: LCSH: Women detectives—Fiction. | Murder—Investigation—Fiction. | LCGFT: Novels. | Detective and mystery fiction.
Classification: LCC PS3608.O4828 B48 2018 | DDC 813/.6—dc23 LC record available at https://lccn.loc.gov/2017042839

Printed in the United States of America
♾ This paper meets the requirements of ANSI/NISO Z39.48–1992 (Permanence of Paper).

For Eddie,

The love of my life, my Anam Cara,

With love

Acknowledgments

I am grateful to three remarkable women who graciously gave their time to read my manuscript and offer helpful suggestions: Judy Soriano, English teacher extraordinaire, for her knowledge of literature and writing; Pam Daoust, author and sister-friend, for her insight into characterization and voice; and Linda Boyden, author and friend, for her understanding of Native characters. Many thanks to Chery F. Kendrick, DVM, for her kind help in understanding animal behavior, and Mark S. Newman, who patiently fielded my many questions regarding all things buffalo.

I am thankful for the candid advice I received from the late Larry Hoklotubbe, my brother-in-law, retired Bureau of Indian Affairs law officer and weapons expert, for the extensive knowledge of firearms he so freely shared with me. Miss you, White Buffalo.

I extend my appreciation to Kathryn Conrad, director, and Kristen Buckles, editor-in-chief, at the University of Arizona Press, for giving me the opportunity to share Sadie's adventures with readers everywhere, and to Susan Campbell, copyeditor, who worked magic with my manuscript. And finally, words cannot express how grateful I am to my husband and first reader, Eddie, for his endless love and support. *Wado.*

BETRAYAL AT THE BUFFALO RANCH

Prologue

Angus Clyborn pulled his Dodge truck into the deserted park that the locals called Old Eucha, killed the engine, and belched. Through his open window, he could hear the waters of Lake Eucha lapping against the shoreline. The town of Eucha, Oklahoma, had once stood there, before being moved to higher ground a half century earlier to make way for the man-made lake that supplied Tulsa with fresh drinking water.

Now, the site of the old town had been reduced to boat launches, permanent picnic tables, and outdoor toilets. Rock walls of the original one-room schoolhouse, partly destroyed by weather and time, rose like a monolith in the shadowy moonlight.

Resting his head against the driver's door, Angus hiccupped. He hoped the night air would help clear his fuzzy thinking and dissipate the odor of alcohol swirling in the air around him. He was already in trouble. His wife, Camilla, would give him all kinds of hell when she got a whiff of the Jack Daniels he'd spilled on his shirt.

He'd tried, promised her he'd never take another drink after the accident three years ago that took the life of a three-year-old girl and left the girl's mother in intensive care for two months. After Angus had made a sizable contribution to the district attorney's reelection campaign, a trick he'd learned from his father, Angus had received a lenient suspended sentence. The judge had also ordered him to get treatment for his drinking and keep his nose clean, which he had done, but the demon of alcohol addiction had been harder to beat than he had originally thought.

The news that his son had been killed fighting in a useless war in Afghanistan had turned his world upside down, throwing him into a desperate search for solace at the bottom of a bottle of Gentleman Jack.

Blue on green, they'd said. Slang to describe the treachery carried out by Afghan troops who, their loyalty turning on a dime, killed their

American trainers. It was unspeakable, incomprehensible, and tomorrow he'd bury his only son, Jason, because of it. But first he would sit in his truck in Old Eucha Park and drench his grief with Tennessee whiskey. To hell with everything else.

Without warning, a blinding light came out of nowhere. The barrel of a gun came through the window of the truck and dug into his neck. The cold metal startled him, and he jerked his head away from the window. Then he felt the end of the barrel press against his cheek.

"Don't move," said a raspy voice. "If you do, I'll finish you off right here."

Still blinded by the light and dizzy from the booze, Angus swallowed hard before he spoke. "Who are you? What do you want?"

"Stop stealing land," the voice demanded, "and give back the land you've already stolen, or I'll come back and erase your drunken ass from the face of the planet. Got it?"

Angus closed his eyes and slowly nodded his head, afraid to move any other part of his body. He tried unsuccessfully to process the voice.

"Please don't kill me," Angus begged. He opened his eyes and slowly turned his head, but the light and the gun barrel had disappeared.

He opened the truck door and fell out onto the ground. Forcing himself to his feet, he steadied his body against the truck and stared into the darkness. His labored breathing overtook the silence. In the distance, he could hear a dog barking and the call of a hoot owl.

He must be hallucinating from too much alcohol, he thought. No one would dare talk to Angus Clyborn like that.

He pulled himself back into the truck, closed the door, and threw the half-empty fifth of Jack Daniels out the window, the glass bottle shattering on a nearby rock. After fumbling with his keys for a few seconds, he started the truck and flipped on the headlights. He searched first in front of the vehicle and then slammed the shifter in reverse, causing the backup lights to illuminate the area behind the truck. He quickly raised the windows and locked the doors while he frantically scanned his rearview mirrors for movement. Nothing.

Fear penetrated his drunken stupor as he drove out of the park and into the night.

★

Angus awoke the next morning with a start. He rubbed his face and tried to remember how he had managed to end up in his own bed. Bright sunlight streamed through the sheer curtains as he fumbled at the bedside clock. Nine fifteen, it read. He turned over to confirm what he already knew. Camilla had left to go shopping in Tulsa, a daily ritual that had begun the day they'd gotten word about Jason. At least it got her out of the house, and they didn't have to share the same space for several hours.

Adrenaline shot through his aching body and words of warning echoed in his head . . . *stop stealing land* . . .

His gaze darted around the room as he sat up. His dirty clothes from the night before lay in a heap on the floor next to the bed. Why couldn't Camilla take care of his clothes the way his mother had? There was no question that his dad was in control in that household. He needed to get Camilla straightened out, he thought, before she got completely out of control.

As he stepped into a clean pair of trousers, his thoughts circled back around to the night before. Who would threaten him like that? Whoever it was obviously didn't know who they were dealing with. Maybe it had been a bad nightmare. Then he remembered what else the voice had said . . . *or I'll come back and erase your drunken ass.*

Grabbing a shirt, he headed downstairs in search of some strong coffee.

Chapter 1

The crack of gunshots caused Sadie to jump. She turned and braced herself for two more volleys from the seven-man honor guard as they fired a twenty-one-gun salute. Afterward, the sound of taps sent a shiver up her spine, bringing up old memories of her father's burial held in the same Eucha cemetery several years before. She pushed loose strands of her long, straight hair away from her face as a tear fell from her cheek, an involuntary response to the death not only of a soldier she didn't know, but of her father, as well.

She and Lance Smith had come to the graveside service of Jason Clyborn out of respect for his wife, Lucy, and her Cherokee family, the Walkingsticks. Sadie had known the Walkingstick family all of her life. They were good people.

As a veteran, Lance had volunteered to take part in the local American Legion Post's honor guard for the twenty-one-gun salute. The riflemen and bugler stood away from the grave under an old oak tree. Even on this sad occasion, Sadie gazed at Lance with pride. He looked so handsome holding his rifle and standing at attention with the other men, his taut, muscular body apparent beneath his deputy sheriff's uniform, and his neatly trimmed coal-black hair peeking from under his Stetson. The vision was enough to make her heart flutter.

Lucy Clyborn looked small and cold, wrapped in a short raincoat as she sat in a metal folding chair and sobbed while members of the American Legion removed the American flag that had been draped on her husband's casket, folded it with great precision, and presented it to her with a salute. She took the flag, held it to her chest, and then placed it in her lap.

Sitting next to Lucy, her mother-in-law, Camilla Clyborn, wore a black trench coat and hat, her face obscured by large sunglasses. Camilla grabbed the flag from Lucy and buried her face in it, wailing loudly. Sadie couldn't believe her eyes.

Wanda Walkingstick reached down and placed a hand on her daughter's shoulder, a calming motherly gesture, while glancing disapprovingly at Camilla's tight grip on the flag. Sadie wondered if Lucy would ever get to touch that flag again. Angus Clyborn, the dead soldier's father, snatched the flag away from his wife and shoved it back onto Lucy's lap, almost losing his ten-gallon hat in the act.

Angus straightened his hat, then stood and caught the arm of the man who had presented the flag to Lucy. "Son, can you get us another one of those flags?" he said, his voice dripping in a strong Texas accent. "His mother wants one."

The man stoically nodded and returned to his place. The service didn't last long, and Sadie felt relieved when it ended.

The cloudy April sky looked threatening and Sadie could smell rain, so as soon as she had offered condolences to the family, she wrapped her sweater tightly around her and walked across the cemetery to her father's grave. She bent down and ran her fingers over his name, Jim "Bird" Walela, engraved in both the Cherokee syllabary and English. His friends had called him Bird, shortened from the English version of the Walela name—Hummingbird. She missed him terribly—his easygoing ways, his quiet words of wisdom, and his no-nonsense philosophy of life.

Sadie glanced at the empty plot next to her dad's grave that had been reserved for her mother, and a mental image of her intruded into Sadie's thoughts. Sadie doubted the woman would ever return to Delaware County again, dead or alive. As a white woman in an Indian community, her mother had never fit in, not because she hadn't been welcome, but because she thought she was better than everyone else. Her abusive words still stung Sadie's heart, and the thought of never seeing her again suited Sadie fine.

Sadie removed the weathered fake flowers from the bronze vase attached to her father's headstone and carried them to her car. When she got in, she placed the flowers on the floorboard and waited for Lance. She tilted the rearview mirror toward her face and used her fingers to comb her bangs and smooth her hair. Removing a beaded hair clip, she held it in her mouth while she straightened her hair behind her neck and clamped it back into position. Before moving the mirror back into place, she checked the rest of her face, admiring her new beaded earrings, a gift from her Kickapoo friend, Leslie. The circular design and bright colors—lime green, brown, red, and yellow—contrasted nicely with her black hair and complemented the oval shape of her face. She smiled and thought of Lance. He loved looking into her blue eyes; he'd told her this so many times she'd lost count.

She watched the people slowly migrate away from the grave and thought the crowd could have been easily divided between two distinct groups—Indian friends of the Walkingsticks and the white folks who had come for the Clyborn side of the family. Even in the middle of the Cherokee Nation, the same cultural divide remained that had been there for centuries: Indian and white, those who lived by modest means and those wearing gold jewelry and expensive clothes.

Angus stopped walking and waved the rest of the family on as he pulled a half-smoked cigar from his pocket and lit it. A man approached Angus and they began to talk. He had gray hair and light skin, and he shook Angus's hand with animation. Sadie could see Angus's hat bobbing affirmatively now and then as he listened.

Sadie scrunched her nose in disgust and strained to see the man as he pulled a can of dipping tobacco out of his pocket and pushed a pinch into his lower lip. She whistled silently to herself when she recognized him as the Cherokee chief, John Henry Greenleaf. It certainly appeared kind of him, she thought, to support Lucy and her family by attending Jason's funeral, but she knew it was simply a public display, appearing to care for Cherokees he didn't even know. He was always the quintessential politician.

Sadie dismissed Angus and the chief from her thoughts when Lance approached her car, his cell phone jammed up against his left ear. She lowered her window and waited for him to finish talking.

He dropped his phone into his pocket, removed his hat, and bent down so he could kiss her through the window. "I've got to run. The sheriff needs me," he said. "I'll call you later." He kissed her again, replaced his hat, and disappeared into the crowd.

"The sheriff always needs you." Her words disintegrated into the damp air.

Lance had recently given up his job as the police chief of Liberty, Oklahoma, to become the deputy sheriff for the Delaware County

Sheriff's Department. Sadie thought it was a good fit for Lance. Being the deputy sheriff meant he was second in command. He supervised two deputies and managed the law enforcement side of the office, leaving the administrative and political part of the job to the newly elected sheriff, Buddy Long. Long was a good politician but knew very little about the day-to-day operations of enforcing the law.

When Buddy Long asked Lance to take the job of deputy sheriff, Lance didn't hesitate. The job carried less responsibility than his former position as the chief of police in Liberty, and he could leave the budget maneuvering and political wrangling behind. The pay was about the same, he'd said, and this job gave him more time for fishing.

But Sadie knew the truth. It also gave him a chance to live closer to her. He'd moved back to Kenwood, the community where he'd grown up, about eight miles as the crow flies across Lake Eucha from her place by way of the dam. She wasn't complaining. He stayed at her house most of the time, and when she wanted to get away, they spent time at his modest cabin, with no Internet or cell phone reception. There were days, too, when they went separate ways in search of their own needed space. It was comfortable, it was convenient—it was perfect. They enjoyed an exclusive relationship, yet retained their independence. What an oxymoron, she thought. She didn't know who was fooling whom. Someday they would marry, she hoped, if she could ever talk herself into taking the plunge again. Her track record with men hadn't exactly been stellar, but for now, she loved having Lance in her life.

Sadie waited for the crowd to disperse before joining the rest of the cars as they slowly crept out of the cemetery. Most of the cars turned north toward Highway 20, but she turned southwest, toward her place.

As she drove, she couldn't shake thoughts of the grieving family. The Walkingsticks had lived near Tahlequah all their lives. Wanda, Lucy's mother, had told Sadie that Lucy had met Jason Clyborn at Northeastern State University, fallen in love, and gotten married shortly thereafter. Two years later, they had moved to Eucha to live with Angus and Camilla, and Angus had helped Jason build a cabin on a corner of the Clyborn ranch. Lucy got a job in the customer service department at First Merc State Bank in Sycamore Springs, but when Jason couldn't find work, he'd decided to join the military. It was the only way he thought he could provide for his wife in a sour economy. He'd left Lucy with her mom and dad, joined the U.S. Army, and volunteered to go to Afghanistan. Wanda said Lucy had been devastated, yet determined to wait for him to come home from war and start a family. Now, cold reality had set in. He'd come home all right—in a box.

Sadie didn't know the Clyborns personally, but she'd seen them around town and had heard stories about them. She knew that Angus and Camilla had moved from Texas into the Eucha area several years ago, after buying a large ranch, and that Angus had begun to build a reputation as a land baron of sorts, taking advantage of every opportunity to buy property, especially land surrounding his ranch. She couldn't imagine what he was going to do with all of it. The profits from running cattle had dried up along with the grass and the ponds—all casualties of the latest drought—except for the parcels that had been blessed with plentiful springs, like hers. Most of the land in the county wasn't fit for growing crops, and oil and gas production was nonexistent in this part of the state, but there were those, she surmised, who just loved dirt.

Sadie didn't much care for Angus Clyborn's abrasive personality. He talked in a loud voice, drove like he owned the road, and strutted like a rooster down the sidewalk. He continually chewed on a half-smoked smelly cigar, wore a Rolex watch and a gold ring, and he combed his thin, unnaturally black hair over a balding head, which was why, she supposed, he usually wore a western hat. She hoped he would be good to Lucy now that Jason was dead.

Sadie drove slowly and for some reason decided to drive past her own place, toward Lake Eucha Dam, which would take her past the Clyborn ranch. When she reached what she guessed was the edge of the Clyborns' property, she was surprised to see some very tall, heavy-duty fencing, with electric wire strung across the top. Why in the world would Angus Clyborn put up a fence like that?

When she reached the entrance to the property, she let her car roll slowly to a stop as she took a quick breath. "Please don't let this be what I think it is," she said quietly, staring at the sign on the large rustic logs arching over the open entryway that read, "The Buffalo Ranch."

Tall fencing flanked the long driveway into the property, dividing the house, barn, and other buildings from the pastures of the ranch. In the distance, she could see three bison—two adults and a calf—grazing on short grass.

"Yanasi," she whispered to herself. Buffalo.

Why was Angus Clyborn running buffalo? The landscape in Eucha seemed impractical for it. It was too hilly, not enough grassland. She knew bison meat was a healthy alternative to beef, much leaner, but it was also a lot more expensive.

She regained her focus when a car sounded its horn as it flew by on its way toward the lake. She turned her vehicle around and headed home. What Angus Clyborn was doing on his ranch was none of her business. She had enough of her own problems without taking on some-one else's.

She drove the short distance back to her own house, and, when she turned off the road, she discovered Lance's truck and a county sheriff's department car sitting next to her house. She quickly parked, got out, and looked around. Where was everybody?

"Sonny?" She whistled for her wolfdog and then walked around the house, from where she could see Lance, Sonny by his side, walking through the pasture toward her house.

Sonny had come to her as a pup when he was only a few weeks old. Her Uncle Eli had seen the mother killed by a car and, realizing she had pups somewhere, had searched until he found them. He gave one pup to his wife's relative and took the other one to Sadie. She named him Sonny and bottle-fed him until he was old enough to eat meat. She had no idea how much wolf blood flowed through Sonny's veins, but it was enough to keep her on her toes. His size intimidated most people who came around, his combination of silver and black fur stole her heart, and his sky-blue eyes reminded her of her own. She loved Sonny and was quite sure that, if the occasion arose, he would die for her without hesitation.

When Sonny caught a glimpse of Sadie, he ran ahead to greet her. Lance followed and gave her a kiss.

"Lance, what's going on?" Sadie said, concerned. "Who's in the deputy car?"

"Deputy Jennings is securing the crime scene, along with your Uncle Eli. Eli found a man at the edge of your property. He'd been shot."

"What?" Sadie exclaimed. "Is he okay?"

"No," Lance said in a matter-of-fact tone. "He's dead."

"Dead?" Sadie grabbed Lance's arm. "Who is it?"

"Don't know. I didn't recognize him, and he didn't have any identification on him. Did you know someone was building a new fence at the northern edge of your upper pasture?"

"No, I haven't been up there in ages." Sadie pushed flighty hair out of her eyes. "I'm sure Uncle Eli would have known if something was going on, though. He's never said anything."

"Whose land is that, do you know?" Lance asked.

Sadie bit on her lower lip while she thought. "It used to belong to George Washington Chuculate. He was disabled and never got around very well. I think he's dead now, but his son's name is Grover, and he lives on Eucha Road between the cemetery and Highway 20, close to the forest service road. He's a real nice guy." She thought for a moment. "He's probably in his late sixties and walks with a limp. My dad told me one time he'd been wounded in Vietnam."

Lance nodded. "I know who you're talking about. I met Grover a couple of years ago at a veterans' gourd dance."

"I remember his daughter from high school," she said. "She was nice too, younger than me." Sadie thought for a minute and then continued. "The land is not that far from where Grover lives now," she said. "They never built on it that I know of, and I'm not sure if there's even a road into it, or not. They never asked for a right-of-way through our property . . . which we would have gladly given," she said, as if thinking aloud. "I think the forest road runs on the back side."

A cool mist formed in the air, chilling Sadie, and she pulled her sweater close around her neck. "Do you suppose it's one of Grover's relatives?"

Lance shook his head. "I don't know. Hopefully, we can identify him before too long."

"Did Uncle Eli say if he heard anything?"

"Nothing to hear. Said he saw Sonny hanging around up there."

"I thought you said he was shot."

"I did," he said. "But it was with an arrow. Looks like it went right through his heart." Lance looked toward the road. "Here comes the medical examiner. Can you control your dog until we can get this taken care of?"

Sadie stared into space and held Sonny by the scruff of his neck as Lance waved the medical examiner's SUV down the lane and toward the house.

Death and the circle of life. Had this mystery man been ready to die? Everyone would face death, Sadie thought, yet she knew of no one anxious to experience it. He had left home, wherever that may have been, to build fence that morning, with no idea he would never return. Did someone have dinner ready, waiting for him to come home? Did he have a lover somewhere waiting next to a phone that would never ring?

Lance disrupted her thoughts. "Lock your doors and keep Sonny close," he said. "I'll be back to check on you later." Then he climbed into the vehicle, and the two men drove slowly into the pasture to retrieve the body.

Lance directed the medical examiner on a worn path through the pasture, and when they had driven as far as they could safely navigate, they got out and walked the rest of the way, carrying the doctor's medical pouch and an empty body bag. Sadie's Uncle Eli and Deputy Drew Jennings stood talking near the break in Sadie's fence. Eli's buckskin horse, still saddled, stood grazing not far away, his reins resting on the ground. Eli raised his chin to acknowledge Lance's return.

The medical examiner placed the bag on the ground, pulled on a set of rubber gloves, and went to work on the arrow protruding from the dead man's back. The other men watched for a minute and then turned away, easing into conversation.

"Well, if this was a hundred years ago, I'd say this cowboy pissed off some Indian," Jennings remarked.

The ME laughed. "Looks to me like that might still be the case."

Lance glanced disapprovingly at both men, and then looked at the body on the ground. He pulled a notebook from his front pocket and made notes about the clothing—the dirty work jeans and gloves, the worn cowboy boots, and the blood-stained shirt. Rolls of wire fencing and a stack of posts were piled nearby; fencing pliers and a fence stretcher lay on the ground closer to the body. Lance couldn't be sure, but the victim looked like a white guy to him—a white guy with no identification. He'd know more as soon as they could run fingerprints through the system.

"Can you put that arrow in an evidence bag for me, Doc?" Lance said.

"Sure thing," he said as he carefully extracted the arrow.

Lance turned his attention to Eli. "Tell me again how you found this guy, Eli."

"It was the horses." Eli rubbed his chin on his upper arm as if trying to wipe away the death in the air. His face reflected a lifetime of working outdoors, and his slim body appeared to be made up of only sinew and muscle. "They were acting up, and when I saw Sonny I knew something wasn't right. It didn't take me but a minute to saddle up. Sonny was standing guard over the body. It was real quiet."

"Did you see anyone else?"

Eli looked at the deputy and the medical examiner and then down at the ground. He backed away, creating some space between him and the others before he spoke again. Lance followed.

"I thought for a minute I did see something," Eli said. "But I'm not sure."

"Who was it?"

Eli looked around at the surrounding area. "It was hard to make out, but I thought I saw a black-and-white paint horse."

"With a rider?"

"Maybe. I couldn't tell." he said. "It was too far away in the trees. There one minute, gone the next."

"Where? Did you try to follow them?"

"No, like I said, it was there and then it wasn't." Eli turned away from Lance and pointed at the abundant oak trees and thick underbrush that covered the hillside before trailing off into a deep ravine, away from Sadie's property. "There," he said, as he pointed with his hand.

Lance walked in the direction Eli had indicated. Even though the hard ground held moisture, he could make out only a few deer tracks. It would be easy to hide in these woods, he thought, and with the large number of the popular black-and-white paints in the county, the rider could have been anyone. This was going to take some digging.

Lance returned to where Eli stood. "I don't see anything," he said.

Eli nodded toward Sadie's house. "Sonny saw him, too," he said, as if the dog could corroborate his story.

"And Sonny didn't go after him?" Lance asked, surprised.

"He started to, but I called him back. Took him with me when I rode back down to the house to call it in."

"You mean that dog minds you?" Lance said, grinning.

Eli smiled, but didn't respond.

"How do you suppose this fellow got this fencing material in here by himself?"

"I don't know." Eli shrugged and shook his head. "Probably a four-wheeler."

Lance searched Eli's strong face for a moment before he spoke again. "Thanks, Eli. If you think of anything else, just give me a call."

Eli nodded.

The medical examiner and Jennings had already zipped the victim into the body bag. "Let's get him loaded before it starts raining," the ME said.

All four men grabbed the body bag and carried it down the hill toward the ME's vehicle.

Chapter 2

After Lance got in his truck and drove toward town following the medical examiner and the other deputy, Sadie went inside and traded her black dress and sweater for a worn shirt, a pair of faded jeans, and boots. Ignoring Lance's advice to lock her doors and hunker down, she walked to the barn and whistled for Joe, her paint horse stallion.

Joe always stood out in a crowd with his brown-and-white markings: a spot on his forehead centered right between his ears, the long fluid marking covering his throat, chest, belly, and flank, cresting just short of his backbone, and a brown tip punctuating his long white tail. Joe raised his head, nickered, and calmly walked to the side of the barn, accompanied by his new best friend, Sir William, the billy goat.

Sir William had appeared in the pasture a few weeks ago, and his mischievous personality immediately stole Sadie's heart. He was a perfect match for Joe with his own brown-and-white markings—a snow-white beard, brown head and ears, and a brown tail. Joe seemed to barely tolerate the goat at first, but now they were inseparable. It wasn't until Sadie saw the gleam in her Uncle Eli's eyes that she'd known exactly where Sir William had come from. Everybody gets lonely, Eli had said, including Joe. Sadie agreed to keep Sir William until such time as he started causing trouble, and then he would have to go live with his benefactor—her Uncle Eli.

She opened the gate to let both animals into the corral. She patted Joe's neck and Sir William's rump. In a few short minutes, she had Joe saddled and rode him into the pasture behind her house, leaving an unhappy Sir William behind.

Sonny ran out front across the open field, sniffing the ground and marking a scrub oak before returning to Sadie's side. Together they slowly climbed the hillside that led to the upper pasture where someone had lost his life earlier that day. Sadie felt a need to see where it had happened, as if that would help her understand, and she felt sure that, with all the activity by Lance and the others, whoever had shot the man with an arrow several hours ago would be long gone. The sun began to sink behind the treetops and the dampness in the air intensified as they rode.

As soon as she could see where the fence had been breached, she stopped and slid off Joe's back. To her left stood newly placed fence posts, familiar-looking wire hanging at one end. It looked identical to the fence she'd seen earlier that day at Angus Clyborn's Buffalo Ranch. That couldn't be a coincidence, she thought. How in the world did someone get these posts and wire in here? And if they had a truck, how did they get the truck up here? "Where there's a will, there's a way," she said aloud. She searched for tire tracks or any other sign that a vehicle had been there, but could find nothing other than where Lance and the others had obviously worked around the victim.

On the off chance that Lance and the others had missed something, she walked the fence line looking for clues. She thought someone might have left a tool, or dropped a cigarette or a gum wrapper, but she found nothing. Sonny sniffed at one of the fence posts and then hiked his leg and marked it.

"Thanks, Sonny," she admonished. "That really helps."

Before she had finished her words, he silently took off back down the hill and into the pasture after a rabbit. She dismissed the wolfdog and the rabbit, climbed back on Joe, and rode through the broken fence and into the wooded area. Joe shuffled his feet, raised his head, and whinnied. She knew by the sound he made and the uneasiness of his movement under her there was an unfamiliar horse not far away—probably another stallion. She patted his neck and spoke in a soothing voice to quiet him. He calmed and remained still long enough for her to stand high in the stirrups and stare into the woods. She thought she saw motion among the distant trees and called out.

"*O'siyo!*" She yelled the greeting in Cherokee. "Hello," she repeated.

There was no answer and no other movement. She remembered Lance's words of warning and then a cold shiver crept up her spine. Maybe the killer was still hiding nearby. What was she thinking?

She whistled and called for Sonny, and after a few minutes he came running from the opposite direction, tongue hanging, fun and happiness reflected in his eyes. She patted Joe on his shoulder. "Come on, boys," she said. "We'll come back tomorrow and look around." She slowly turned Joe back toward the barn and nonchalantly headed toward home, hoping if someone was watching, they would not become alarmed at her sudden exit from the area.

By the time she reached the barn, unsaddled Joe, and fed Sonny, the sun had disappeared and a bright moon had begun its ascent into the sky. She patted Joe on his neck and Sonny on his head, and went inside.

Her clothes felt cold from the damp evening air, so she changed into a long tee shirt and shorts and then searched the refrigerator for something to eat. After constructing a ham and cheese sandwich with extra helpings of lettuce and tomato, she pulled out a bag of potato chips and a bottle of low-calorie beer, proceeded to the couch, and flipped on the television. She tried to focus on the twenty-four-hour-a-day news channel until her sandwich, chips, and beer were gone. Then she carried her empty plate into the kitchen and opened the back door for Sonny to come inside. After sniffing the air and checking for loose crumbs on the floor, he curled up in front of the couch. Sadie returned to the couch and put her bare feet on Sonny's side, massaging his thick fur with her toes. Eventually, she lay back and closed her eyes, surrendering her thoughts to the day's events.

Jason Clyborn's sad funeral brought forth uncomfortable feelings about an unnecessary war—one that had cost countless lives for no good reason. And for each life lost, pain and misery crawled back home like an evil spider, spinning its web around everyone the young warrior ever knew or loved.

Her thoughts wandered and eventually moved to Angus Clyborn, the dead soldier's father. How would he treat Lucy now that Jason was gone? Probably the same way he planned to treat any animal hemmed inside the electrically charged fenced-in enclosure he'd named the Buffalo Ranch. Not very well.

And now an Angus-like fence had appeared between hers and Chuculate's property, which led her thoughts to the death that had taken place there. She didn't know who the dead man was or where he'd come from. Why was he building a new fence? Had the property sold and she didn't know about it? And, why would she? All of it made her feel uneasy and vulnerable. She reached down and touched Sonny's head with her fingers. She would always feel safe as long as her wolfdog lived. A fleeting thought of living without Sonny pricked her heart, and she clung to his fur for a moment before letting go.

Then there was Lance. He'd protect her if she'd let him. She loved him and their happy, easygoing relationship, but she clung to her complete independence as if she might lose herself without it.

She curled up and allowed herself to drift further into unconsciousness, feeling Joe's bare back and his gait under the weight of her body and hearing Sonny's happy howl in her dream.

Cloudless blue skies turned gray and cold air surrounded her as if someone had turned on an air conditioner. She looked in the distance and saw a man riding a black horse coming toward her, his identity obscured by shadows. Suddenly, an arrow passed so close to her ear she could hear the feathers whistle as it glided through the air. Joe reared, but she grabbed his mane and held on, trying to control the powerful stallion with the grip of her legs. She could hear Sonny growl and attack something or someone, but everything was a blur. Then the rider and the horse came back into view, running toward them at full speed.

Sonny yelped a cry of pain and Joe reared again. She could see Sonny lying on the ground. Something was wrong; he wasn't moving. She jumped from Joe's back and ran to Sonny's lifeless body just as Joe began to fight with yet another horse. She fell on the ground next to Sonny, searching his body with her hands, trying to determine what was wrong. The stallions screamed and bit at each other, their hoofs pounding.

"Sonny! Joe!" she shrieked, jarring herself from the nightmare. She gasped for air and sat straight up, shaking. Sonny stood and growled, then began licking her face. She grabbed him by the scruff of his neck, buried her face in his fur, and sobbed. Rarely did a dream seem so vivid, and this one had shaken her entire being.

After regaining her composure, she went into the bedroom and pulled her late father's Remington 30.06 from the closet. She checked to make sure the rifle was loaded, even though she knew it was, slipped on her shoes, and opened the back door. Adrenaline flooded through her as she flipped on the floodlight and quickly looked around. Sonny ran through the door into the yard and marked the gatepost. She walked out onto her back porch and whistled for Joe. The horse ambled around the barn and snorted. Sir William quickly followed. What was she doing, besides overreacting to a dream that had no existence in fact? She called Sonny back inside and locked the door.

Through her kitchen window she saw headlights turn off the road and move toward her house. When she looked closely, she recognized Lance's truck. She smiled as the tension began to slowly drain from her. She waited for him to park and approach the house before opening the door for him.

"What's this?" he said, nodding to the rifle in her hand. "Is everything okay?"

"I'm fine." She looked down as if she'd forgotten about the gun. Without saying a word, she stowed the rifle in the corner behind the door where she could get to it quickly if she needed it again.

Lance handed her a brown paper sack and walked back into the yard. "Lock the door," he said, as he flicked on a flashlight. "I'll check around the house."

She took the paper sack and opened it to discover several foil-wrapped cylinders that she recognized as Lupe's tamales. She put the bag on the table, checked to make sure all her windows were locked, and went back to the door.

Lance moved through the doorway and gave her a quick kiss. "Everything looks okay," he said.

After parking his cowboy hat on an empty peg by the door, he dropped into a chair next to the sack of tamales. He picked up the paper sack, opened it, and inhaled. "Lupe came by the sheriff's office with these tamales and asked me to bring them to you," he said. "They're still warm. You want one?"

Sadie smiled and reached for a couple of plates and tore off several paper towels. "Are you still on call or do you want a beer?"

"No, I'll take a Pepsi if you've got one."

Sadie rummaged in the refrigerator, pulled out two cans of Pepsi, and handed one to him. "I always have Pepsi for you, my dear."

They sat at the kitchen table and devoured Lupe's delicious tamales. Sadie ate one and left the other three for Lance.

"Have you seen or heard anything else since I left?" he asked as he ate.

"No. I rode Joe up to where they tore down the fence, but I didn't see anything."

Lance stopped eating and stared at her for several seconds. Sadie could practically hear his thoughts leaking out into the air around them. *Why did you do that? I told you to lock your door, but you never do what I tell you. You think you're invincible, but you're not. Just because you have a wolfdog doesn't mean someone can't shoot you both.*

But instead of saying anything, in true Lance Smith style, he slowly finished off the last tamale and took a long swig of Pepsi before he spoke in an even tone. "Thought you were going to lock the doors and stay inside." After finishing off his Pepsi, he added, "I wouldn't be very happy if I came here and found you with an arrow sticking out of your chest."

Sadie forced a grin, grateful for his sweet tactfulness. "I should have stayed home," she conceded. "Joe acted like there was another horse around. I felt uneasy, so I came back home fairly quickly." Wanting to change the subject, she added, "Speaking of arrows, did you find out anything about the guy who was killed?"

Lance leaned back in his chair and stretched his legs out into the room and crossed his feet. "He didn't have a lick of identification on him, but the ME took his fingerprints, which we ran through the national system. We got a hit in Texas, a little town called Sweetwater Creek, about twenty miles west of Denton. Evidently, he'd done a little time in the Denton County Jail—twice for DUI and once for grand larceny. We still haven't figured out what he was doing around here. Jennings is supposed to be running down the next of kin."

"Oh." Sadie didn't know what to say. Why was a mystery man from Texas dying so close to her home? "What's his name?"

"Kenny Wayne Sanders, forty-three years old, but don't go spreading his name around until we can find some of his family. You don't know anyone who makes their own arrows, do you?"

Sadie thought for a moment. "No, I don't think so. Why?"

"Sanders was killed with a handmade arrow, but you need to keep that to yourself, as well."

"That's a skill you don't see much anymore," she said. "Are you sure?"

"Pretty sure." Lance wadded the paper sack, stood, and dropped it in the trash along with his empty Pepsi can.

"None of this makes any sense, Lance."

"I know." He moved behind her chair and put his arms around her.

She pulled herself out of the chair and fell into his embrace.

"But I promise you we'll figure it out," he said. "Okay?"

"I'm glad you're here," she said.

"Don't worry," he said and grinned. Pushing her hair out of her face, he kissed her again. "I'm going to keep a personal eye on you tonight."

"Okay," she whispered.

Chapter 3

Rebecca Silver sat down at her makeshift desk, picked up a letter opener, and slid the blade under the flap of the envelope. She already knew what the letter said, but she decided to give it her full attention anyway.

The opening line angered her. *Dear homeowner,* it said.

"You'd think they could at least acknowledge my name," she said aloud. She stopped reading for a moment, trying to absorb her situation, and then continued reading.

This is the final notice of foreclosure for the property located at 22165 Slate Street NE, Bakersfield, California. The property will be auctioned thirty days from the date of this letter. Please vacate the property by that date or you will be removed by force.

"You have such a way with words," she said, as if the writer of the letter could hear her.

If you have any questions, please feel free to contact the foreclosure department at . . .

Rebecca let the letter slip from her hand, watched it fall onto the wooden floor, and then looked at her surroundings. She and her ex-husband, Levi Silver, had moved into this house ten years earlier when they moved from Oklahoma. Levi took a job with the Bakersfield police department, but as a rookie police officer, hadn't brought home a very large paycheck. She remembered being astounded that the city asked him to put his life on the line every day for such a measly salary. It kept food on the table, but Rebecca had grown weary of clipping coupons for bare necessities, shopping for the cheapest cuts of meat, and buying sale clothing from last season.

That's when she'd decided to take a job at a nearby convenience store to bolster the family budget. The store was close to home and one she used frequently to pick up last-minute items and buy gas. She liked the friendly manager, and it felt good to help make ends meet. Once they got on their feet financially, they planned to start a family. She took the late-night shift to coordinate with Levi's work hours so they could spend time at home together during the day.

To improve his pay grade and bring a little excitement to the job, Levi volunteered for undercover work. That had been a big mistake. In order to make his cover believable, he'd gotten a little too friendly with the crowd he was trying to infiltrate. One thing led to another, and before he knew it, he had become one of them—selling and using cocaine and heroin.

Things went from bad to worse. Rebecca involuntarily shivered as a horrendous memory resurfaced. One of Levi's drug-crazed friends followed him into the convenience store one night and overheard his conversation with Rebecca. She inadvertently busted Levi's cover when she told him that his sergeant had called and left a message.

After Levi left, the man returned to the deserted store, forced Rebecca into the back room, and knocked her to the floor. She fought him as hard as she could, and told him her husband would kill him. But it didn't matter. He held a switchblade to her face and, with drug-induced strength, violently raped her. The few minutes it took for Rebecca to endure this horrific act turned into a lifetime of shame for her. She would never be the same.

Rebecca reported the rape to the police and identified the rapist, but before he could be arrested, he was killed during a well-orchestrated drug raid. She often wondered if he'd been targeted by the officers because of her. She didn't care if he had. When she tried to quit her job, her employer agreed to lay her off so she could apply for unemployment.

Once Levi's cover had been broken and the state of his drug addiction uncovered, the police department placed him on leave and sent him to drug rehabilitation. After his limited success in the program, the department gave him a desk job answering the phone and filing papers. Levi hated it. He told Rebecca how he could see disgust in the eyes of the other police officers. He was no longer one of them. The bond he'd had with his fellow officers was shattered.

When the City of Bakersfield decided to cut back on the budget and lay off police officers, Levi's position was one of the first to go. His severance check lasted for one month, and then he stood in the unemployment line with her. The meager income from two unemployment checks wasn't enough to survive in Bakersfield, California. Humiliation turned to anger and the couple began to fight over everything.

Rebecca knew Levi blamed himself for the rape, and if she dared be honest with herself, to some extent, so did she. She felt dirty and pushed him away. She couldn't stand for him to touch her. He started falling asleep on the couch, never bothering to get up and turn off the television or go to bed. When he began spending most of his time at a local bar, Rebecca assumed he was trying to numb the pain of losing not only his job, but also the love of his wife. So she wasn't completely surprised when he came home late one night and dropped divorce papers in her lap.

She had stared at the pages for several moments before she could find her voice. "Why can't we try to work it out first?" she said, with reality setting in, fear and humiliation spilling out through the tears streaming down her face.

"Tina's pregnant." He dropped his head at the weight of the words.

"Tina?" she repeated. "Who the hell is Tina?"

"She's the bartender," he said, and then added, "I don't even know if I'm the father . . . but, probably." He turned and walked toward the door.

Anger swelled inside Rebecca as she took off her shoe and threw it at him, hitting him squarely in the back of the head as he walked out into the darkness. After he had been gone for a while and Rebecca realized he wasn't going to return, she scribbled her name on the papers and sealed the envelope. Giving herself no time for second thoughts, she walked to the corner and let the envelope fall into a blue mailbox next to the convenience store where she had once worked. As she closed the door on the mailbox, a weight lifted from her shoulders. That's when she knew she'd made the right decision. She hadn't seen Levi since.

Now here she sat, holding a letter demanding she vacate her home. She wondered if she would have to file bankruptcy, and for a short moment, thought maybe she should tell Levi about the letter. After all, his name was first on the mortgage. But then she realized she didn't care. He'd find out eventually. Right now she needed to focus on herself and decide where, at the age of thirty-six, she was headed on her life's journey.

Rebecca got out of her chair and walked across the room to a bookcase that held more junk than books. She picked up their wedding photo and deliberately dropped it on the floor. The glass broke in a jagged line across Levi's face. The location of the crack amused her, bringing a moment of levity.

Another photo on the bookcase caught her attention. It was of her father and mother, Grover and Marie Chuculate. She picked up the picture frame and wiped the dust off the glass with the palm of her hand. The picture had been taken five years ago, the last time she'd seen her mother alive. She ran her finger across her parents' faces, and then looked at her reflection in a nearby mirror, trying to imagine which of her facial features came from them. The high cheekbones, the strong jawline, and her dark chocolate-brown hair all resembled her father's. Her hazel eyes, slender fingers, and perfect nails came from her mother.

Shortly after the photo was taken, her mother had died from a deadly mix of too much alcohol and a smoldering cigarette. Rebecca hadn't been back to Oklahoma since her mother's funeral.

She picked up the phone and dialed the familiar number. Her father answered, and his quiet voice tugged at her heart when she heard it on the line.

"Daddy," she said. "Yes, I'm fine. I've got some extra time off. I thought I might come back to Oklahoma and visit, if it's okay."

She smiled when she thought she could hear a tiny bit of excitement in her father's voice.

"No, Levi isn't coming," she said, realizing she would eventually have to break the news to him, but not now. She changed the subject. "How are you feeling?" she asked.

She listened while he repeated the canned speech he always gave her about doing fine, never mentioning the diagnosis of leukemia the VA hospital had given him several months before. It was a result of being sprayed with Agent Orange in Vietnam, they'd said, and offered him little hope of beating it without endless rounds of chemo and a bone marrow transplant, which he had promptly refused.

"It will be good to see you, too," Rebecca said, as she hung up. She thought about her childhood in Oklahoma. Her father had been gone most of the time, traveling to Indian communities all over the country for the Bureau of Indian Affairs. But Rebecca always cherished what little time she'd had with him.

She sat back down and began to make plans. She had a friend who might let her store the larger household items in her garage until she could figure out what to do with them. The rest of the stuff, she'd leave for the bank to dispose of. They wanted it; they could have it.

After straightening things out in her mind, she returned her thoughts to her father and tried to piece together the words she would need to tell him that she no longer had a home or a husband in California. She knew he'd have the words of wisdom she needed to hear. He always did.

Chapter 4

The day after Angus Clyborn buried his son, he drove into town, got out of his one-ton dually Dodge truck, and made his way into the First Merc State Bank on Main Street in Sycamore Springs. He almost collided with an elderly lady leaving the bank, caught his balance, and continued toward the elevator. Knocking the ashes off the end of his cigar, he snuffed out the burning embers on the bottom of one of his alligator boots before placing the half-smoked stogy into his shirt pocket and pushing the elevator button. The doors parted and he joined two other men for the elevator ride up one floor to the trust department.

The décor on the second floor differed greatly from that of the lobby. In contrast to the economy tile on the first floor, Angus's exotic boots sunk into the lush, royal-blue carpeting of the trust department. He entered a large open area with several desks arranged in perfect order, flanked by six offices on three outer walls.

Angus walked past the young receptionist, ignoring her request for him to wait, and continued straight to Fred Lansing's office, where he pushed the office door open without a word or a knock, intruding on two women signing papers across the desk from the trust officer.

"Oh, I'm sorry, Fred," he said, with a loud voice. "I didn't know you were busy. I'll wait right outside your office for you to finish."

Without bothering to reclose the trust officer's door, Angus pulled a chair away from a nearby empty desk and sat down. He retrieved his half-smoked cigar from his pocket and stuck it, unlit, in the corner of his mouth. An employee, a woman dressed in an expensive-looking suit and stiletto heels, walked past him and gave him a don't-you-dare look. Forcing a smile, he took the cigar out of his mouth and stuck it back into his pocket.

Lansing ushered the two women out of his office, smiling, shaking hands, and offering his future services. After they walked toward the elevator, he shifted his attention to Angus. "Come on in, Angus," he said, with a dry tone.

Angus strode into the office and settled onto a plush upholstered chair across the desk from Fred. He leaned back and rested the heel of his right boot on his left knee.

"What can I do for you today, Angus?"

"I'd like for you to draw up some legal papers for me, Fred—a trust agreement. I've accumulated quite a bit of land now, and I'd like to make sure no woman ever gets her hands on it."

"I'm not quite sure what you mean, Angus. Your properties are all in title with your wife, as joint tenants, aren't they? Are you saying you want to change that?"

"Yes, I am. What if something happens to me? They'll all be yapping at her window like a pack of wolves, fighting over who gets my land."

Lansing stared at Angus. "But, you'll be dead, Angus. What do you care?"

"It's the principle of the thing, I guess." He uncrossed his leg and pulled himself up straighter in his chair. "And then there's Lucy—Jason's wife. Now that he's gone, I don't want her thinking she can marry someone else and give away part of my land to her new husband."

"I thought you deeded part of your land to Jason and Lucy. You can't exactly renege on that now, Angus."

"Never filed it. Gave them a copy and kept the original in the safe. All I've got to do is put a match to the corner of it." Being in control was Angus's drug of choice, especially when it concerned his ranch.

"Oh." Lansing sat for a moment as if thinking through Angus's request, and then pulled a sheet of paper out of his drawer and began to take notes. "Exactly what do you want this trust agreement to say, then?"

Cory Whitfield held her cell phone between her shoulder and ear, talking while she filed miscellaneous documents in a row of filing cabinets filled with trust files. She eyed the area around her, making sure no one was close enough to overhear her conversation.

"Lucy, I am so sorry I couldn't make it to Jason's funeral. Old man Lansing wouldn't give anyone time off to go, except I'm pretty sure he went. Did you see him?" Cory closed one filing cabinet and moved to the next while she listened. "Hang in there, girl. I know it's going to be hard. When are you coming back to work?" She watched as Lansing opened his office door and stood talking to Angus. "If you need anything, call me," she said. "I've got to go."

She quickly hung up and dropped her cell phone into her pocket as Lansing and Angus turned and walked in her direction. She looked up, acknowledged the two men, and smiled.

"Cory," said Lansing, "I've drawn up a trust agreement for Mr. Clyborn. Take this file and type it up for me. I'll need it by the end of the day."

"Yes, sir," she said, taking the manila folder from him. "I'll get right on it."

The two men walked toward the reception area, stood talking for a moment, and ended their conversation with a customary handshake. Angus got on the elevator and Lansing returned to his office.

Cory sat down at her desk and, pulling out the form Lansing had completed, turned on her computer. Once the template displayed on her screen, she began to fill in the blanks from the information in the file. When she got to the end of the document, she added the customized points Lansing had spelled out in detail. She stopped typing, took in a deep breath, and looked around. She couldn't believe what she was typing. When she was finished, she hit the print command—for two copies.

After pulling the printed pages from the printer, she slid one copy in her top drawer to read again later, and placed the other copy in the front of the file and carried it toward Lansing's office. One of Lansing's protégés, dressed in the obligatory navy three-piece suit, burst out of his office and slammed into Cory's arm, sending Angus's file flying into the air.

"Watch where you're going," growled the young man, who then continued down the hallway and out of sight.

Cory's anger flared. The offices were full of men who had recently graduated from college with business degrees. They jockeyed for positions with wild abandon, trying to impress Lansing enough to win that all-important title after their name so they could move on to a bigger bank somewhere besides Sycamore Springs.

Cory had an associate's degree in accounting from Northeastern Oklahoma A&M, the two-year college located forty miles north in Miami, Oklahoma, but when time had come to transfer to a four-year school to get her bachelor's degree, the grants and scholarships had dried up, so she took a job at First Merc State Bank until she could save enough money to continue her education. She had no doubt that she could do the same job as the snobbish males in their fancy suits and outlandish ties, but at this point, she just wanted to bide her time until she could find another job somewhere else.

She dropped to the floor and started picking up all the papers, trying to remember the correct order in which to replace them in the file. A tax bill had landed near her left foot. She picked it up, looked at it, and wondered why anything dealing with taxes would be in one of their files. She figured it wasn't any of her business, so she grabbed it and put in the back of the folder.

Once she had collected the rest of the papers from the floor, she smoothed all the pages, placed the file in Lansing's incoming box, and returned to her desk. She pulled out the trust agreement copy she'd hidden in her drawer earlier, folded it, and, when no one was looking, carefully slid it into her purse. She would be glad when this day was over.

Chapter 5

Sadie drove into Sycamore Springs and parked behind Playin' in Paradise Travel, the travel office she'd promised to run for a friend three years ago. Since then, the friend had bowed out, and Sadie had signed a contract with the Maui-based parent company to manage the office. She loved to book happy vacations for folks from around the Sycamore Springs area, and business had picked up so much that she had hired LaDonna Bean to help in the office.

LaDonna didn't like her given name, so she had become known to all of her friends simply as Beanie. She stood tall and thin, with curly reddish-brown hair, emerald eyes, a smattering of freckles across her nose, and a vibrant personality. Sadie thought the nickname fit her perfectly.

Beanie opened the office every morning at nine o'clock, and Sadie usually arrived around eleven-thirty to relieve her for lunch. Then they spent the afternoon working together.

When Sadie walked through the back door, Beanie turned and waved, holding the telephone smashed up against her right ear. After a few minutes, she hung up.

"Hi, Sadie," she said. "Can I have a little extra time for lunch today? I'm going to meet Cory and Squirrel."

"Squirrel?"

"I'm sorry. I mean Lucy. We call her Squirrel."

"Lucy Clyborn? Jason's wife?"

Beanie nodded her head. "It's awful, isn't it?" she said, her voice taking on a sad tone. "I can't imagine how terrible she must feel. Cory thought it would be a good idea for her to get out, and I agreed." Then she smiled, lighting up her entire face.

"I think that's a great idea, Beanie. Take as much time as you need. I'll be here."

Beanie swiveled in her chair. "We were college roommates in Tahlequah, at Northeastern," she said.

Sadie smiled.

"We called ourselves the Three Sisters—Cory for corn, Squirrel for squash, and of course I'm the beanstalk." She laughed. "You know about the Three Sisters, right?"

"Yes," Sadie said, as she continued to smile at the girls' clever correlation of names with the vegetables that made up the Cherokee tradition of planting corn, squash, and beans, vegetables that grew together, each depending on the others for support. "The corn provides a structure for the beans to climb, eliminating the need for a pole," she said. "The beans balance the richness of the soil for the other plants, and the squash covers the ground, preserving moisture and preventing the growth of weeds. The three vegetables together provide balanced nutrition."

"Wow," Beanie said, her eyes wide with surprise. "You really do know."

"I'm not sure I get the connection between squirrel and squash, but it's cute."

Beanie giggled. "I don't know either, but that's how it turned out."

Sadie loved the conversations she regularly shared with Beanie. They always brightened her day.

"If you girls have a Three Sisters kind of relationship," Sadie said, "then I'd say you have some very special friends. Have a good lunch."

"Thanks, I will." Beanie grabbed her purse, headed for the door, and then turned around. "I love working for you, Sadie."

Sadie blushed and waved Beanie out the door as the phone rang. After a short conversation with a prospective traveler, she clicked on the Internet and typed in the name of Kenny Wayne Sanders. She groaned when her browser returned 2,770 hits. "Talk about the proverbial needle in a haystack," she said aloud.

She began eliminating sites. She read about doctors, athletes, politicians, sex offenders, Canadians, Norwegians, and Australians, all with the name of Kenny Wayne Sanders, or a variation thereof. Before she knew it, Beanie had returned from an hour-and-a-half lunch.

The cheerful girl breezed in through the front door of Paradise Travel, bringing the spring sunshine with her. "Oh, Sadie," she said. "Thank you so much for giving me some extra time today. It was so good to see Lucy and Cory. I miss those girls so much."

Sadie leaned back in her chair and rubbed her eyes. "It's good to have friends like that," she said. "Don't let them slip away, or you'll be sorry."

"We have a new project," Beanie said with excitement. "We are going to start buying lottery tickets and pooling our winnings. When we get enough money, we're going to bid on some property."

"Bid on what property?" Sadie asked.

"Cory's boyfriend works in the county treasurer's office. He told her that when people get behind on their property taxes, the county seizes the property and sells it to get their money for the delinquent taxes. If the taxes aren't that much, we could bid on the property and then turn around and sell it to make money. He calls it 'flipping.'"

"Flipping?" Sadie tried to hide her amusement. "I think it might be a little more complicated than that."

"We're going to call us the Three S Group—you know, for the Three Sisters."

Sadie laughed. "That's perfect."

Beanie held up a pink lottery ticket. "This is a winner. I just know it will give us enough money to bid at least on something. But we've got several months before anything goes up for sale."

Sadie laughed. "Well, good luck, Beanie. In the meantime, could you call Mr. Winton? He wants to book a trip to Oʻahu for his family. The number's on that yellow sticky note on your phone."

"Of course." Beanie stored her purse and went to work.

Sadie returned to her search for information on the man who had been inconveniently murdered so near her home. She scrolled down the list of sites and clicked on the next one that looked promising. Up popped a website for a winery in California. The next link returned information on a high school track star in Georgia.

After a while, she decided to refine her search. When she entered the name together with Sweetwater Creek, Texas, the browser returned no hits at all, so she went back to her original search criteria.

Growing weary of her lack of success, on a whim, she entered Angus Clyborn. Once again, nothing. She backspaced out the name and went back to her original search for Sanders. This time she got a completely different list of sites. Then she realized she had only erased Angus, not Clyborn, and had ended up with a search for Clyborn and Sanders.

The first site pointed to an article about a court record in Denton County, Texas. She clicked on the article and began to read. After a few seconds, she picked up the phone and dialed Lance's familiar cell phone number. The call went straight to his voice mail.

"I found some information on the dead guy," she said, feeling excited. "Call me."

She hung up, hit the print command on her computer, and then returned to her screen to continue her search. She was finally getting somewhere. By closing time, she had a stack of papers to take home to show Lance. She placed them in a folder and gathered her things.

"What in the world are you working on?" Beanie asked. "You're taking work home?"

"That's a good description." Sadie grinned. "Let's call it homework."

"Okay, boss. See you tomorrow."

Lance drove toward Eucha after a call came into the sheriff's office about a group of people blocking the entrance to Angus Clyborn's ranch. Lance couldn't imagine what the ruckus was all about, but when he turned off Highway 20 onto Eucha Road, he found himself following two vans, both with attached satellites and identifying call letters from Tulsa television stations.

He followed the vans past Sadie's place to the entrance to Angus Clyborn's ranch, where he found a similar van already parked, a camera man, and a woman in high heels walking around with a wireless microphone in her hand.

"What the . . . ?" Lance let the rest of the sentence fall away as he parked in the middle of the road, turned on his flashing red lights, and got out of his truck.

A group of ten to twelve protestors stood in front of the entrance into the Buffalo Ranch. As soon as the cameras began to fire up, the protestors held their signs high and marched in a small circle, chanting.

Lance walked into the middle of the circle and spoke in a loud voice. "Who's in charge here?"

A woman who appeared to be in her early sixties pulled down her sign. "We're on a public right-of-way," she said, "and we have a right to assemble here."

Lance motioned for one of the reporters to kill the cameras. "What exactly are you protesting?" he asked, returning his attention to the woman.

"The senseless killing of innocent wild animals," she explained, with what Lance thought was an excess of animation. "Deer. Elk. Buffalo. They don't have any chance to escape these savage hunters." She motioned toward the high fence. "It's like shooting fish in a barrel, wouldn't you say?"

"Yes, but it's on private land, ma'am."

"I don't care. Someone needs to speak up, and that's what we're here for."

"Who exactly is 'we?'" he asked.

"The Tulsa office of COWA," she said, pronouncing the acronym as if it were a common word.

"Excuse me?"

"Caring for Our Wild Animals," she explained. "COWA."

Lance stuck out his lower lip and nodded slowly. "Okay, you've got fifteen minutes to make your point," he said, "and then I expect you to leave Delaware County and hotfoot it back to Tulsa. Got it?"

The woman motioned to one of the reporters. "I can make my statement here," she said.

The reporters with their microphones and cameras moved in and the circle began to move again. Lance stepped back, shaking his head, and surveyed the small crowd. One sign read "Stop the Slaughter" and another read "Animals Have Rights, Too."

He looked at his watch and climbed back into his car. Protesters were few and far between in this part of the state, and he didn't have much tolerance for these. Most people in Delaware County let their neighbors be, and as a lawman, he liked it that way. He doubted these city slickers knew much about animals, wild or otherwise, but at the moment, he had to agree that "shooting fish in a barrel" didn't sound too pleasing to him, either.

Pulling his cell phone out of his pocket, he noticed he'd missed a call from Sadie. He dialed her number, but the signal strength was too weak to carry the call. He closed his phone, put it back in his pocket, and looked at his watch, again. They had twelve minutes left.

Chapter 6

Grover Chuculate climbed down the steps of his mobile home and used his walking stick to steady himself as he ambled down a well-worn path, about five hundred feet, to a narrow spring-fed stream. He knelt at the water's edge and scooped a handful of water onto his face and the back of his neck. He looked into the sky and splashed water on his face again. Then he began to sing the chorus of one of his favorite hymns in Cherokee—"Heavenly Home."

Di gwe nv sv, wi ji ga ti
Ta li ne yv, ga ji yo u
Hna gwu a se, wi ji ga ti
Ta le ne yv, ga ji yo u

When he had finished singing, he prayed, and then meditated for several minutes to the sound of the rushing water. Then he used his stick to steady his aching body as he rose to his feet. He took his time, relishing the early morning sunshine, always amazed at how the sunlight struck the trees, the rocks, and the grass, and how the shadows fled as the sun crept into the sky, continually transforming the landscape throughout the day. He heard the distinct call of a cardinal before he spotted the crimson bird take flight from a nearby tree. Grasshoppers sang to each other, hopping out of the way with each step Grover took.

Eventually, Grover returned to his trailer and settled into a wooden folding chair sitting outside the front door. He laid his walking stick on the ground next to his chair and reflected on the helpful piece of wood. He'd carved it by hand from the branch of an oak tree that had fallen one night during a storm. He considered it a gift from the Creator—a gift for which he was thankful.

He pulled a worn handkerchief from his pocket and wiped his face. He was getting soft, he thought, preferring the shade of red oaks and the green-and-white striped awning attached to the side of his little home instead of the intense heat of the Oklahoma sun. Something that came with getting older, he guessed. Grover's thoughts shifted to his daughter, Becky. She would be arriving soon from California. It seemed like an awfully long drive to make alone, but that's what she had decided to do. It would be good to see her.

Grover wished he'd had the opportunity to be a bigger presence in his daughter's life before she'd left Delaware County for the big city lights in California. He'd thought her move was just a stage she was going through when she married a cop named Silver, moved to Bakersfield, and started using the more formal version of her name—Rebecca. She was still Becky to him.

As Grover considered Becky and her choices so far in life, he blamed himself for her marrying a lawman. He, himself, had spent thirty years working as a police officer for the Bureau of Indian Affairs. He liked the job, even though it had taken him all over the country, leaving little time to spend with his family. He traveled from one Indian reservation to another, supervising the resolution of continual conflicts, relishing each and every battle, addicted to the adrenaline. When he finally got too old to keep up, he retired and came back home, only to find he'd missed the little blessings of family that most people cherished daily.

He discovered that his wife, Marie, had learned how to entertain herself in his absence. She had become a drinker and a smoker, and gorged on bags of cookies and potato chips until she became not only obese, but diabetic as well. Unfortunately, her careless lifestyle would be her demise. Grover came home one night to find the house ablaze. Marie had gotten drunk and set her bed on fire with a cigarette. Grover managed to pull her out of the burning house alive, but she never recovered from the burns.

After Marie died, Grover found himself alone, but he was okay with that. He bought a mobile home, dragged it down Eucha Road and set it up beside the concrete slab where the other house had stood, and called it home. Grover didn't have much to begin with, so starting over wasn't that hard. He decided to focus on himself for a change—balancing his mental, spiritual, and physical health. However, with the distraction of the deadly disease of leukemia, he'd had minimal success.

Grover's time on earth had grown short, and there were many things to talk about. He hoped he had the right words to share and, more importantly, that Becky would want to hear them. His thoughts shifted to his only son, who had been gone for more years than he could count. His name was George, having been named after his grandfather George Washington Chuculate. Everyone called him Gee for short.

Gee had been a good-looking kid, with intense brown eyes, strong facial features, and coarse black hair that he wore pulled tight at the nape of his neck—a spitting image of himself, Grover thought, when he was young, before time and disease had turned his black hair gray, clouded his brown eyes, and streaked his tanned face with wrinkles, stealing his good looks.

Grover had raised Gee at a time when imparting wisdom simply wasn't in his grasp. Gee had been rebellious, always getting into trouble. It was that kind of trouble that had landed him in front of a judge who had given him two choices—jail or the military. Grover suggested the army, so Gee flew to Fort Hood, Texas, and became part of the 1st Cavalry Division.

Gee liked the structure of the army, and Grover began to think maybe it had been a good choice for the boy. That is, until Gee deployed to the Gulf War in 1991 for Operation Desert Storm to protect the U.S. interest in the Kuwaiti oil fields from invading Iraqi troops. By the time the "100 Hour War" had ended, it had taken Gee Chuculate's life with it.

Grover never forgave himself. Having spent almost a year crawling through the jungles of Vietnam in the late sixties, he knew firsthand what it was like to dodge bullets and roadside bombs, and he wouldn't have wished it on anyone, especially his son. If he'd been a better father, he thought, maybe he could have kept Gee out of trouble and he'd never have had to go to war. Maybe he'd still be alive. But maybes were just that—fleeting thoughts of what could have been. He could see no point in dwelling on them now.

Grover had his horses, four of them, to tend to. They made his life complete. He could throw his cane to one side, climb onto a group of precisely placed rocks, and hoist himself up on one of their backs. It was then that life eased into focus. He'd made a lot of decisions on the back of a horse, and every one of them had been good.

He sat in the shade and sipped iced tea, hoping he could spend what time he had left with his daughter. Maybe he could convince her to stay in Oklahoma for a while. *Osda*, he thought. Good. After all, other than his horses, she was all he had left.

Chapter 7

While she waited for Lance to return her call, Sadie pulled out the papers she'd printed at her office earlier and arranged them on the kitchen table. She had three stacks—one for Kenny Wayne Sanders, one for Angus Clyborn, and one for both. Then she sat down and organized the papers in chronological order, trying to sort the events in her own mind so she could explain it to Lance so he wouldn't have to read everything she'd brought home.

Sadie startled when Sonny jumped up and ran to the door. Lance had turned off the road onto the lane that led to her house. When she saw his truck, she unlocked the door and walked into the yard to greet him.

"Come inside and see what I've learned about the dead guy," she said, after giving him a welcoming kiss. She walked toward the back door, stopped, and turned. "Can we say his name yet?"

"Just to yourself," he said. "We haven't found his next of kin."

They entered Sadie's house through the back door into the kitchen. Sadie kicked off her shoes by the door and nodded toward the table. "Wait until you see this stuff." She grabbed two cans of Pepsi from the refrigerator and handed one to Lance. "Have a seat."

Together they thumbed through the sheets of paper that covered Sadie's table. Finally, Lance looked at Sadie. "What does all this mean, Sadie?"

Sadie took a deep breath and then exhaled. "Well, the way I see it, Kenny Wayne Sanders, if that really is who died up on the hill, is connected to Angus Clyborn from way back. In one of these documents, he's referred to as 'Anton Clyborn,' but I'm pretty sure it's the same person. The fence that Sanders was installing—or, I guess it was him that was doing that—matches the fence that appeared recently around Clyborn's ranch."

Sadie thumbed through the papers, pulled out several pages, and handed them to Lance. "According to these depositions, which were taken over ten years ago, Kenny Wayne Sanders and Angus Clyborn both used to work at a hunting ranch near Brownsville, Texas. When that ranch went under, they both moved to Sweetwater Creek, Texas, and went to work at another hunting ranch specializing in pay-to-hunt big game such as elk, white-tailed deer, and bison."

Lance took a swig of Pepsi and continued to listen attentively.

"Look at this newspaper article," she said, pulling a page from the stack on the table. "The two got crosswise with one another," she continued, "over one of the bison kills. When two paying customers fired simultaneously at a buffalo, Clyborn said his client made the kill, and Sanders said his customer made the fatal shot. The argument turned into a scuffle that escalated into a full-blown fistfight. Evidently, the hunters don't have to pay if they don't make a kill, and the fight was basically over who would collect money from which hunter. It appears the hunters were arguing over who got to cart home the buffalo head." Sadie shook her head. "Sanders came away with a broken nose and Clyborn suffered two broken fingers. They settled that case out of court."

She picked up another sheet of paper and handed it to Lance. "The second set of court case documents came from Denton County, Texas. Sanders was arrested for drunk driving and leaving the scene of an accident." Sadie looked at Lance. "Guess who the other person was involved in the accident."

Lance grinned, as if amused with her detective work, and shrugged his wide shoulders. "Go ahead and tell me."

"None other than Angus Clyborn," she said. "Sanders had rear-ended Angus in a fit of rage over a woman they had both been trying to pick up at a local bar. Angus dropped the charges, but it was too late. Since Sanders already had two prior arrests for driving under the influence, he ended up serving three months in the Denton County Jail."

Lance picked up one of the papers and began to read. "We already have that," he said.

"The two men obviously have a history," Sadie continued. "Maybe Sanders was working for the Buffalo Ranch. But with such a rocky history between the two, why would Sanders follow Angus Clyborn to Oklahoma?"

Lance rubbed his forehead and then began to shuffle through Sadie's papers. "People do weird things," he said.

"And why was Sanders installing wild-game fencing at the edge of my property?" she asked. "Or maybe he was doing something else. Whatever it was, it cost him his life."

Sadie walked to the refrigerator and pulled out a stick of string cheese. "Want one?" she asked, allowing enough time for all she'd said to sink in. Lance declined and she sat back down, took a bite of cheese, and continued to talk.

"And, based on what I've read here," she said, "I'd say my worst fears have been realized. The Buffalo Ranch is a place that Angus Clyborn is going to let rich city folks come and pay inordinate amounts of money to shoot buffalo, and wildlife that isn't wild anymore . . . inhumanely trapped inside a ten-foot fence." Sadie searched Lance's face. "This all makes me sick," she said.

Lance dropped the pages he'd been reading on the table and leaned back in his chair. "Let's not jump to any conclusions about Clyborn and Sanders. I'll do some background work tomorrow. But I'm afraid you're right. I just left a group of folks from Tulsa who drove all the way down here, news reporters in tow, to protest Clyborn's hunting ranch."

"Really," Sadie said, surprised.

"They were from COWA—something about caring for wild animals. They were definitely putting on a show for the six o'clock news because there was no one else around to witness their little demonstration, except me, and I sent them on their way as soon as the cameras stopped rolling."

"Was Angus there?"

"No. After I write up the report for the sheriff tomorrow, I'll drive out and have a talk with him," he said. "Hopefully, I'll be able to see if his explanation bears out any of your theories." He began to collect the papers together in one pile. "You don't mind if I borrow your handiwork, do you? You'd make a pretty good detective."

Sadie smiled. "Help yourself."

Lance stared at her with his intense coffee-colored eyes for a moment before speaking again. "Sadie, I'm worried about you, and I don't want anything happening to you. Try to keep the doors locked when I'm not here. Okay? I can be here at night, but it doesn't appear that daylight prevented Sanders from getting killed."

Sadie got up, sat on his lap, and put her arms around his neck. "Don't worry about me," she said, and gave him a quick kiss. "Sonny's a pretty good protector when you're not around."

"Yes, but as smart as you think that dog is, he can't shoot a gun," Lance quipped.

Sadie laughed. "No," she said, "but I can," nodding toward the long gun leaning in the corner near the door.

"Just be careful," he said.

Chapter 8

Rebecca Silver turned off the highway and drove toward Eucha. It had been a long time since she'd driven the roads of her childhood, but she still knew every nuance of the journey—the homes, the landscape, the unique feeling of Delaware County. The countryside remained the same; it was she who had changed.

Living in California had forever altered her life, in some good ways and some bad, but she couldn't help but wonder where she'd be, what she'd be doing, if she'd stayed in Oklahoma. She lowered her car window and released her fleeting thoughts into the rush of the evening air.

Old feelings grew in her as she remembered driving these roads after staying out too late as a teenager, trying to organize her thoughts, her excuses, in advance. She found herself doing the same thing now. It was going to take a lot of careful words to explain away a failed marriage and a repossessed home.

Apprehension morphed into excitement when she reached the crest of a familiar hill from which she could see the lights glowing from her father's little trailer. As she dropped into the last curve and turned into the driveway, the fatigue from her long trip slipped away. She was happy to be home.

Grover Chuculate stood waiting in the doorway, and as she got closer she could see his familiar barrel chest, his gray hair parted in the center and pulled into a slender braid that fell down his back, and his eyes dancing with delight. He grinned, but said nothing.

"Hi, Daddy," she said, as she approached.

He held out his hand and she took it. Hugging had never been a part of their lives and she didn't expect it now.

"Can I help you get your things?" he asked.

"I'll get them in a little while," she said. "I'd rather just look at you."

She brushed her bangs out of her face, hoping she didn't look too bad after the long drive. He smiled and together they walked inside.

Grover sat down in what appeared to be his favorite chair, comfortable and well worn. Finally, he spoke. "It is good that you are home, Becky," he said. "After you bring in your things, we will find a place for everything. I hope you will stay a while."

Rebecca walked over to her father and patted him on the shoulder. "Me, too," she said, accepting that she was once again Becky, Grover's daughter, instead of Rebecca, Levi's wife. "I'm going to freshen up a bit."

She walked into the small bathroom and suddenly felt claustrophobic. How on earth would she be able to stay here in her father's trailer? It was barely big enough for him. She splashed water on her face and then used a fresh washcloth to dry. The cloth smelled like fabric softener, and she realized her father must have been preparing for her visit. He didn't seem like the type to use such an amenity for himself. Her mother's facial features stared back at her from the reflection in the mirror, and the rest of her face looked haggard, dark circles under her eyes magnified in the harsh light. She smoothed her limp, brown hair behind her ears and returned to the living room.

"I'm going to grab my bag." She walked into the evening air, stopped, and gazed into the clear night sky. "Oh, my," she said.

Grover spoke from the top of the steps behind her. "You can see the dippers tonight," he said.

A giggle escaped at the memory of her dad teaching her about the stars. The first things he always pointed out were the dippers—the big one and the little one. She could hear crickets singing around her and a bullfrog bellowed in the distance. It was good to feel the heartbeat of the countryside.

She pulled her overnight bag from the back seat of the car and carried it back inside, leaving the rest of her things locked securely in the trunk. Grover quickly took the bag from her and carried it into the bedroom.

"You can sleep in here," he said. "I'll take the couch."

"No," she protested. "I'm not going to take your bed. I'll be fine on the sofa."

Grover wouldn't take no for an answer. "It's getting late and I'm not going to argue with you," he said, speaking with the same tone of authority he'd used when she was a child.

Knowing she would never win an argument with him, she relented. By morning, she would have to figure out what she was going to do. She realized she simply couldn't intrude on her father's life. He didn't have room for her. Why hadn't she thought this through? Knowing her father slept right outside her bedroom door allowed her to surrender to the exhaustion that had been creeping around the edges of her life for months. She felt safe and she slept hard.

Becky awoke to the aroma of strong coffee, but when she opened her eyes it took her a moment to gain her bearings. The small room and everything in it looked foreign to her in the morning light, but then she could hear her father's familiar voice humming right outside her open window. She rolled out of bed and peeked through the screen, but the only thing she could see was a leafy tree branch.

She pulled on a pair of shorts and a tee shirt and fumbled for her tennis shoes. By the time she stepped out onto the porch, the humming had disappeared and so had her father. She went back inside, rummaged in the cabinet for a clean mug, and poured herself a cup of coffee. It was strong, it tasted good, and it was just what she needed.

She picked up the week-old local newspaper and went back outside, where she found a place to sit on one of the lawn chairs her father had set up around what appeared to be a campfire. It was apparent that her father spent most of his time outside in the shade of the tree instead of cooped up inside the small trailer. Was he happy here?

A horse nickered, catching her attention. She set her coffee cup on the ground and walked to the fence where four horses stood, swishing their tails at horseflies while they drank from a huge tank of water. It had been a few years since she'd seen her father's gentle giants, so she walked quietly through the gate hoping she wouldn't cause alarm. She walked among them, scratching their necks and rubbing their backs, and as her father had taught her to do in her younger days, she hummed softly. It lets them know you are one of them, he'd always said. She rubbed her face against Blackie's neck. The smell and feel of the stallion brought back childhood memories like a movie on auto-rewind. She had forgotten how wonderful horses made her feel.

48

Leaving the horses, she returned to the shade tree where she'd left her coffee, sat down, and proceeded to read the newspaper, marveling at what made headlines in small-town Oklahoma. She couldn't help smiling. Pictures from the Lake Eucha Gigging Tournament, men and boys holding strings of fish and gigging spears, covered the front page.

The headline on page 2 caught her eye—"Meeting Held at Lake Eucha to Discuss Bigfoot Population." "Seriously?" she wondered aloud as she scanned the article, laughed, and quickly moved on through the paper to the classified ads. The ads were sparse, made up mostly of foreclosure notices, houses for rent, and a few job listings. One by one, she eliminated the job offerings. She couldn't drive a truck, had no nursing skills, and the teacher's aide job wouldn't start until August. Then she read the very last ad on the page. It was for a housekeeper/cook for a hunting lodge. How hard could that be? The pay wasn't listed, but it provided room and board. She could make some money, have another place to stay, yet be close enough to spend some time with her dad. Once she got on her feet, she could do something else.

Grover rounded the corner of the trailer, walking stick in hand, his head and shirt dripping wet.

"Morning swim in the creek?" she teased.

He acknowledged her comment with a nod of the head and sat hard on the other lawn chair. "See you found the coffee."

Becky retrieved her cup and took a sip. "Yes, and it tastes good. I'll get you some." She hopped out of her seat, went inside, and returned with a cup for him.

Watching him drink coffee, she realized how much he'd aged. His face appeared drawn this morning, and as she studied him more closely than she had the night before, she noticed he'd lost weight. "How are you feeling, Dad?" she asked.

"Can't complain," he said. "Every day I wake up is a good day." He sipped his coffee. "And now that you're home, it is even better."

"I've decided to stay a while, Dad." She placed her foot on one of the rocks encircling the dead campfire. "Levi left me. I can't go back to California. Not right now, anyway." She silently marveled at the ease with which the words had streamed from her mouth.

Grover's face showed no emotion. "It's good that you are home. You can stay with me."

Becky grabbed the paper. "There's a job in the paper, Dad. It supplies room and board. I'm going to call about it." She handed the paper to him.

Grover read the ad and then grunted. "The only hunting ranch I know about around here is that crazy *yonega* down by the dam. You do not want to work for him. He is evil."

"Daddy, what makes you say that?" she said. "What has he done to make you say that?"

"You do not want to work for him," he repeated.

"Well, I'm going to call and see what he has to offer. It can't hurt to check it out." She swallowed the rest of her coffee, got up, and went inside. It couldn't be any worse than what she'd been through in California. It was a start. That's all she needed.

Chapter 9

Lance prepared to leave the sheriff's office and make a visit to Angus Clyborn at the Buffalo Ranch to see if he could shed any light on the deceased man, Kenny Wayne Sanders. So far, no one wanted to claim Sanders as next of kin. Deputy Jennings had been successful in locating the man's ex-wife, who now lived in Arizona, but she wasn't interested in hearing about her ex-husband's demise. As far as she was concerned, he probably had it coming, and he had ceased to be her problem five years ago, she'd said, when she signed the final divorce papers. She had no idea where his relatives were and didn't care what happened to his remains.

Nothing like the scorn of an ex-wife, Lance thought as he chuckled to himself. He hoped Angus could shed some light on Sanders. The documents Sadie had gathered the day before certainly indicated they had known each other in the past. He would drive out unannounced and see what he could find out.

The door to the sheriff's office opened and two men walked inside. Lance recognized them as locals—Roy Carter and his son, Robert. They both wore working ranch clothes—well-worn cowboy boots, jeans, shirts, and hats. Their faces had seen too much Oklahoma sun, and the nicks and callouses on their hands reflected heavy outdoor work.

Lance walked over and shook hands. "What can we do for you, Roy?"

Both men nodded and removed their hats. They appeared to be uncomfortable in the office surroundings. "We've got a problem brewing," Roy said. "We'd like to nip it in the bud before it gets out of hand."

"Have a seat," Lance said, as he flipped open two metal folding chairs and placed them facing his desk. Then he sat down, took out a notepad, and recorded their names, the date, and the time. "Okay, now, what kind of problem are we talking about?"

"Bang's," Roy said.

"Bang's? Like in, the cow disease, Bang's?" Lance asked.

"Yes, sir." Roy nodded his head in a definite affirmation. "Bang's."

"If you've got cattle in your herd with Bang's, you're going to need to notify one of the local veterinarians, and I'd guess the Oklahoma Department of Agriculture is going to want to know. I'm not sure there's anything we can do to help you here."

"We don't have Bang's yet, but it's only a matter of time. There's a man bringing buffalo into Eucha, and everyone knows they carry brucellosis." Roy stopped for a moment and then added clarification, "That's the same thing as Bang's, you know."

Lance nodded, showing that he understood.

"It doesn't affect the buffalo," Roy continued, "but they can spread it to cattle, and it'll wipe out the whole herd." The man nervously fingered the hat in his hands. "We can't afford to lose our cattle to Bang's. We came here to ask you to stop that man from importing those wild animals. His ranch is down by Eucha Dam, which isn't real close to our cattle ranch, but once it's in the area, it can be spread by dogs and everything else." Concern crossed his face. "We just can't afford it."

Lance made another note and pushed the notepad to the side. "I guess you're referring to Angus Clyborn." It was a statement more than a question.

"Yes, sir. You might want to know he's bringing in all kinds of wildlife. I've seen truckloads of elk, too. Can he do that? Legally?"

"Give me your phone number," Lance said. "I'll look into it and let you know what I find out."

Roy rattled off his phone number as the two men rose. They shook hands with Lance and started for the door. Roy positioned his hat on his head, turned toward Lance, and spoke with authority. "I'm not a man who makes threats, but I'll promise you one thing—if that disease creeps into my herd, I'll take things into my own hands. Just so you know." He nodded and walked out the door.

Lance stood with his right hand on his hip and shook his head. "You sure are making a lot of enemies, Angus."

Sadie arrived early at her office at Paradise Travel. Beanie had a man and a woman sitting across from her desk, eyes shifting from one brochure to another.

"I just don't know," the woman was saying. "The Big Island is the biggest. Wouldn't there be more to do there?"

"Not necessarily," Beanie said. "It depends on what you want to do. The Big Island is definitely the biggest island, but it's also the quietest. It does, however, have a volcano that's been erupting for over thirty years—Kilauea. You can book a helicopter tour and fly over it, and actually see the lava flowing into the ocean." Beanie flipped another brochure out for the couple and pointed to the photos of Kilauea. "Isn't this spectacular?"

The couple scanned the pictures with interest as Beanie mentioned some of the other sights to see on the different islands. "The Pearl Harbor Memorial is on Oʻahu," she said, "but there's a lot more people there and it's a smaller island. That's where Honolulu is. It's the state capital."

Sadie listened quietly, allowing Beanie to control the sale. She was proud of Beanie and how she'd grown into her position at the travel office. She'd studied hard and learned all the details travelers needed or wanted to know. If she continued to do well, Sadie planned to surprise her with a trip to Maui in a few months. One thing was for sure, the bookings to Maui would quadruple after Beanie experienced for herself the magic of the Valley Isle.

The door opened and Angus Clyborn stood in the doorway for a moment before walking in and allowing the glass door to slowly close behind him. He took a stubby cigar out of his mouth, knocked the ashes to the floor, and held the cigar in his hand.

Sadie stood and walked over to meet him near the door, hoping he wouldn't disturb Beanie and the conversation she was having with the potential travelers.

"May I help you with a Hawaiʻi vacation?" Sadie asked, noticing that he was a lot shorter than she had previously thought.

"Are you the girl that lives out toward Eucha?" he asked.

"I'm Sadie Walela," she said, offering her hand. "And, I believe you're Mr. Clyborn. My condolences on the loss of your son."

Angus shook her hand with an iron grip. "Yeah, Walela, that's it," he said, ignoring her words of sympathy.

Sadie pulled her hand away. "How can I help you, Angus?"

"I want to buy your place," he said in a loud voice. "And I don't want you to cheat me with an exorbitant asking price, either. How much would it take?"

Sadie tried to smile as she teetered between mild amusement and undignified offense at his ludicrous comments. "Well, Angus, I'd love to help you, but my place is not for sale. There's a real estate office two doors down." She nodded with her head. "Maybe they can help you find some land."

"No, I want your place," he barked, "and I'd prefer not to have to pay a realtor, either." He stuck the stogy back in the corner of his mouth.

Sadie's amusement in the conversation dwindled as Beanie's customers stopped talking and began to stare.

"Let's step out on the sidewalk, Angus," Sadie said, as she waved the cigar smoke out of her face, "so our conversation won't disturb others."

Angus turned on his heel and pushed through the door. Sadie followed.

"Now," Sadie began in a stern voice, "perhaps you didn't understand what I said. My place is not for sale. If you want to buy more land, I suggest you look somewhere else."

Angus grinned. "Everything is for sale, honey, for the right price. I'm sure we can come up with an equitable amount."

Sadie took a deep breath. "No, Angus, everything is not for sale. And, please do not refer to me as your 'honey.' This conversation is over. Have a good day." She turned toward the door.

"We'll see, little lady," he said. "We'll see."

The condescending tone of his voice crawled up the back of Sadie's neck, causing her to bristle. She shot him a back-off-buddy look and walked back into Paradise Travel.

Inside, Sadie returned to her desk and watched Angus stand in front of her business and revive his cigar. Pushing his western hat off his forehead, he blew smoke rings into the air, brushing ashes off the western shirt that strained to cover his plump belly. Then he placed one of his fancy boots on the bumper of someone's parked vehicle and leaned on his knee. His behavior irritated Sadie, and she decided if he didn't leave soon, she'd call Lance and have him move him on down the street.

She took a deep breath and jiggled her mouse to awaken her computer screen. About that time, the couple Beanie had been helping rose and shook Beanie's hand.

"This will be delightful," the woman said. "Thank you so much for all your help."

"I know you're going to have a great time," Beanie said and smiled.

Sadie gave Beanie a thumbs-up and smiled at the couple as they left through the front door, and then sighed with relief when she realized Angus had disappeared.

"Good job, Beanie," Sadie said. "What did you book for them?"

"They're going to spend three days on the Big Island, four days on Maui, and a week on Oʻahu," she said. "That's a nice trip, don't you think?"

"I think so." Sadie grinned. "Two weeks in Hawaiʻi should give anyone enough time to decide they don't want to come back to northeastern Oklahoma."

Beanie laughed.

"Maybe before long we can send you to one of the islands so you can see firsthand what you're peddling."

"Oh, Sadie. That would be wonderful." Beanie glowed with excitement.

"Okay, we'll work on that." Sadie looked at the clock on the wall. "It's about time for your lunch. How's the Three Sisters project coming along?"

"So far, we've only won twelve dollars."

Sadie could hear the disappointment in Beanie's voice. "Well, I'm sure you'll hit a big ticket before long. Hang in there."

"We will." Beanie picked up her sweater. "You want me to bring you back something to eat?"

"No, thanks. Have a good lunch."

Beanie disappeared out the front door and Sadie decided to tidy up the office. She pulled out a dusting cloth and cleaned the computers and printer, and then retrieved a dust mop from the closet and swept the painted concrete floor. When she got to the ashes Angus had deposited near the door, her thoughts returned to the annoying man. Why did she allow everything he did to get under her skin?

A faint odor of the man's cigar still hung in the air, so Sadie propped the door open to let fresh air in the small office. After a few moments, she closed the door, put the mop away, and sat at her desk.

Why would Angus want her land? Was he just a jerk, or was there some unknown reason he was targeting her place? She ran the events from the last few days through her mind—specifically, the death of Kenny Wayne Sanders. Could Angus have done that? And, if so, why? She wondered about the fate of the buffalo trapped inside the tall fence at the Buffalo Ranch. She hated to think they were on display for an easy kill so that some rich person could hang a trophy head in the family den. The fence left behind by Sanders linked him to Angus, she thought. But that land belonged to the Chuculates.

Heat suddenly rushed to her face. He'd made the same pushy offer to them, she thought. He'd bought that land and had begun to connect parcels of land together like a puzzle. That's why he wanted her land, so he would have road access to the Chuculate property. Why didn't he just ask for an easement?

Her Uncle Eli popped into her mind. If Angus used the same approach with Eli that he had with her, he would end up staring down the end of a double-barreled shotgun. Her uncle did not contain his anger as well as she did. She'd better give him a call.

She'd just hung up from a long conversation with her uncle, who had been dismissive and uninterested in anything about Angus Clyborn, when Beanie returned from lunch.

Beanie waved a pink lottery ticket in the air. "This is a winner," she said. "I can feel it in my bones."

Sadie laughed. "Good luck," she said. "I'm going to walk over to the courthouse and do a little bit of research. If you need me, call me on my cell."

Beanie agreed, and Sadie took off for the courthouse.

Chapter 10

A few hundred feet from the courthouse steps, Sadie stopped and observed Angus walking out the front doorway, followed by an elderly Indian man. Angus turned around, shook hands with the old man, and strode off toward a black Dodge truck with dual rear wheels. He got in and drove off.

The Indian man walked down the steps and stood on the sidewalk, looking at a piece of paper. When Sadie got closer, she recognized him as one of her late father's friends.

"*O'siyo, tohitsu,*" she said, saying hello and asking how he was in Cherokee.

The old man grinned and exhaled a gravelly laugh as he held a check in the air.

Sadie could see he was missing several front teeth. After the customary inquiry of his family, she said, "What brings you to the courthouse today?"

"I sold eighty acres of land for five thousand dollars." He grinned proudly. "*Yonega* needed it for his elk," he said, referring to Angus as a white man. "I guess that's all right if the animals need it. I don't need it that bad."

Sadie made a quick calculation in her head. That was less than sixty-five dollars an acre. "That was what Angus paid you? Five thousand dollars?" she said in a tone so as to not alarm the old man. "That's a lot," she lied.

"We need the money," he said.

Sadie nodded, and the old man walked away from her, down the sidewalk.

Tears pooled in her eyes. She was so sick of white people taking advantage of Indians. They'd been doing it since they set foot on this continent, and she supposed it would never end. Most of the land that had been allotted to the tribes in Indian Territory had been swindled away from the Indians with the stroke of an X on a piece of paper, a deed. Indians didn't understand the European concept of owning land; land was a gift from the Creator just like the air. No one can own the air, the Indians reasoned, so how could anyone buy and sell the earth? She regained her composure, climbed the steps, and entered the courthouse.

Once inside, she stopped at the first office on her right—the county clerk. She approached a high counter where a young girl, wearing black-framed glasses too big for her face, rose from her desk and offered her assistance.

"I'd like to look up the name of some landowners of some adjoining property," Sadie said. "Can you help me?"

"Sure." The young girl motioned for Sadie to follow her through shelves of thick, dusty books to another counter where three computers sat lined up side by side. "Here's how it works," she said. She showed Sadie how to access the database. "You can use names or legal descriptions." She pointed to a large map on the wall. "You can find the section numbers on this map. My name is Renny, if you have any questions."

Sadie thanked her, pulled up a chair, and began to punch in names. She started with her own. The screen filled with information about her property. She used one of several blank notepads strewn across the counter to write down the legal description. Then she rose and looked at the giant map, where she could easily trace the outline of both her property and her aunt and uncle's next to it.

She returned to the computer and entered the name of Chuculate. The inquiry prompted several properties under that name. It took a while, but she checked every one of them. Nowhere could she find the property behind hers, where Kenny Wayne Sanders had died.

After an hour, she asked Renny to help her again. Returning to the giant map, Sadie pointed to an area on it. "This is my property," she said. "How do I find information about this land directly behind mine? I thought it was under the name of Chuculate, but I can't find it."

Renny adjusted her glasses, stared at the map, and wrote on the palm of her hand with a pen. Then she went to the computer Sadie had been using and punched in several letters and numbers. When the screen returned the information, Sadie gasped.

"Are you sure that's right?" Sadie asked.

"Yes, ma'am, I'm pretty sure. This guy's been buying up land like nobody's business. He's all over the place." She rose and returned to the large map. "Look. All of this is in his name now." Her hand floated over the map, indicating a wide swath of land from the main entrance of the Buffalo Ranch up the valley, behind her uncle's place and her own.

Sadie stared in disbelief. "You mean Angus Clyborn owns all of this land?"

"Yes, ma'am. I think his legal name is Anton Clyborn, though. Angus must be a nickname."

Sadie realized her mouth was gaping. She closed it and swallowed hard. "Thank you," she said. "You've been lots of help." She gathered her notes and her purse and quickly left the clerk's office.

Sadie's mind raced wildly as she hurried back to her office. Angus was a monster gobbling up every bit of land in and around Eucha. What was he going to do? An image popped into her head of a wild animal park where people shot animals from their cars as they drove through and picked up their trophy-head mounts as they left.

When Sadie got back to the travel office, she decided not to share her new information with Beanie. Angus Clyborn taking over the countryside seemed surreal, too bizarre to repeat. Maybe the girl in the clerk's office was wrong. It had to be a big mistake. Together they closed the office and Sadie decided to stop by the grocery store on the way home.

The locally owned IGA bustled with afternoon business. Sadie grabbed the last grocery cart and pushed it toward the corner of the store filled with fresh vegetables and fruit. Still distracted by thoughts of Angus's land grab, she sideswiped another shopper's cart.

"Oh, I am so sorry," Sadie said, pulling her cart backward. "I'm a terrible cart driver."

The other shopper, a woman about her own age, looked up and smiled. "No harm," she said.

The woman's facial features—hazel eyes, brown shoulder-length hair, and pretty smile—triggered Sadie's memory. "I'm Sadie Walela. Do I know you?"

"It's been a while," the woman said. "We went to school together. You were in the class above me. My name is Rebecca Silver, but please, call me Becky. You would probably remember me as Becky Chuculate."

"Of course," Sadie said. The name Chuculate echoed in her head. "I do remember you, and it has been a while. Do you live around here?"

"No, I've been in Bakersfield, California, for the last several years. I drove in yesterday to visit Dad and came in today to pick up some groceries."

Sadie looked in Becky's cart at organic lettuce and tomatoes, a variety of fruit, low-fat cottage cheese, skim milk, and fat-free yogurt. "Yes—I'm going to go out on a limb and say if your dad is like most of the men I know around here, he probably doesn't eat too much Greek yogurt." They laughed together.

"We're having wild onions for dinner," Becky said with a smile. "I thought I might need something to balance it out."

"What's your dad's name?" Sadie asked.

"Grover. Grover Chuculate."

"I think your family used to have land next to mine. Is that right?"

"I really don't know. I've been gone a long time. I have no idea about Daddy's land."

"How long are you going to be here?" Sadie asked.

"I'm not sure yet," Becky said.

Sadie reached into her purse and pulled out a business card. "If you would like to have coffee or lunch before you go back to California, give me a call. I'd love to visit with you."

Becky looked at the card before dropping it into her purse. "I will," she said. "It was nice seeing you again."

"You, too."

Sadie watched as Rebecca Silver, or Becky Chuculate as she had known her, pushed her cart toward the checkout counter. She had a gut feeling that the woman walking away from her had a story to tell. She hoped she'd get to hear it, and she wanted to find out more about how her father's land had turned into Buffalo Ranch land.

Sadie gathered a half-gallon carton of milk, a six-pack of Pepsi, a nice bunch of bananas, a freshly baked loaf of bread from the bakery, and some sliced ham and turkey for sandwiches. As she headed toward the front of the store, she compulsively grabbed a bag of potato chips and dropped them on top of her other items, rationalizing that she could walk off the extra calories tomorrow.

She lined her cart up to check out, and while waiting her turn, she picked up a copy of the *Delaware County Journal*, the weekly local paper. A headline on the front page caught her attention: "Cherokee Nation Acquires Buffs, see page 3." She let the paper drop open to reveal a photo of a man with short, jet-black hair and bulldog jowls she thought to be the Cherokee Nation tribal councilor, Eugene Hawk, and two other men she didn't recognize standing in front of a tall fence with several buffalo in the background.

"Are you ready, Sadie?" The young cashier flashed a pleasant smile.

"Oh, yes." Sadie refolded the paper and pushed her cart through the checkout. The article would have to wait.

In no time, Sadie had paid the cashier, offered her shopping cart to another shopper, and carried her groceries through the automatic sliding doors and into the parking lot. She placed her bags in the back seat of her car, and as she opened the driver's door to get in, she noticed a huge cattle truck flying down the highway. At first, the truck didn't seem unusual, until three more followed closely behind. When Sadie looked closer, she realized the trucks weren't hauling cattle at all. They were full of buffalo.

She jumped in her car and pulled out onto the highway not far behind the caravan of trucks. "Please," she whispered to herself. "Please don't let the *yanasi* be on their way to the Buffalo Ranch."

When she reached the place where Highway 20 veered west toward Eucha, she watched the trucks continue to speed south on Highway 10. Relief flooded Sadie's mind. If they were going to Angus's place, they would have turned west, not south.

"You've got buffalo overload on the brain," she said to herself.

She dismissed the trucks from her mind, turned west, and headed toward home.

Chapter 11

After Roy Carter and his son left the sheriff's office, Lance spent an hour in conversation with Sheriff Buddy Long and Deputy Drew Jennings about the conundrum Angus Clyborn had begun to create with the local ranchers and COWA.

The sheriff sat comfortably reclined in his chair behind an oversized desk, his short legs crossed and propped on its corner. His round pink face and partially bald head made him look like he had a permanent sunburn. "I don't think it's illegal to shoot buffalo, or whatever else, on your own land," Sheriff Long said, "supposing you own whatever it is you're shooting."

Deputy Jennings, dressed in his usual attire of worn jeans and boots, offset with a starched shirt, stood casually next to the window, staring into the world as if someone had put him in charge of observing everything taking place in the street. He shifted his weight and crossed his arms. "Wouldn't it be just like butchering a cow?" he offered. It was more of a stated opinion rather than a question.

Lance stood leaning against the wall. "I don't know. But I think we're sitting on a powder keg that's about to explode. I've got a feeling something isn't right out there, and I think it starts with the connection between Angus and the dead man found next to the Walela ranch."

The sheriff lowered his feet to the floor and leaned forward in his chair. "Are you saying Angus Clyborn had something to do with the murder of that Kenny Wayne Sanders fellow?"

"No, I don't have any proof of that, Sheriff," Lance said. "I was on my way out there to ask him some questions when the Carters showed up complaining, afraid his buffalo might be carrying brucellosis."

"Well, let me know what you find out," the sheriff said, relaxing again, "but I think old Angus is just looking for a way to make a buck, and it wouldn't exactly be in his best interest to be importing a cow disease . . . or for that matter, committing murder."

"Were we able to get any prints off of the arrow?" Lance asked.

The sheriff shook his head. "Haven't heard anything yet."

"Do we know where the arrow came from?" Lance continued.

"Like, a brand name?" Jennings asked.

"There was no way to trace where it came from," the sheriff explained. "It was handmade."

"Handmade?" Jennings sounded surprised. "Nobody makes their own arrows, do they?"

"Evidently, they do," Lance said.

Jennings shifted away from his station at the window. "Doesn't that mean it was an Indian?"

Lance shot an unfriendly glance at the deputy. "Not necessarily. Arrow-making is a talent not many people have anymore, but I'm sure anyone could learn how to do it, regardless of ethnicity. And judging by the number of hunters who take part in bow season every year, there's a good amount of people who might make their own arrows." Silently dismissing the deputy with his eyes, Lance adjusted his hat and addressed the sheriff. "I'll let you know what I come up with." He nodded and walked out of the office and into a sunny spring day in Sycamore Springs, Oklahoma.

When Lance reached the entrance to the Buffalo Ranch, he let his vehicle roll to a stop. There would be no hiding his identity with the freshly applied law enforcement logo emblazoned across the door of the truck he was driving. He preferred to move through the community with less fanfare, but he hadn't had a choice. The sheriff didn't like him driving his personal vehicle, so Lance reluctantly gave in to the new protocol.

He drove on toward a two-story house, a giant barn, and a structure that appeared to be a hunting lodge. A small herd of bison grazed in the distance behind a tall fence that divided the pasture from the buildings. Lance parked behind a black Lexus displaying Cherokee Nation plates, got out, and approached the front door of the house.

The door opened and two men walked out, but their conversation immediately stopped when they saw Lance. Lance recognized both Angus Clyborn and Eugene Hawk. Angus looked different without his western hat, his thin black hair clinging to his balding head.

Hawk, a lawyer and Cherokee Nation tribal councilor, wore his short, coal-black hair slicked away from his pockmarked face and sported ostrich boots, gray slacks, a white tailored shirt, and an expensive-looking watch. Lance knew the man had law offices in both Tahlequah and Sycamore Springs, and from what Lance had heard, the unscrupulous man spent most of his time trying to finagle money out of anyone he could.

Hawk transferred his briefcase and black leather jacket to his left hand so he could shake hands with Lance. Lance introduced himself as deputy sheriff to both men.

Angus shook hands with Lance and then removed the cigar from his mouth. "What can I do for you, Deputy?" he asked.

"I was looking for the owner of this place. Would that be you?" asked Lance, knowing the answer before Angus spoke.

"Angus Clyborn," he said. "The one and only."

Eugene Hawk backed away. "I see you have business to tend to, Angus. I'll be in touch."

Lance quickly spoke. "If you don't mind, could you wait a second, Mr. Hawk?"

Hawk hesitated.

"Now, what's this all about, Deputy?" Angus asked.

"We're checking with everyone in the area, trying to identify a body we found two days ago not far from here."

Angus replaced the cigar in his mouth and took a drag. "Yeah, I heard about that," he said. "Who was the unlucky bum?"

"Well, we're not sure. I'd appreciate it if you could both take a look at this photo and tell me if you've ever seen him around here?" Lance pulled a photo out of his shirt pocket and handed it to Eugene Hawk first.

Hawk stared at the photo for a second and, without so much as a blink, passed it to Angus. "No, I'm sorry. I don't know this man. I can't help you."

Angus took the photo, glanced at it, and held out for Lance to take back. "No, I've never seen him, either."

"It was nice to meet you, Deputy." Hawk nodded, walked past Lance, got into the Lexus, and drove off.

Lance waited to take the picture back from Angus. "He's a white male, we think about six foot. But we don't think he's from around here. We don't have any reports of missing people." Lance nodded at the photo still in Angus's hand. "Are you sure you've never seen him? Can you take another look?"

Lance tried to make eye contact with Angus, but Angus looked away, contracting his jaw muscle.

"No, I have no idea who he is," Angus said. "Now, if that's all you want, I'm kind of busy."

Lance glanced past Angus's shoulder through the wide open front door. He could see several animal-head trophies hanging on the wall above a large rock fireplace. "That looks like quite a collection of hunting trophies you've got on display."

Angus turned and looked inside the house as if he didn't know what Lance was talking about, and then turned back around. "I like to hunt," he said.

"That's fascinating," Lance said. "Do you ever hunt with a bow and arrow or a crossbow?"

Lance continued to gaze into the house, but he could feel Angus's penetrating stare.

"I prefer a large-caliber hunting rifle for most kills," Angus said. "It's not quite so messy."

Lance nodded. "I know what you mean. If you don't hit them squarely in the heart with an arrow, it can take them a while to go down."

"So you're a hunter?" Angus immediately changed to a friendlier tone. "We're going to be offering guided hunts for some trophy wildlife, if you'd be interested."

"Really?" Lance tried to sound surprised. "I saw some buffalo when I drove in. Is that part of the program?"

"We've got elk, white-tailed deer, and buffalo." Angus stuck out his chest. "It's a lot of fun. We guarantee a kill or you don't have to pay."

"I'll keep that in mind," Lance said.

Suddenly, Angus's defensive tone returned. "Is that all?"

Lance took the photo and returned it to his pocket. "Thanks for your help," he said.

Angus turned and walked back inside, quickly closing the door behind him.

Lance grinned when he climbed back in his truck. "You're a terrible liar, Angus."

As he drove out of the Buffalo Ranch, Lance let his truck slow to a stop so he could appreciate the grandeur of several bison and a calf grazing in the distance. Lance thought the magnificent animals embodied the struggle for survival of all American Indians. The people had used every inch of the buffalo for something—from the hide, the meat, and the bones to the hair, the horns, and the innards. When Indians harvested a buffalo, absolutely nothing went to waste.

When the white man moved west, they slaughtered buffalo to the point of extinction simply for the thrill of the kill, allowing the majestic animals to decay where they fell. Sadly, many Indians met the same fate. The buffalo had survived it all, and so had the Indians. The sacred connection between buffalo and Native people would never be broken. Obviously, Angus didn't know that.

Lance drove northeast toward Eucha, where he hoped to talk to Grover Chuculate. According to Sadie, Grover's father, George Washington Chuculate, had owned the land behind her house where Kenny Wayne Sanders had met a violent death at the hands of someone wielding either a crossbow or a bow and arrow, and Lance wanted to know if Grover knew anything about it.

As he drove, Lance thought about when he'd met Grover at a gourd dance to honor veterans a few years back. A Vietnam veteran, Grover wore with pride the badge of the Electric Strawberry, a strawberry-shaped emblem with a lightning bolt through it representing the 25th U.S. Army Division. Vietnam was an experience they had in common, and they had talked for a short time about where they'd been "in country." The conversation had given Lance a special appreciation for the man. Anyone who had survived the battles Grover had in Southeast Asia had to be an honorable man. He hoped Grover had the right answers to the questions he was about to ask.

Lance stopped at the mailbox that read "Chuculate" and turned into the long driveway. He parked and waited. A dog appeared and announced Lance's arrival as only a hound dog could. Lance lowered his window. He could see Grover sitting in front of a mobile home, working on a project with two buckets. After a minute, Grover called his dog to his side and motioned with his head that it was okay for Lance to get out.

Lance slowly rolled out of his truck and approached Grover. "*O'siyo, tohitsu.*" He spoke the Cherokee words of greeting, secretly hoping Grover wouldn't want to converse in Cherokee. If he did, Lance would have to admit his limited knowledge of the language.

"*Osda.* Good." Grover nodded and continued in English as if they were good friends who had just seen each other earlier in the day. "Pull up a chair," he said. "You like wild onions?"

Lance grinned, introduced himself, and offered his hand to Grover.

"Yes, I remember you," Grover said.

Grover looked older than Lance recalled. He had lost weight and looked tired. They shook hands, and Lance retrieved a lawn chair from a nearby tree and sat down facing Grover. Grover nodded as if giving his approval of his guest and then continued working with his arthritic-looking hands, separating the wild onions, dipping them in a bucket of clean water before transferring them to a plate on a small wooden table.

"These are some good onions," he said, "and I've got plenty."

He leaned over and lit a well-used campfire with a wooden kitchen match and allowed the fire to grow. After a few minutes, he balanced the skillet on a couple of rocks at the edge of the fire and spooned grease from a nearby can. "Can you get me some eggs out of the refrigerator in there?" Grover pointed with his chin at the open door of his trailer.

Lance obliged and retrieved a small bowl of eggs and handed them to Grover. He could smell the bacon grease heating in the skillet and suddenly his stomach growled. Grover broke six eggs, one by one, into the skillet and added the onions while Lance returned the rest of the eggs to the refrigerator. He was beginning to really like Grover Chuculate.

Grover scooped wild onions and eggs onto paper plates, and the two men ate with plastic forks in silence. After they had finished, they laughed and talked about digging wild onions next to the creek, hunting deer on the wildlife refuge, and fishing in Lake Eucha. Finally, Lance began to ask the questions he'd come to ask.

"Can you tell me about your father's land?" Lance asked. "It's the land that sits behind the Walela place."

Grover thought for a moment before answering. "Yes," he said. "I know about my father's land. He has been dead a long time."

"Did you ever transfer it into your name?"

Grover sat back in his chair. "It was my father's. Now it is mine to use as I see fit. When I die, it will be for my daughter to use, if she wants."

"There was a man killed there a few days ago."

Grover frowned.

"Have you been to that property lately?"

"There's no road," he said. "You have to ride a horse."

Lance nodded. "I know." He looked past Grover's house, where four horses stood brushing flies into the air with their tails. Finally, Lance pulled the photo of the victim from his pocket and handed it to Grover. "Have you ever seen this man before?"

Grover took the picture, held it, and looked at it a long time. He nodded. "I saw him walking along the road a couple of weeks ago when I went into town for groceries. I offered him a ride, but he didn't want to sit in the seat next to my dog." Grover turned his head and spit in the yard. "Thought he was too good, so I left him there." Then he added, "It was raining that day, too."

"Where did you see him?" Lance asked. "Along what road?"

"On the highway, before the Eucha Road turnoff."

"Did he say what his name was?"

Grover handed the photo back to Lance. "No," he said.

Lance returned the picture to his shirt pocket, pulled out a business card, and handed it to Grover. "If you remember anything else about this man, would you give me a call?"

Grover took the card and slid it into his pocket.

"*Wado*." Lance stood and rubbed his belly. "Thank you for the wild onions and eggs. They were delicious."

"*Osda*." Grover grinned. "It's good. Come on back sometime. We'll talk some more."

Chapter 12

Sadie dropped her grocery bags on the table and proceeded to put her food away. She hadn't heard from Lance so she kicked off her shoes, made herself comfortable on the couch, and began to read the paper.

She turned to page 3 and looked at the photo again. She had been right about Eugene Hawk. The caption under the photo identified Hawk and another Cherokee Nation council member, Marshall Lee, as well as the caretaker of the herd, Jack Foreman.

"Cherokee Nation Bringing Bison to Kenwood," read the title of the article.

> After considerable interference by Care for Our Wild Animals, a group known as COWA, the Cherokee Nation has acquired eighty surplus bison from Yellowstone National Park. Twenty buffalo have already arrived in Kenwood where the tribe will run the herd, and sixty more are scheduled to arrive this week, according to Jack Foreman, who will oversee the operation for the tribe.
>
> The tribe plans to grow the herd and use some of the meat to supplement food for the elders in the tribe, according to Foreman.
>
> "The Cherokee Nation has invested in this herd for the nutritional value of the meat and the monetary value of the hides and other by-products," said Cherokee Nation councilman Marshall Lee. "Buffalo are good for the tribe," he said.

"The purchase took longer than we thought it would," Councilman Eugene Hawk said. "We had to work around a fanatical and powerful organization called COWA that tried to stop the transfer because they don't want any buffalo leaving Yellowstone. I guess they don't know that American Indians were living one with the buffalo long before Yellowstone ever existed, and that's a heck of a lot longer than their petty organization has been around. And if Yellowstone lets the bison population get out of control, they have to kill them. What sense does that make? We're just happy that everything worked out. The Cherokee Nation has its own buffalo herd now."

The Cherokee Nation will run the buffalo herd on four hundred acres of tribal land that has been set aside in Kenwood. Approximately $200,000 has been invested for special perimeter fencing and supplies to hold them, according to the councilmen.

Yellowstone bison are available only to Native American tribes, and the transfers are handled by a Wyoming bison ranch. The bison must be raised for commercial use.

"If we do this right I think the tribe could make some money," Hawk said.

Sadie let the paper fall into her lap. Relief set in when she realized the truckloads of buffalo she'd seen on the highway were obviously on their way to Kenwood. She approved of the tribe's new operation. Raising buffalo to supply meat to elderly Cherokees seemed like a good idea to her. Then her mind shifted to Angus's Buffalo Ranch. If he had hunters paying for a trophy buffalo head, then what happened to the meat? Could he sell it? Did it have to be inspected? Once again, she reminded herself, what Angus Clyborn did was none of her business.

That is, she reasoned, unless it had something to do with Kenny Wayne Sanders's murder.

She wanted to see the Cherokee herd. It would take only twenty to thirty minutes to get to Kenwood from her place, and it couldn't hurt to look. But dusk had fallen. It was that time of night when, for some unknown reason, deer and other country animals drew themselves to the roadways as if playing a game of chicken with nighttime drivers. She would wait until morning.

After lowering the ramp, the man unlocked the padlock on the back of the cattle truck while the bison inside rocked the trailer. One of the buffalo pushed against the gate with its rump, and the man reached in with a livestock prod and shocked the animal, causing it to move away from the doorway. The man pushed two levers up with his hand and then used his worn and dirty cowboy boot to slide the bottom bar.

Using his body weight, he pulled the gate backward. He didn't want to be anywhere near the ramp when the bison discovered freedom from the confinement they'd endured for two days. It only took a few seconds for five bison to rumble their way out of the truck, onto the ground, and into the darkness.

"There you go," he yelled. "Sealed and delivered. Bonus included."

A man's voice came out of the darkness from the front of the truck. "What kind of bonus?"

"One of them cows is expecting," boasted the driver. "Looks to me like she's ready to drop."

"Well, that truly is a bonus," replied the voice. The man, still invisible in the moonless night, approached and transferred several bills into the palm of the driver as he shook his hand. "Thanks, my friend," he said. "This, I believe, should pay for the bonus *and* your silence."

"Yes, sir," the man said as he slid the money into his shirt pocket.

The faceless voice quietly disappeared into blackness as the driver climbed into the cab of the truck. The diesel engine groaned as the truck moved off into the night.

The clock read eleven thirty-three. Sonny raised his head when the phone rang, looked around, and then closed his eyes and rested his muzzle on his paws when Sadie answered Lance's call. She'd already gone to bed and had to fight to erase the sleep from her voice.

"I'm sorry I didn't call earlier." His voice carried through the phone line. "I've been working an accident on the highway between Jay and Sycamore Springs. It took longer than I thought. I wanted to make sure you and Sonny were safe inside the house."

"We're fine," she said. "I don't think whoever killed Sanders is coming back around here. I think it had more to do with Sanders than where he happened to be." Then she spun the conversation in a different direction. "Are the people in the accident going to be okay?"

She sat up in bed and propped a pillow behind her back while Lance talked. Everyone would be okay, he assured her, but the wreck had happened on a curve and he'd had to direct traffic around it until the wrecker service finished another call and arrived to untangle the vehicles and get them off the road.

"I've got to finish writing the report on this accident before I can get away, and I need to run by my house. Are you going to be okay?"

"Go on home and get some rest," she said. "I promise I'm fine. I have some more information for you, though. You won't believe what I found out at the county clerk's office today about Angus Clyborn and all the property he's been buying." She propped the phone against her ear and listened to the exhaustion in Lance's voice. "There's more, but don't worry. It can wait until tomorrow."

She hung up and tried to go back to sleep, but it took her mind a few minutes to stop running. When she finally slipped into unconsciousness, she dreamed of being on Joe's back, Sonny at her side, surrounded by a herd of buffalo. Her mission: to protect the herd at all costs.

★

When Sadie awoke the next morning, she skipped breakfast and dressed in a hurry, anxious to see the new Cherokee Nation buffalo herd in Kenwood. After she fed Joe, Sir William, and Sonny, she jumped in her car and drove west toward the Eucha Dam on the road that would take her to the small Cherokee community of Kenwood, stopping twice—once to avoid colliding with a small herd of deer, and again to miss a raccoon that was so fat it could hardly waddle across the road. When she reached the Buffalo Ranch, her stomach churned as she saw several vehicles parked near the large house. She hoped they didn't belong to buffalo hunters.

She dismissed Angus from her mind and continued south, allowing the coolness of the morning air to refresh her spirit. She loved the countryside in spring, before the Oklahoma summer heat came along and scorched everything into oblivion. For now, the oak and maple trees had new leaves, a few redbud trees still clung to their purple blooms, the dogwoods dotted the roadside with beautiful white flowers, and she could smell the fragrance of the tall pines.

As the winding road uncurled in front of her, she made her way below the Eucha Dam and beyond, past the turnoff to Groundhog Hollow Road in the Spavinaw Hills State Game Refuge, and ended up on Kenwood Road. Kenwood consisted of a couple of churches, several small homes, a grocery store and gas station, and no stoplights. Sadie parked in front of the Kenwood Store and went in.

Inside, she found a young Indian man stocking shelves. The rest of the store was deserted. She retrieved a bottle of water from a freestanding container filled with a variety of soda pop and water covered in crushed ice.

"*O'siyo*," she said.

The young man stood, acknowledged her with a nod, and walked to the cash register.

Sadie pulled a couple of bills out of her purse and dropped them on the counter. "Say," she said. "You don't happen to know where the tribe is running their new buffalo herd, do you?"

The young man smiled. "Go about a mile in that direction," he said, pointing with his head, "and take the dirt road back to the right. Can't miss it."

Sadie opened her bottle of water and took a drink. "Have you seen them?"

The clerk shook his head. "Not yet."

"Sounds like a good deal for the tribe."

The young man smirked. "We'll see," he said.

Sadie smiled, thanked him, and returned to her car. She secured her bottle of water and drove west. She followed the young man's directions and found herself staring at yet more high fencing, the same as the fencing surrounding Angus's ranch and the same fencing Kenny Wayne Sanders had been installing on her property line. The fence led her to a metal gate, where she found two parked trucks with two horses standing next to them. She pulled in behind the second truck, killed the motor, and got out. She could see the herd clustered together in the distance.

One man worked on the saddle of one of the horses. The other appeared from the first truck and confronted her. "May I help you?" he asked, in an unfriendly voice.

"Hi," she said. "I read about the Nation bringing in a buffalo herd and I just wanted to see them." She stepped forward and offered her hand.

"You're not with that COWA group, are you?" He sounded apprehensive.

"Oh, no." Sadie laughed and introduced herself. "Sadie Walela, just a harmless Cherokee citizen watching our tribal money at work. You're Jack Foreman, right? I recognize you from your picture in the paper," she explained.

He reluctantly shook her hand. "Yes, ma'am. The herd is growing." He turned and pointed at the herd. "Got another shipment in yesterday."

"How many do you have, now?" she asked.

"I'm getting ready to verify that today. I was late getting here to meet the trucks yesterday and they just backed up, unloaded them, and took off. I guess when there's no money to change hands, you take what they give you."

"No money?"

"Yellowstone gave these buffs to us because of some agreement the tribe made. I don't really know all the details. I just run buffalo; I don't keep track of the politics attached to them." He pulled his cowboy hat down over his eyes. "Nice to meet you," he said. "There they are. Look all you want." He returned to the other man, took the reins of one of the horses, climbed on, and let himself through the large metal gate. The other man followed.

Sadie got back in her car and watched as the two men rode toward the herd. The buffalo began to fan out when the riders approached, and Sadie tried to count them, but they were too far away. She estimated the herd to be about sixty-five to seventy. Not sure why it mattered, she finally gave up and headed back to Eucha.

As she drove, she thought about the new buffalo herd. She was glad the tribe was investing in something besides casinos, and as a Cherokee citizen, it gave her a sense of pride.

Chapter 13

After stopping at the Kenwood Store again for a snack to replace the breakfast she'd skipped earlier, Sadie left Kenwood and headed home. The morning had dwindled away, and she would have to hurry in order to make it to Paradise Travel in time to relieve Beanie for lunch.

Her Explorer hugged the curves she'd driven in the opposite direction earlier that morning and her mind wandered. Why all of a sudden had so many buffalo appeared in Delaware County? Wouldn't they be happier roaming wild on the western plains instead of cooped up in the hills of northeastern Oklahoma? She hoped the new Cherokee buffalo herd would be happy.

Enjoying the spring morning, she drove back through a corner of the Spavinaw Hills State Game Refuge toward the Lake Eucha Dam. When she reached the Buffalo Ranch, she noticed the vehicles she'd seen earlier were gone, and that made her feel better. She hated the idea of hunters mercilessly murdering animals—wild or not. She had no problem with those who hunted and harvested the meat for sustenance, but to kill an animal simply to display its hide or hang its head on the wall was dead wrong, in her opinion, and smacked of arrogance.

As she turned the corner, she noticed a lone buffalo on the ground near the corner of Angus's property. Sadie slowed her vehicle, keeping an eye on the animal. Thinking it might be ill, she pulled to the side of the road and watched. It didn't take her long to realize the cow wasn't ill at all; she had found an isolated corner to give birth. The big animal lay on her side and heaved several times until the calf dropped onto the ground. Then the cow immediately sprang to her feet and began to lick and clean the new arrival.

Sadie sat in her car, trying to be as quiet as possible so as to not distract the new mother. She'd witnessed the miracle of a foal being born, but this was her first buffalo. The cow cleaned the calf, licking the new-born to stimulate its new muscles, and then she nudged it, urging it to stand on its own. The little one wobbled, tried to stand, and fell. The mother encouraged it and the calf tried again. Gaining its bearing, it finally stood and nosed its way to its mother's milk.

Sadie couldn't believe her eyes. It was white. She'd just witnessed the birth of a white buffalo. Trying to contain her excitement, she fumbled for her phone to call Lance, but it slipped from her grasp and fell. After fishing it from between the driver's seat and the console, she dialed. Nothing. She looked at her phone and realized the battery was dead. Dropping the phone on the seat next to her, she pulled her vehicle out onto the road and continued toward town and Paradise Travel.

As she drove, she couldn't stop thinking about the white buffalo calf. What would happen to it? It would generate a lot of interest among American Indians across the nation. Angus would never understand how important the birth of this calf was to Indians who considered the white buffalo calf sacred. Knowing Angus and his arrogance about life in general, things were going to get complicated at the Buffalo Ranch.

That afternoon, Eugene Hawk guided his Lexus through the entrance to the Buffalo Ranch and parked in front of the house. Angus was sitting on the porch with a beer in one hand and his trademark cigar in the other, looking as if he had won the lottery.

"I thought you were on the wagon, Angus." Hawk nodded toward the beer in Angus's hand.

"I am," Angus retorted. "I gave up whiskey because the court said I had to, but this is beer. It doesn't count."

"You might want to do some more research on that, Angus. I think alcohol is alcohol regardless of what form it takes." Hawk climbed onto the porch and took a seat in one of the teak deck chairs.

"We've just hit the jackpot, Gene." Angus threw his head back and snorted. "Can you imagine how much someone's going to pay to kill a full-grown white buffalo? Why, we'll have to stuff the whole animal instead of mounting its head. Hell, we might as well put it on display and let people pay to see it."

Hawk sat forward in his chair and stared at Angus. He couldn't believe what he was hearing; his stomach muscles tightened.

"Do you know what the odds are of having a white buffalo?" Angus emptied his beer bottle and tossed it into the yard.

Hawk didn't respond.

"One in ten million," Angus said. "You want to see it?" He sounded excited. "I put them up in the back pasture to keep it out of sight. I'm keeping it a secret. Don't need no gawkers, just yet. At least not until I can figure out what to do."

Hawk swallowed hard to keep the acid from climbing into his throat, struggling to grasp what Angus had just said. "Hold on, Angus. We need to talk about this. Do you have any idea what a white buffalo means to Indian people?"

"No, and I don't rightly care. It doesn't belong to the Indian people, it belongs to me. I can't help that it was born to one of my cows."

Hawk spoke louder, as if that would help Angus understand. "Wait, Angus. Listen to me," he said. "White buffalo are sacred to all Indian people. As soon as word gets out that there's a white buffalo on this ranch, you're going to have Indian people from all over the country coming here to pay homage. Do you really want that kind of attention?"

"Well, word isn't going to get out just yet," Angus said. "I'm going to start the bidding at $50,000."

"For what?" Hawk struggled to keep his voice under control. He couldn't believe his ears. How on earth was he going to explain to this *yonega* the consequences for his proposal to hunt down and kill a white buffalo. Angus wasn't just white. He was white and stupid. The weight of their business arrangement began to bear down on Hawk's shoulders.

"The highest bidder, Hawk." Angus raised his voice. "The highest bidder gets to kill the white buffalo. It will be a few years before he's full grown, so we'll have plenty of time to get ready. We'll call it the 'Buffalo Hunt of the Century.'"

Hawk could feel the heat rising to his face. "No, Angus. You can't do that." He rose and walked to the edge of the porch. "You need to understand something, Angus. If you put a price on the head of this white buffalo, there will be an even bigger price on your own head." Hawk jumped off the porch and opened the car door. "Think with your brain for a change, Angus, instead of your greedy ass."

Angus stood up and spit into the grass. Hawk got in his Lexus and roared down the driveway and out of the Buffalo Ranch.

Angus could hear the phone ringing inside the house. When it stopped, he listened for Camilla to call his name, which she did. He walked into the kitchen and picked up the receiver.

"Angus Clyborn here," he said. "Yes, ma'am. Do you have any experience working as a housekeeper?" Angus listened to the woman on the other end of the line. "Well, that sounds good. Come on out. Do you know where the ranch is?" He gave the caller directions, hung up, and then reached into the refrigerator for another beer.

Becky nosed her car out of Grover's driveway and headed toward Eucha Dam. The man she'd talked to on the phone when she called the number in the newspaper ad had told her how to get there. You can't miss the sign for the Buffalo Ranch, he'd said. He would meet her at the main house.

Becky knew the back roads around Eucha. Growing up as a teenager in Delaware County meant you burned a lot of gasoline in an attempt to kill time. During the school year, there was always a sporting event—football, basketball, or baseball—to attend. Shopping malls, movie theaters, bowling allies, and skating rinks were a couple of hours away. The rest of the time, kids had to create their own entertainment. As a result, a lot of girls ended up pregnant after an evening spent in the back seat of their boyfriend's car. Feeling extremely lucky that she hadn't been one of those girls, Becky pushed memories of her teenage years out of her mind as she drove.

The countryside had changed very little since she'd left Oklahoma and moved to California. She recognized a house where one of her former classmates lived. The same tired, rusty vehicle sat propped up on cement blocks, a symbol of perpetuity that spoke volumes about her decision to move away. She was convinced that if she stopped and knocked on the front door, an older version of the boy she'd known twenty years ago would appear. She nudged the accelerator and sped past the house as if he might in some way know it was her driving by.

The man on the phone had been right. The entry and sign were unmistakable. She drove up the long driveway and parked in front of the house. A man smoking a cigar walked out onto the porch and introduced himself as Angus Clyborn, the owner of the Buffalo Ranch.

"Come on in, little lady," he said, "and let's talk about cooking and housekeeping."

Becky reluctantly followed him around the house toward another building, wondering why her father had described him as evil. When they got closer, she could see a sign above the full-length concrete porch that read, "Bunkhouse." Angus held the door for her and then followed her inside. The wooden floor creaked under their footsteps.

Angus walked to one end of the huge open room and motioned for Becky to follow. "This is the kitchen," he said.

Becky peered through the doorway into a large kitchen filled with commercial appliances and fixtures. Everything looked brand new.

Angus walked through the kitchen to another doorway and Becky followed. "This will be your quarters," he said.

Intrigued, Becky walked into a small one-room apartment with a twin-sized bed, nightstand, a wooden rocking chair, and a flat-screen television attached to the wall.

"You can have visitors after all your chores are done. What you do in your off time is of no concern to me. There's no phone, but there's one in the main room of the bunkhouse. You'll have to pay for any long-distance calls you make."

Angus retreated back through the kitchen into the open room. Silently, Becky followed.

"When the hunters arrive, we'll set up a cot for each one of them in here. There's a large bathroom with showers at the other end." He took an unlit cigar out of his mouth and pointed with it. "Now, your job will be to cook breakfast and dinner for the hunters, clean the bathrooms, and wash the towels and sheets after they leave, to get ready for the next bunch of hunters. I hope you can cook." Angus put the cigar back in his mouth. "What'd you say your name was?"

Becky felt small in the large empty room. "Becky Silver," she said.

"Well, Becky, can you cook? It won't need to be anything fancy. We'll probably feed beans and cornbread, stew, chili, stuff like that. You know, food that makes them feel like hunters. You'll have to do the shopping and make sure you have what you need. I'll give you a company credit card to use."

Becky licked her lips. Her mouth and throat had gone dry. Was this something she could do? Wanted to do?

"I'll pay you $500 a week to start, and if it works out for both of us we can talk about a raise after about three months. I don't pay the government. You'll have to figure out the taxes on your own."

Becky quickly did the math in her head. Two thousand a month with no expenses for rent would add up in no time. She could work here for a while and if she didn't like it, she'd have time to look for something else.

"Well, what do you say, little lady?"

Becky thought for a moment. He hadn't asked for any references, where she came from, or anything. Should she ask for the offer in writing? What if he refused to pay her? Then she looked at her surroundings. Everything screamed money. It wouldn't hurt to give it a try, she thought. Then her father's words echoed in the back of her head—*You do not want to work for that man. He is evil.*

"Well?"

Make a decision, she told herself. "Okay," she said, and held out her hand. "When do I start?"

Angus's belly jiggled when he laughed. "First thing in the morning. Bring your things and we'll get you settled. We don't have any hunters scheduled for a few days. That'll give you time to get situated."

Becky shook hands with Angus and retreated to her car. "What have I done?" she said aloud as she drove out of the Buffalo Ranch and onto the road. Her gut was full of excitement and apprehension at the same time. She felt good that she had made a decision for herself, yet something gnawed at the edges of her psyche. It was that feeling she had when her head said "yes" and her heart said "no." She hoped she hadn't made a mistake.

Chapter 14

Angus stopped on the road and looked left toward the hills. There were still two parcels of land that he wanted, situated in the middle of the massive area that would eventually make up all of the Buffalo Ranch. He unfolded the tattered map and laid it across his steering wheel. The Indian woman in town had been stubborn about selling, but he could wear her down, like he did every other woman he'd ever had to deal with. This one, however, might just be a little harder.

The mailbox bore no name, just a number, but the records at the courthouse had listed the owners as Eli and Mary Walela, relatives, he presumed, to the obstinate woman at the travel agency. He drove his massive truck across the cattle guard and parked in front of the modest home. He got out of the truck and walked into the yard. Beyond the house he could see a barn and an empty corral.

When no one appeared, he reached through the open truck window and sounded the horn for a few seconds. On the hillside behind the barn, at least a dozen horses raised their heads and stared in his direction. The door opened and an older Indian man stepped onto the wooden porch. He wasn't a big man, but stood straight as an oak tree in work jeans, boots, and a plaid shirt, projecting an air of confidence Angus hadn't seen in a while. "Can I help you?" the man finally said.

"Yes, sir," Angus said as he introduced himself. "Are you Eli?"

Eli nodded his head once but did not invite the man to come closer.

"Well, Eli, I'd like to buy this place. How much would you take for it?"

Eli stared at Angus. "You must be lost. This place is not for sale."

"Aw, of course it is." Angus spoke louder, thinking it might add a bit of needed intimidation. "Everything can be bought for the right price. What do you say we sit down and talk about how much it'd take?"

"No, sir. You need to leave my property now."

Angus gazed into the pasture and then turned back to Eli. "I'll even give you extra for those mangy horses you got. I'm sure you could use the money, looking at how old your house is and all."

Eli spewed a string of Cherokee words at Angus.

Taken aback by his reception, Angus decided to use another tactic. "I don't know what you just said, but it didn't sound too friendly. It's just a business proposition. That's all."

A woman appeared in the doorway behind Eli and handed him a rifle. Eli slid the lever back as if checking to make sure it was loaded, and then he stuck the butt of the gun against his side and under his elbow, with the barrel pointed straight at Angus.

"You need to leave my property now," Eli said again.

"Are you threatening me?"

"Take it how you want. Get off my property." Eli's voice remained calm.

Angus climbed back into his truck. "We'll see about that," he said, as he started the engine and drove down the lane and away from the house.

When Angus reached the road, he got out, pulled a knuckle-busting lug wrench from behind his seat, and walked around his truck to Eli's red mailbox. "Nobody talks like that to Angus Clyborn," he said aloud as he took the tool with both hands and swung at the mailbox like he was a baseball player aiming for a fastball. When he made contact, the metal receptacle and the wooden post flew in different directions, both landing in the nearby ditch. He walked over and smashed the mailbox again before throwing the tire tool in the bed of his truck.

Angus laughed, turned toward the house, and caught a glimpse of Eli aiming his rifle in his direction just as the taillight on his truck exploded, throwing tiny pieces of red plastic in the air. The sound of the second rifle shot came quickly, and when the bullet made contact with its target, the back window of the truck shattered into a thousand pieces. Angus, too scared to make a sound, threw open the truck door and jumped in, keeping his head low in case the next shot happened to be aimed at him.

His hands were shaking in such a way that he could hardly turn the key in the ignition, but when the engine roared to life, he shoved the gearshift in drive and took off, the tires throwing gravel as he sped away.

By the time Angus arrived at the sheriff's office, his hands had quit shaking, but he was livid. Who the hell did that old Indian think he was, shooting at Angus Clyborn? His classmates might've bullied him in high school and on the varsity football field, but no one would do that now. His daddy had taken him into the woods and beat him until he fought back. That's when he vowed never to be beaten again—physically or otherwise. He learned how to come out on top no matter what it took. His daddy taught him to be a winner, and he'd never forgotten that lesson. He'd show that country Indian who had the most clout in this county, and it wasn't going to be Eli Walela.

Angus threw open the door to the sheriff's office and almost tripped over the threshold. He caught himself and stomped up to the sheriff, pushing his nose so close to Buddy Long's face that the sheriff immediately backed away.

"What's wrong, Angus?" Long said.

"Buddy Long, I'm mad as hell, and I want to file charges against a man who just tried to kill me." Angus couldn't contain the anger reverberating in his voice.

Deputy Jennings came from behind his desk with a worried look on his face.

"It's okay, Jennings," Long said. "Where's Smith?"

"He left a while ago. You want me to call him?"

"No, but come in my office and take this man's complaint." The sheriff turned his attention back to Angus. "Why don't you come in and have a seat, Angus, and we'll talk about it, okay?"

Angus could feel himself getting angrier as he sat down and waited for both lawmen to arrange themselves with paper and pen. This was the price he had to pay to live in the obscurity of Delaware County, he thought. Incompetence at every turn.

The two men sat and listened to Angus recount what had happened at the Eli Walela place, spinning the story in his favor. He told them how he'd stopped to make a neighborly visit, that's all, and how Eli had threatened him, and when he went to leave Eli had tried to kill him for no reason at all.

"Attempted murder, that's what it was," Angus said. "I want that savage thrown in jail, and I want it done before the day is over."

Long looked at Jennings and then back at Angus. "That's a pretty serious charge, Mr. Clyborn. Were there any witnesses?"

"I don't need witnesses," Angus shouted. "I've got proof." His heart raced and he could feel his face getting warm. "Just come out here and look at my truck."

Angus felt the chair falling backward as he stood and stormed toward the door. Long and Jennings followed, and together the three men inspected the damage to Angus's truck. Finally, Long turned to Jennings and said, "Take his report, and we'll have Lance take care of it when he gets back."

After turning Angus over to Deputy Jennings, the sheriff disappeared. It took Jennings almost an hour to finish writing up the incident report, as Angus kept adding first one thing and then another. Jennings looked exasperated when he finally handed the report to Angus.

"That's it, Mr. Clyborn. Sign here and I'll make you a copy."

Angus signed the complaint and handed it back to the deputy. "So when are you going to arrest him?"

Jennings walked over to the copy machine, placed the report on the glass, and punched a button. Once the machine spit out a copy, he turned and handed it to Angus. "When Lance Smith, the deputy sheriff, gets back, he'll talk to the district attorney and decide what happens next."

"We'll see about that," Angus said, as he marched out the door and let it slam shut behind him.

The slow-turning wheels of justice in this one-horse town were akin to prehistoric, in his opinion. He'd take care of it himself.

Angus turned right and walked straight down the sidewalk to the county courthouse, where he entered, walked past the man at the front desk, and headed straight toward the office of Lloyd Davis, the county district attorney.

When Angus pushed through the door, he could see Davis seated in a leather chair behind a large wooden desk, with the phone nestled between his shoulder and ear. His skinny, colorful tie divided his wide chest like the spine of an open book. He leaned forward, ended his phone conversation, and hung up. When he stood, his black horn-rimmed glasses slipped to the end of his nose as he offered his hand to Angus.

Angus ignored the district attorney's friendly gesture and slammed the copy of the incident report in the middle of his desk. "Do something," he demanded.

Davis frowned and picked up the report. "What's going on, Angus?"

"I want you to issue an arrest warrant for this heathen. He tried to kill me."

Davis sat back down, glanced at the report, then looked up at Angus and said, "Sit down, Angus."

Angus sat, pulled his cigar out of his pocket, lit it, and propelled blue smoke across the desk at Davis.

A frown formed across Davis's face as he read the complaint. "Angus, I know Eli Walela, and this doesn't make any sense. What did you do to him?"

"Made him a friendly offer to buy his land, that's all. He went berserk and shot out the window of my truck. I tell you he's dangerous, a menace to society. I want you to throw him in jail and throw away the key. Maybe he'll reconsider my offer then."

Davis shook his head. "I'll talk to the sheriff and get back to you, Angus."

"Don't take too long to think about it. Or, do I need to remind you that my money put you behind that desk?" Angus forced the chair back, dropped his cigar on the floor, swiveled the tip of his alligator boot on top of it, and tromped out.

Roy Carter leaned against the gate of his corral and watched Dakota Scott, the veterinarian the locals referred to as Doc Cody, examining one of his cows. The animal had aborted her fetus three days earlier. The cow squirmed in the cattle chute, and the veterinarian waited a minute before adjusting the wooden piece that held the cow's head in place.

Roy's stomach churned. He chewed on his lip and then spit in the grass. He already knew what Doc Cody was going to say, and the more he thought about it the angrier he got.

Doc Cody walked to his truck, pulled out a box that resembled Roy's fishing tackle box, and extracted a syringe. He adjusted the straw cowboy hat on his head and nodded at Roy. "You want to give me a hand here?"

Roy walked to the head of the chute and talked quietly to the cow, unsure if the calming effect was for the cow or for him. "It's okay," he said. He held the head restraint tightly while the doctor worked.

Doc Cody quickly extracted a sample of blood. "Okay, that's it."

Roy loosened his grip and released the cow from the chute. Following the doctor to his truck, Roy spit on the ground again.

"It's Bang's, isn't it?" Roy growled.

"I won't know for sure until I get the blood work back, but that's my suspicion. Was this cow vaccinated?"

"We've never had Bang's around here before."

"What about the others?"

Roy shook his head.

"Have you introduced any new cattle into the herd?"

"Bought a couple of heifers from my neighbor about six months ago, but that doesn't have anything to do with it." Roy couldn't control the anger in his voice. "I'll tell you what does, though. It's that damn Texan that's moving wild game into the area. He's got elk and buffalo and who knows what. That's where this came from, and he's going to be sorry he ever set foot in Delaware County by the time I get through with him."

Doc Cody shook his head. "You don't know that, Roy. Let's wait and see what happens."

"I'll tell you what's going to happen. I'm going to lose my entire herd because of that son of a bitch. And, he's going to pay for it."

Chapter 15

Eugene Hawk saddled his horse, a black-and-white paint gelding named Pepper, and let the reins fall to the ground. The horse stood in place, snuffled, and swished a horsefly away from his belly with his white tail.

Hawk climbed in the Ford F-350 diesel truck and backed up to a sixteen-foot covered stock trailer, both of which he'd borrowed from his friend, rancher Bobby Boyles, under the pretense that he was looking to buy four horses and needed the means to transport them from the sale barn in Tahlequah to his ranch north of Liberty in Cherokee County. With the gooseneck firmly attached, he led Pepper inside the trailer, secured the horse with a rope attached to his halter, and slid the lock into place at the rear.

Hawk carefully nosed the truck and trailer out onto the highway and began the forty-five-minute drive north to Eucha. Once he rounded the Lake Eucha Dam, he drove north and east to the small community of Eucha, turned left at the three-way intersection, and followed the road for several minutes before turning left again onto an obscure dirt road the forestry department rarely used. The only tracks he could see were the ones he'd made the night before. He pulled to the side of the road, got out, and opened a makeshift gate halfway, then retrieved Pepper from the back of the trailer and led him inside the fenced area. Using the same halter rope he's used earlier, he tied the horse to the low-hanging limb of a sycamore tree, patted his neck, and assured him he'd be back soon. Hawk's soothing voice seemed to satisfy Pepper, who began to nibble some nearby grass.

Hawk closed the gate, got back into the truck, and pulled the trailer back toward Eucha, where he turned south and then west. After several minutes that felt like hours, he let the truck and trailer roll to a stop at the entry of the Buffalo Ranch and scanned the area. The ranch was supposed to be deserted, something he was counting on so he could get in and out unnoticed. The two ranch hands that helped Angus with the animals had left the night before to check on a small herd of elk they were hoping to pick up from another hunting ranch in Colorado. Angus had told him on the phone that morning that Camilla had gone shopping in Tulsa, and while she was gone he intended to talk some unsuspecting landowner into selling him some more land. Dirt cheap, he'd said.

Hawk spit in the weeds through the open window of his truck as if trying to rid himself of a bad taste in his mouth. Angus was rude and crude, and now Hawk regretted becoming entangled with the man as a business partner. Angus had no scruples, and the deeper Hawk became involved with him, the more that became apparent. Hawk realized his hands weren't exactly clean in this operation, and unfortunately, he had already passed the point of no return, but maybe he could do one last thing right before it was all over. He had to save the white buffalo calf from the monster Angus Clyborn. And he hoped it wouldn't cost him his life.

Hawk guided the truck and trailer up the driveway, then slowly drove beyond the house and the bunkhouse to a large metal gate in the tall fencing next to the barn. He opened the gate, drove through, and closed it behind him before driving into the valley where the road disappeared into a worn path that must have been there for decades. So far, so good. He had encountered no one.

After he'd driven deep into the heart of Angus's Buffalo Ranch, he could see what he came for. A buffalo cow stood in a temporary round pen watching Hawk approach. Her cream-colored calf stopped nursing and looked his way as well. Both appeared to be curious, but not scared. That was a good sign. He knew this particular cow hadn't come from Yellowstone. It had been raised on a ranch that had a good reputation as far as the treatment of buffalo was concerned, but that didn't negate the fact that they were wild. He didn't think someone could simply domesticate buffalo like you could beef. Buffalo demanded a strong hand, and suddenly he had no idea how he was going to pull off this mission.

It took him three tries to get the trailer backed up and aligned with the gate. He slid out of the truck and opened the tailgate of the covered stock trailer. This could be tricky, but he'd handled a lot of cattle in his day and hoped his instincts would be right.

Angus had imprisoned this poor cow and calf in a small area, and the grass had already been picked to bare earth. The feed bin and the water trough were empty, meaning the mother buffalo was probably hungry and thirsty. That would put any animal in a bad mood. He took some grain out of the cab of the truck, climbed into the trailer, and spread it on the floor of the trailer next to a pile of hay he'd already arranged.

Hawk cursed under his breath. He'd reacted impulsively. He hadn't thought this through completely and hoped he wasn't creating a bigger problem than he already had, but he couldn't allow a white buffalo to be here, not on Angus Clyborn's Buffalo Ranch.

The sides of the round pen weren't as tall and strong as the other fencing, and he knew the buffalo cow could walk right through it if she desired. He certainly didn't want her to think he represented a danger to her calf. That could be deadly.

Hawk went back to the cab of his truck and retrieved a suede bag, withdrew from the pen, and sat down on a large stump. He took the leather pouch of tobacco and held it for a minute as he tried to collect his thoughts, tried to remember what his grandfather had taught him. The lessons of his youth were dim, fleeting, so instead he began to sing. But he'd forgotten all the Cherokee words to the song he'd learned as a child, and eventually resorted to humming. He raised his face to the sky and spoke aloud, asking for a blessing on what he was about to do. After several minutes, he took a pinch of tobacco out of the pouch and placed it on the stump. Then he retied the pouch and pushed it into his shirt pocket.

Hawk moved cautiously around the outside of the pen and, just as he'd hoped she would do, the large animal and her calf slowly lumbered in the opposite direction. He took off his hat, held it to his chest, and watched a miracle unfold before his eyes. The buffalo and her calf maneuvered away from him and into the alley, stepped into the low trailer, and began to eat the grain he'd scattered there. He'd been right; she was hungry. He stood there dumbstruck for a moment until he regained his composure, ran to the trailer, and slammed the door shut.

The buffalo eyed him through the small slits in the side of the stock trailer and a bolt of adrenaline shot through his veins. It was a sign. She knew he was there to help her, to save her and her calf from Angus. He looked toward the sky and spoke a word of thanks. If his luck held, Angus would never know he had taken the white calf. His knees were shaking as he climbed into the cab of the truck. Then he made another request to the heavens above—just get him and his cargo out of there alive.

Hawk tugged the shifter into drive and eased the truck and trailer away from the round pen and through the pasture. Relieved that no vehicles had returned to the house or the bunkhouse, he negotiated the metal gate and drove steadily toward the main entrance, but his heart began to race when he saw a vehicle approaching on the road. He held his breath while a man wearing a white cowboy hat ignored him completely and drove a battered pickup truck toward the dam.

Carefully, Hawk passed through the entryway, turned left, and drove in the opposite direction the cowboy had gone. He checked his rearview mirror and watched the Buffalo Ranch fade into the distance. He drove slowly, cautiously, back the way he'd come, back to the narrow forestry access road and the gate where he'd left Pepper. When he arrived, Pepper was standing right where he'd left him. The horse lifted his head and whinnied.

Hawk left the engine running while he got out and opened the gate, wide this time, and then returned and pulled the truck and trailer through. He could feel the weight of his cargo shift, and he looked toward the sky. "Just a little bit longer," he said. He continued driving the truck into deep weeds and circled so that the front of the truck now faced the gate he'd just come through. He killed the engine, jumped out, and ran to the gate and closed it. So far, everything was going as planned, and adrenaline pumped through his body.

Technically, this was part of the Buffalo Ranch—a hundred and sixty acres of land that had belonged to the Chuculate family until Hawk had done the dirty work necessary to make it part of Angus Clyborn's empire. George Washington Chuculate was dead and had been for a long time. By rights the land belonged to his heirs, but no one had ever bothered to claim the land and change the title. Hawk knew how to draw up the paperwork and quiet the title, forge the necessary documents to turn ownership over to the bogus organization he'd created on paper, and transfer the land to Angus for a nominal cash fee that he'd immediately deposited into his own bank account.

If anyone ever found the cow and calf, Angus couldn't say they had been stolen, because they were still on Buffalo Ranch land. He just hoped that the death of Kenny Wayne Sanders didn't draw attention to the area. The top of the steep ridge, above where the cow and her calf now stood, happened to be where Sanders had been building fence when he was killed. The adjoining land belonged to the Walelas, and Angus had said he was in the process of acquiring both ranches. He'd have to wait and see, but Hawk didn't think Eli Walela was the type of man who would fall for Angus's smooth talking.

Hawk untied Pepper, stuck his cowboy boot into the stirrup, and lifted himself atop the horse. He began to sing in a low and soothing tone as he approached the trailer. He and Pepper waited by the truck for a while, hoping the buffalo cow and her calf would relax. Finally, Hawk reached over and pulled the lever on the back of the trailer, allowing the gate to open. The cow and her calf burst out of the trailer and ran exactly in the direction Hawk had hoped they would, toward the ravine, toward the creek, toward the area he hoped they would settle into until he could figure out what to do with them.

Hawk followed on Pepper, keeping his distance, as the cow found the hay and grain he'd left for her the night before. With the nearby creek, the animals should have what they needed, for now.

Hawk climbed off Pepper and kneeled near a large rock. He pulled the leather pouch from his shirt pocket, took a pinch of tobacco, and laid it on the rock.

"*Wado*," he said. "Thank you."

Then he remounted Pepper and rode back to the truck and trailer; he and Pepper would travel back home breathing a little easier.

Chapter 16

Sadie had been out of touch with Lance all day. It had taken three calls for her to detail how she'd witnessed the birth of the white buffalo calf, because his voice mail kept cutting her off. Then she'd been with a customer when he called back and left a message on her cell phone, telling her to repeat her story about the buffalo calf to absolutely no one. He was transporting a prisoner to Tulsa County and would call after he got off work. Tell no one, he repeated.

She parked next to her mailbox, got out, and pulled several pieces of mail out of the box and thumbed through the envelopes. Looking up, she could see her uncle in the distance, digging with a posthole digger where his mailbox should be. She got in her car and drove to where her uncle worked, lowering her window and quietly watching while Eli finished off a hole about two feet deep and at least a foot in diameter.

Without explanation, Eli spoke to her as if she had been there from the beginning of the project. "Come here and help me a minute, Sadie."

Sadie immediately turned off the engine and got out to help.

Eli picked up a metal pipe with a mailbox welded to the top of it and dropped it in the center of the hole. "Hold this steady for me, would you? And, keep it straight."

Sadie did as her uncle requested and watched while he retrieved two five-gallon buckets of water he had sitting on the ground near his truck. He poured some of it in the hole and waited. After he seemed to be satisfied that the water was holding, he took a sack of concrete mix and what looked like a broomstick handle out of the bed of his truck. He poured the contents of the sack and the water into the hole a little at a time and used the makeshift tool to mix it together until it came to the right consistency.

"Aren't you supposed to mix that together in a wheelbarrow or something?" she asked.

"Don't worry about it."

After a few minutes, she spoke again. "Uncle, why are you putting up a new mailbox?"

"Other one broke." He spoke with little emotion and pointed at the ditch with his chin.

Sadie looked at Eli's crumpled red mailbox that had obviously been vandalized.

"Who in the world did that?" she asked.

Eli continued to smooth out the top of the concrete around the pipe Sadie was holding. "Buffalo Man."

"Buffalo Man?" Sadie frowned. "You mean Angus Clyborn? Why would Angus vandalize your mailbox?" Then the conversation she'd had with Angus two days before flashed through her mind. "Did he approach you about selling your land? He's just an old blowhard, you know."

"That's okay," Eli said, as he continued to make sure the pipe was stable. "I don't think he'll try it again, but if he does, his swinging arm is going to hurt." Eli backed up to admire his handiwork. "You can let go, now."

Sadie released her grip and studied her uncle's face. "I think you'd better tell me what happened."

Eli retrieved the old mailbox and threw it into the back of his truck. "Nothing to tell. He broke my mailbox; I broke the window in his truck. Now, we're even."

"Oh, no." Sadie rolled her head. "Tell me it isn't so."

"Don't worry about it. It's done. The mailbox is fixed. Why don't you come over for dinner? Mary would love to see you. She's got a pot of beans on."

"Okay, I'll be over in a bit."

Eli got in his truck and nosed it toward his house. Sadie got in her car and sat quietly thinking for a few minutes. This sounded like nothing but trouble to her.

When Sadie got home, she put away the groceries she'd bought and went through her mail. She changed into a pair of worn jeans and a tee shirt, and after checking on Joe and Sir William, she invited Sonny to join her on the trip to dinner. Sonny took his place of honor in the front seat of the truck Sadie had inherited from her late father, and sat there looking straight ahead through the windshield like a satisfied passenger while the truck bumped through the pasture from Sadie's house to her aunt and uncle's.

Sadie maneuvered the truck past the corral and the barn and then hit the brake when she saw Lance's truck sitting next to the gate. What was he doing here? She hadn't heard from him all day. Why would he be here before stopping by her house? She got out and held the truck door open for Sonny, who quickly jumped out and ran to the edge of the barn to mark it.

When she walked through the kitchen door, she found Lance and Eli sitting at the kitchen table in a serious discussion while her Aunt Mary, apron strings trailing down her backside, bent to retrieve an iron skillet full of cornbread from the antique oven. The aroma of beans filled the homey kitchen.

"Come on, Eli. You can't go around shooting at people just because they piss you off," Lance said, sounding irritated.

Eli spit out a string of Cherokee words and Lance looked at Sadie with a please-help-me look on his face.

Sadie shrugged and smiled. "The gist of what he said was 'bullshit.'"

Mary threw two thick potholders in the middle of the table and deposited a plate of cornbread on one and a pot of beans on the other. "Take a break, you two. Everything looks better over a good meal."

Sadie gave Mary a hug, pushed curly silver hair out of her aunt's round face, and kissed her on the forehead. "You can solve all the problems in the world with food, can't you, Auntie?"

"I wish I could, dear," Mary said, her blue-gray eyes sparkling.

Sadie walked behind Lance and kissed him on the neck, and he pulled out the chair next to him for her to sit. "I see you made it home from Tulsa," she said, sending the unspoken message, *Why didn't you call me first?*

Lance leaned over and kissed her on the cheek. "Technically, I'm still working," he said and grinned.

Mary joined them at the table. "Hand me your bowls," she said, and ladled beans out for everyone. Eli picked up a jar of jalapenos and used his fork to drag several out, letting them fall in the middle of his beans. Then he crumbled a piece of cornbread on top.

Sadie quietly buttered her cornbread, calculating what to say. Finally, she decided to jump in with both feet. "What exactly is the problem, Lance?"

Lance took a bite of beans and spoke with his mouth full. "Angus filed a complaint against Eli for shooting at him."

"What?" Sadie's butter knife clanked against her plate.

"If I'd been shooting at him," Eli growled, "somebody would be digging a grave in the Sycamore Springs cemetery . . . if anyone would even allow the arrogant *yonega* to be buried there."

"Eli," Mary admonished her husband.

Sadie glanced sideways at Lance, who showed no response to Eli's statement. "I take it this has something to do with the new mailbox," she said.

Lance continued to eat. "Yes, and Angus failed to mention that minuscule detail when he sold his story to the district attorney."

"The DA?" Sadie said, alarmed.

"Angus made a visit to the DA before the ink was dry on the complaint. I think Angus must have something on the DA, otherwise he would have let us handle it first."

"First?" Sadie asked.

"The DA issued an arrest warrant for Eli."

"A warrant? Is that why you're here?"

"What about arresting him for destroying our mailbox?" Mary asked.

Sadie jumped in. "Yeah, isn't vandalizing a mailbox a federal offense?"

Eli put his spoon down. "He started this. I told him to leave my property. He's mean and I won't put up with his nonsense. Sometimes you have to get down on their level before they understand you mean business. That's all that happened. We're even."

Lance let out a long sigh. "I know, Eli, but most judges don't take lightly to someone shooting at another person. What if you'd missed the truck and hit him? You'd be facing murder charges."

"I didn't miss. I aimed at his taillight and hit it. Then I aimed at his window and I hit it. Hell, he wasn't even in the truck."

Sadie looked at Lance with concern. "What happens with the arrest warrant, Lance? You don't have to arrest him, do you?"

Lance pushed back from the table. "In light of the additional information, that Angus provoked Eli, I think I'll pay a visit to Mr. Clyborn and see if we can't come to some amicable understanding."

"Can I go with you?" Sadie asked with excitement.

"No." Lance's answer was quick and definitive as he shot her a glance that silently said, *And, don't be telling anyone about that calf.*

Sadie sighed, indicating that she understood. "Okay," she said.

Lance stood and nodded at Mary. "Thank you, ma'am, for the meal." Then he turned his attention to Eli. "And, you sir, could you lay low until I get this straightened out?"

Eli put his spoon down and looked at Lance, grinned mischievously with his eyes, and then made an affirmative grunt.

Chapter 17

Lance drove through the entrance to the Buffalo Ranch and continued up the hill toward the house. Sometimes he felt like half his job consisted of refereeing adults who acted like they were still teenagers. Angus was nothing but a bully who had run up against someone with a backbone. Lance thought this situation between Angus and Eli could easily explode out of control, and he planned to stop that from happening.

Lance pulled up next to Angus's truck, near the barn where Angus stood bent over the engine of a riding lawn mower. The ranch looked deserted except for six buffalo cows and a calf, all the normal color of buffalo brown, standing in the distance behind a tall fence.

Angus ignored Lance until he got out of his vehicle and approached. Lance stood for a moment and surveyed the ranch before he finally spoke.

"Evening, Angus. How's the buffalo business?"

Angus gave Lance an inquisitive look. "Fine, Deputy. It's going just fine. Why do you ask?"

Lance scanned the landscape again. "Heard a rumor that you might've had a special calf born—a white buffalo calf. Is that true?"

Angus frowned. "I have no idea what you're talking about, but the color of my buffalo is none of your business."

Lance eyed Angus. "White buffalo are an anomaly, and they're sacred to American Indians, so if anything like that should ever happen, I hope you'd give us a call. If people hear the same rumor I've heard, they're going to descend on this ranch faster than you can say 'squat.' Do you understand?"

"Is that why you're here? You want to know about my buffalo? Why aren't you out arresting the man who tried to kill me?"

"Oh, yes. I wanted to talk to you about your complaint."

"What about it? Can't you read? It ought to be pretty self-explanatory." Angus pulled a handkerchief out of his back pocket and wiped sweat from his face.

"I'm wondering if you might be able to shed some light on Mr. Walela's vandalized mailbox."

Angus returned to the lawn mower, picked up a screwdriver, and began tinkering with a clamp on the mower. "No, I don't know anything about any mailbox. All I know is that crazy Indian tried to kill me." Angus stopped working and stared at Lance as if only at that very moment had he realized Lance was Cherokee. "No offense," he added.

Lance leaned against Angus's truck and glanced in the bed. "Mr. Walela says you destroyed his mailbox, and I wanted to make sure you knew that the U.S. postal inspector treats mailbox vandalism very seriously. It's a federal offense and carries a six-figure fine and possible prison time."

Angus threw his screwdriver to the ground. "You can't prove nothing," he snarled.

"That's true," Lance said. "Just like you can't prove Mr. Walela tried to kill you. Do you have any witnesses?"

"I don't need any." Angus picked up another screwdriver and pointed with it. "Look at my truck. The DA believes me, and he's more important than you are, anyway." Angus shoved his nose in the air. "You don't have any witnesses to any mailbox vandalism either, do you?"

Lance took a handkerchief out of his pocket, reached into the bed of Angus's truck, and retrieved a lug wrench with traces of red paint on one end.

"This witness will do just fine," Lance said. "When we match the red paint on this tire iron to the red paint from Eli's mailbox, why, I'd say that will suffice better than any eye witness."

Anger flooded Angus's face. "You can't take that without a search warrant."

"Oh, yeah? Watch me."

Angus shook his finger and pointed toward the road. "Get off my property and don't come back."

Lance pulled an envelope and a pen out of his shirt pocket and handed them to Angus. "I'll be gone just as soon as you sign this release. It cancels your complaint against Mr. Walela. That's what you want to do, isn't it, so he doesn't have to file a complaint with the postal inspector?"

"You damned Indians all stick together, don't you?"

Careful to show no emotion, Lance nodded toward the paper.

Angus signed the release and threw it, and the pen, on the ground.

Lance picked them up, took his time folding the paper, and then returned the pen and paper to his pocket. "Thank you, sir. It's been nice doing business with you today." Lance started to walk away with the tire iron still in his hand, and then turned back and pointed to his chest. "Oh, yes, just so we're clear. This badge says I can come back anytime I want."

"What about my lug wrench? You can't take it now. I signed the paper."

"Insurance, Angus. Insurance."

Lance returned to his vehicle, threw the lug wrench on the floor, and drove out of the Buffalo Ranch.

Angus seethed with anger while he watched the deputy sheriff exit the Buffalo Ranch and disappear down the road toward town. This white buffalo calf would be a fitting way to say good riddance to all the hicks in Delaware County. He'd been working at building up this hunting ranch for a while now, and a prize trophy like a white buffalo could fetch as much as a quarter of a million dollars. Why, he knew rich oilmen who would gladly pay that or more to hang the head of a white buffalo in their den. It wouldn't hurt to have more money in his pocket when he finally left this place behind.

Angus dropped the wrench next to the lawn mower and entered the barn. He came back lugging a square bale of hay and pitched it into the bed of his truck, then returned to the barn and carried out two sacks of cube feed and dropped them next to the hay. He got into his truck and drove toward the round pen that held the mother cow and her precious calf.

As he bounced through the pasture and into the valley, Angus began to envision where he might go once he was done with this place. Hawai'i sounded good. He and Camilla had gone there when they got married, but that had been so long ago he imagined it would have changed a lot. He'd heard of the Parker Ranch on the Big Island. Maybe he could buy it, or a place similar, and live in paradise.

He'd sell this ranch to the highest bidder—and there'd be lots of bidders, because everyone would want to own the Buffalo Ranch after he'd made it famous. Drawing up the trust for the ranch had been a good idea. It would make it easier to get rid of Camilla. Her behavior was getting on his nerves. She'd never been cut out for life with him. It wasn't his fault she got pregnant, but he'd manned up and married her anyway. He had to admit, the best thing she ever did was give birth to their son, Jason, but now he was gone. She might as well be, too. Maybe he could send her back to her mother. Then, on the other hand, he didn't even know if her mother was still alive. He'd work it out, one way or another.

Angus's thoughts shifted as he continued on the path to the place where he'd hidden the cow and calf. How did that cop know about the white calf? As soon as it had been born, he'd herded both animals to this secret place. No one could have seen it here.

He slammed on the brakes and let out a grunt. The pen was empty. He stopped the truck, got out and looked all around. How had they gotten out? They must be nearby. Where were they? He knew the pen wasn't very strong, but the cow had seemed happy enough to stay put. She had only stamped the ground once when he got too close to her calf. After that, she'd seemed fine.

He walked completely around the pen. Someone had been there. He could feel it. And the grass near the gate had been flattened. He checked the ground carefully but couldn't see any tracks on the hard dirt.

He turned away from the enclosure and looked around, eventually zeroing in on a nearby stump. He walked over and picked up what was left of a small pile of tobacco. He smelled it and threw it on the ground. What in the world was tobacco doing here? Then it hit him. Indians used tobacco in their ceremonies. The Indians had stolen his calf. That's how that Indian lawman knew about the calf. He probably knew all along.

Angus jumped back into his truck and careened away from the pen toward the house. Those Indians were not going to get away with this. He parked next to the house and entered through the kitchen just as Camilla came from the garage into the living room. She dropped several shopping bags and an oversized leather purse next to the sofa.

When she saw Angus, she used her long nails to fluff her bangs over a wide headband that matched the black-and-white pantsuit she wore, and then removed her designer sunglasses, revealing dark circles under her eyes. The movement of her arm caused her bracelets to clank and her diamond rings to sparkle.

"Wait until you see what all I bought," she sang.

Angus barked in her direction while he picked up the phone and began to dial. "I don't care what you bought," he said. "Someone stole my white calf."

Her face took on a sour look. "Oh, you and your damned buffalo. I don't get it." She picked up her packages, climbed the stairs to the loft, and slammed the bedroom door.

Angus left a message for Eugene Hawk to call him immediately and then slammed the phone down on the counter. Hawk should know what to do.

Angus couldn't report the cow and calf as stolen, because he didn't have any papers of ownership yet. Hawk was supposed to be taking care of that. He didn't make a habit of branding his animals because it spoiled the hides. He knew the buffalo had metal identifying ear tags, but he had no idea if the animals had any other unique markings. Acquiring the buffalo was Hawk's responsibility, and Angus wasn't exactly sure where they had even come from. Up north, Hawk had said. Hell, that could be anywhere from Kansas to Canada, he muttered to himself.

Angus hadn't considered needing to prove ownership. Hunters didn't much care about that when they looked down the sights of a heavy-duty hunting rifle and pulled the trigger. All they wanted was a trophy to hang on the wall. But the arrival of the white buffalo had changed all that. The calf meant there was a lot of money to be had in the trophy hunting world, so his main priority now was finding that white buffalo calf.

Lance drove away from the Buffalo Ranch lost in thought. Angus Clyborn was beginning to be a problem.

Lance was convinced that Angus knew the man who had been killed near Sadie's ranch, but so far the murder investigation was moving slower than a slug on a sidewalk. Sadie's research had shown that the two men had known each other in the past, but that didn't prove anything. All it meant was that Angus was a liar, something Lance had known from the first day he'd talked to him. Unfortunately, Lance couldn't haul him in for lying.

Angus was also a bully, but that didn't necessarily make him a murderer, even though he obviously thought he could get away with trashing someone else's property. Eli Walela wasn't a good choice to try that on. Eli was a good man, but Lance didn't think it was in anyone's best interest to back him into a corner.

If Angus really did have a white buffalo calf, Lance was going to have a giant headache trying to keep the crowds under control. He couldn't even imagine how many people would show up to see it. Once again, Angus had to be lying about the calf. Either that or Sadie was wrong about what she'd seen. That was unlikely.

Angus reminded Lance of a rogue bull he'd once owned. No matter how many times Lance reinforced the fence, that ornery bull walked right through it and mated with every cow he could find before Lance could get him rounded up and returned to his own pasture. The bull had turned into such a pain, Lance had loaded him up one Saturday morning from his neighbor's pasture and hauled him straight to the Delaware County sale barn, where he sold him for next to nothing to get rid of him. He wished he could do the same with Angus—ship him off to some other lawman's jurisdiction.

Chapter 18

Saturday morning gave Sadie a chance to relax. Beanie had volunteered to work for some extra money, and Sadie gladly accepted.

Sadie lay in bed thinking about the man who had been killed at the edge of her property. She had an uneasy feeling about the whole thing and felt in her heart that Angus Clyborn had been connected in some way. She stiffened when she remembered how the girl in the county clerk's office had slid her hand across the map indicating the land Angus had gobbled up.

Her thoughts drifted to the Chuculates, and she wondered why they had sold their land to Angus. She wasn't aware that they'd ever used the land, so maybe it was a good way for them to make some money from selling land they didn't need.

The phone beside her bed rang and she grabbed it before the second ring, thinking it might be Beanie needing help. It was Lance.

"Morning, Sunshine." His voice boomed through the receiver.

Sadie smiled, propped a pillow behind her head, and settled in for a lengthy conversation.

"Good morning to you, too," she said. "I'm glad you called. I discovered the Chuculates sold the land behind my house to Angus, so that means Sanders was killed on Buffalo Ranch land."

The silent phone line meant Lance was thinking. "Are you sure?" he finally said. "I talked to Grover Chuculate, and he didn't say that."

"That's what the records show at the county clerk's office."

More silence. "I'll check on it," he said.

"I can't wait to hear all about your visit to the Buffalo Ranch," she said, moving the conversation in a new direction. "What happened?"

She listened while Lance proudly explained how he'd convinced Angus to drop the complaint against Eli and he hoped that would put an end to the conflict.

"Well, I'm glad you got that taken care of," she said. "I don't see Eli angry very often, but he was definitely angry." Before Lance could say anything else, she changed the subject. "What about the white calf? Did you see it?"

She couldn't believe it when Lance explained that, according to Angus, there was no white buffalo calf.

"Lance, there *is* a white calf. I saw it. Did you look around for it?"

No, he said, explaining he couldn't search for something that wasn't connected to an investigation. If Angus had a white calf, it would show up eventually. Until then, it wasn't any of her concern.

Sadie reluctantly agreed, and after several minutes of small talk and making plans for dinner, she hung up. Angus was lying about the white calf, and she wondered what else he was lying about. She didn't trust Angus; he was a jerk. She had to concede the affairs taking place on the Buffalo Ranch were none of her business, but the murdered man had been found uncomfortably close to her property, which made it her problem. She intended to uncover the truth.

She felt an immediate need to get out of the house, away from people, and breathe some fresh air. After making a quick call to the travel office to make sure Beanie didn't need anything, she dressed, grabbed an apple and a bottle of water, and headed for the barn, with Sonny following close behind. In a few short minutes, she'd saddled Joe, got on, and reined him through the gate and into the pasture behind her house.

She pulled Joe to a stop and waved when she saw her Uncle Eli working with a horse in his corral. He used his hat to return the gesture. Sadie nudged Joe with the heels of her boots and continued to climb the hill to the place where some stranger had met his maker. Everything looked the same as it had the last time she'd been here.

She slid off of Joe's back and looked around, hoping she might have missed something before, anything that would shed some light on what had happened that day. Sonny ran from post to post, sniffing and marking, and then trotted through a break in the fence away from Sadie.

"Okay," she said. "We'll go in that direction."

She hoisted herself onto Joe's back and followed slowly, looking for something, anything of interest, along the fence line that led away from her land. Technically she was trespassing, but she didn't think anyone would mind. After all, she was just out for a morning ride and didn't see any "no trespassing" signs posted.

The land Sadie rode on did not lend itself to grazing buffalo, but it was perfect for deer. She noticed a few trails that had been cut through the brush with four-wheelers. Hunting on gas-powered vehicles didn't sit too well with Sadie, but she realized it was the new way of doing things.

She had been riding for more than an hour when she came to a clearing at the top of the ridge she'd been following. She got off Joe and dropped his reins to the ground, indicating to the horse to stay where he stood. She whistled for Sonny and the wolfdog appeared, panting as if he'd just run a fast race. Sadie dug in Joe's saddlebags and pulled out a pair of binoculars along with the apple and water. She found a place near the edge of a drop-off overlooking some buildings in the valley below and sat down. She had no idea she had ridden so far. The Buffalo Ranch lay sprawled below.

Sonny plopped down beside her, sniffing at her food. She bit off a piece of apple and handed it to him. He moved it around in his mouth and then spit it out. Sadie chuckled. "What?" she said. "You don't like fruit?" She reached over and scratched the top of his head.

The sunshine broke through the few lonely clouds, and Sadie leaned against a large rock, soaking in the warmth of the sun. She took another bite and washed the sweet taste down with water. Suddenly, Sonny's ears pricked and he stared into the valley. A low rumble grew in his throat.

"What is it, Sonny?"

She finished off the last bite of apple and dropped the core on the ground. Lifting the binoculars to her eyes, she tried to focus in on what interested Sonny. It took her a few minutes, but she finally found the source of his angst. Angus Clyborn and another man stood in an open area, shooting a crossbow at a round target attached to two rectangular bales of hay stacked against the back of the barn. First Angus would shoot and retrieve his arrows, and then the other man would do the same. She wished she could see the arrows they were shooting. Maybe Angus and his friend had killed Sanders.

Sadie's late dad had taught her how to handle a longbow when she was young, a bow that had been handed down to him from his uncle. Sadie and her dad used to practice shooting arrows at a bale of hay, in much the same manner as the two men in the valley below. Her dad hunted deer during the annual bow season, but she didn't like to hunt and had lost interest. She still had her dad's bow and thought for a moment that she should get it out and either use it or give it to Lance. Either way, she'd think about that later.

Sadie sat back down next to Sonny and patted his head. "It's okay, boy. They're not going to bother us and we're not going to bother them. Be quiet."

She rested her elbows on her knees and continued to spy on the men through her binoculars. She could see the small herd of buffalo in the distance behind the barn. She looked in earnest for the white calf with no luck. Where had it gone? Returning her attention to the target shooters, she tried to focus on the other man with Angus. He wore a red long-sleeved shirt and jeans, and had short black hair; she thought he looked a lot like the Cherokee councilman, Eugene Hawk. What would he be doing at the Buffalo Ranch?

What appeared to be an argument broke out between the two men, and Sadie wished she could hear what they were saying. For a minute, she thought Angus was going to hit the other man, but instead, the red-shirt man turned on his heel and disappeared around the barn and out of sight.

Sadie stood and stretched her legs, and Sonny trotted into the brush. She put the binoculars back into Joe's saddlebag, drank the rest of her water, and added the empty water bottle to the bag. The sunshine felt good on her face, and she sat back down to enjoy the warmth. Suddenly, she intuitively felt a presence behind her. Her heart pumped and her mind raced. They hadn't seen her, had they? Red-shirt couldn't get to where she was that fast, could he? Where had Sonny gone?

Quickly, she turned. Eli stood about ten feet away from her, holding a rifle. He didn't look happy.

"Uncle Eli," she said, relieved. "You scared me. Why are you sneaking up on me?"

"You shouldn't be here," he said in a stern voice.

"Why not?" she protested. "I'm not doing anything wrong."

"This is not our land. Come on, let's go." He turned and walked away from her. A few moments later he reappeared on the back of a buckskin horse. He nodded his head for her to follow and began to ride away.

Sadie climbed onto Joe's back and whistled for Sonny. The wolfdog raced ahead as she reined Joe in behind her uncle's horse. This didn't seem like a good time to tell him about Angus's accumulation of land, which included the very trail they were on. After several minutes of silent riding, Eli pulled his horse to a stop until Sadie could come alongside him.

"Did Lance tell you that Angus dropped the complaint against you?" she asked.

Eli ignored her comment. "One man has already died in these woods," he said, looking into the distance.

"Okay, I get it," she said, accepting her uncle's protective nature. "Let's go home."

Sadie fell in behind her uncle again and followed him back along the ridge toward home. When they approached the break in the fence at the edge of her property, she could see two men working on the fence. They stopped working and eyed Eli and Sadie.

Eli nudged his horse and trotted up to the men. Sadie remained behind her uncle, yelled for Sonny, and commanded him to stay close to her, which he did.

Eli began to talk to the men and Sadie moved closer. The two men spoke broken English and Eli replied in a mixture of English, Spanish, and Cherokee. Sadie couldn't follow the conversation, but it seemed friendly enough. She heard the words *el bisonte Americano*, and was convinced they were talking about American bison; since they were working on Angus's fence, that meant they probably worked for the Buffalo Ranch.

Eli climbed off his horse and showed the two men the stakes that indicated Sadie's property line, and the two men nodded with great animation. All three men shook hands, and Eli climbed on his horse and motioned for Sadie to follow him back through the break in the fence toward her house. Sadie commanded Sonny to stay close and waited until they were far enough away from the workers to speak.

"I guess they came to finish the job Sanders started," she said.

Eli nodded. "When they get that fence up, it would be a good idea for you to stay on your side of it."

"We were just out for a ride, for heaven's sake. Angus couldn't even see us up there. I don't see that it's a big deal."

"That man and everything he does is a big deal. He spreads trouble everywhere."

"I'm not afraid of Angus," she retorted.

"You don't have to be afraid of him, but you need to be smarter than him. There's no reason to stick your nose where it doesn't belong." Eli had an intense look on his face. "We don't have to let him run over us, but we need to stay away from him so he cannot drag us down to his level."

Sadie smiled and thought maybe he was repeating words he himself had heard earlier in the day from Aunt Mary. Regardless, he spoke good words and she took them in the spirit with which he offered them. Ever since her dad had died, her uncle had been a protector of sorts to her, and she loved him for it. She considered herself smart enough to take care of herself, but she appreciated him and her Aunt Mary for always supporting her, anyway.

"Don't worry, Uncle. I'll be careful," she said, as she turned Joe toward her corral. Eli broke off toward his own property, tipped his hat to her, and nodded. Sonny ran ahead and gulped water from the nearby creek.

After removing Joe's saddle and bridle, Sadie brushed him from head to toe before releasing him into the pasture with his friend, Sir William, the billy goat. The sun had crept high in the afternoon sky, making a beautiful spring day. She returned to the house thinking about what to fix for dinner. Lance wasn't a picky eater, but she wanted to make something special for him.

Inside the kitchen, she opened the refrigerator and surveyed its contents, and then turned her attention to the counter. Based on what she had, it would be pork chops, green beans, fried potatoes and onions, and for dessert—leftover brownies. She hurried off to clean up and prepare to see Lance.

Roy Carter rode his horse north into the pasture where his cattle meandered in and around a small pond. Bandit, the cow dog, ran out front, making a beeline toward the small herd of Herefords. At last count, Roy owned forty-three cows, twenty-nine calves, ten steers, and one bull. Not too shabby, he thought, for a part-time electrician and part-time rancher. His steady work as an electrician helped support his love of raising cattle, and each year his profits grew from the sale of yearlings. White-faced Herefords grazing on emerald-green Bermuda grass looked like a picture postcard to him. The idea of losing this herd hurt like a knife stabbing him in the gut.

Roy reined his horse to a stop and whistled. Bandit barked as if answering his master's command and rushed to round up the animals. As the dog circled the herd, nipping at their heels, the cows and their bawling calves moved south. As Roy watched, anger grew in the pit of his stomach as any profit he had counted on from this fall's sale trotted toward the corral where a stock trailer waited to haul them all away. He contemplated his situation as he balanced himself in the saddle.

After the vet had confirmed what he already knew, that his herd had been infected with brucellosis, the man from the agriculture department had come out and declared that his herd had to go. He might have to sell his animals for next to nothing, but if that's what he had to do, he'd do it. He'd already decided he was not going to let Angus Clyborn get away with destroying him and his herd. He'd warned the deputy sheriff to stop this before it happened. Obviously, his herd of cattle didn't rank very high on the lawman's priority list. He thought the deputy sheriff, just like the rest of the people in the county, feared Angus Clyborn, but Roy wasn't the least bit intimidated. The overweight blowhard had to pay.

When the cattle had been loaded and the stock trailer pulled away, Roy unsaddled his horse and released him into the pasture, and then retrieved his Winchester rifle from the house. After securing the rifle in the gun rack of his truck, he climbed in and followed.

Chapter 19

Lance swept through the kitchen door, gave Sadie a kiss, and then tickled her ribs, causing dredging flour to fly into the air. She playfully slung a bit of flour in his direction and he quickly retreated, laughing.

"Do you want a beer, or are you on Pepsi duty tonight?" she asked.

Lance opened the refrigerator and poked around. "I'd better stick with Pepsi," he said, as he retrieved a can, popped the top, and took a seat at the kitchen table.

After depositing the pork chops into the hot grease in the iron skillet, she washed her hands and retrieved her own drink—a low-calorie beer. "I'm going to splurge," she said.

"Do you miss cooking at the American Café?" Lance asked, grinning.

Sadie gave him a sideways glance as she used a fork to turn the meat. "No," she said. "And, I think that's an experience I don't care to repeat. At least one good thing came out of it, though. I did learn a lot about cooking from Emma."

"My gain," he said.

"Well, I like selling vacations better." She scooped an apple out of a woven basket on the counter, washed it, and began to slice it into irregular pieces. "Don't you think we're overdue for a vacation? Where would you like to go?"

"Right now I'd like to go anywhere to get away from your neighbor."

Sadie transferred the pork chops from the skillet into a baking dish, piled the apples on top, added some beer, and placed the baking dish in the oven. She dropped her pot holder on the counter and sat down at the table.

"I'm going to let that bake for a few minutes," she said, and then responded to Lance's comment. "What's the matter? The buffalo man causing you problems?" Sadie laughed. "That's what Uncle Eli calls him—the 'buffalo man.'"

"He is definitely a piece of work."

"What about Kenny Wayne Sanders? Have you tied him back to Angus?"

"No more than you did. I confirmed what you found out. I also talked to Grover Chuculate, and he recognized him in the picture I have. He said he saw him walking on the highway a few days before he was found dead. Chuculate offered him a ride, but Sanders refused, which is kind of strange since it was raining."

Sadie returned to the counter and began to peel potatoes and chop them into bite-sized pieces. Then she did the same thing with a medium-sized onion.

"What does that prove?" she asked.

Lance took a swig of Pepsi. "Nothing," he said. "But I'm pretty sure Angus and Eugene Hawk lied to me about knowing Sanders."

"How do you know?"

"Instinct."

Sadie lit the fire under the same skillet she'd fried the pork chops in, and when it was hot she slid the potatoes and onions off the cutting board and into the hot pan. The sound of sizzling grease and the aroma of onions filled the kitchen.

"Did Mr. Chuculate say why he sold his land to Angus?"

"I don't think he did. He said the land belonged to his father and now it belonged to him, and when he was gone it would belong to his daughter."

"Then why is it in Angus's name at the courthouse? And, why is the trademark fence of the Buffalo Ranch going up around it? Uncle Eli and I saw a couple of men working on the fence again today. They were friendly. Eli showed them where the correct property line is and they seemed grateful."

Sadie opened a jar of home-canned green beans and dumped them into a saucepan before returning to stirring potatoes and onions.

"I don't know, Sadie."

"Don't you think we need to ask him?"

"Ask who?"

"Mr. Chuculate."

"I didn't have time to check on it today, but I will. In the meantime, I suggest you keep your nose out of it."

Sadie retrieved the pork chops from the oven and served them along with the potatoes, onions, and beans. Lance dug in like he hadn't eaten in a week.

"Did I tell you I ran into Becky Chuculate in the grocery store? She came home from California to spend some time with her dad." Sadie began to eat. "Maybe I'll mention it to her."

Lance ate in silence.

Sadie changed the subject. "What about the arrow? Any luck on finding out where it came from?"

"Not yet," Lance said. "All we know is, it is handmade."

"I saw Angus and another man target shooting with arrows this morning."

Lance frowned. "Oh, yeah? And, where was this?"

"I went for a horseback ride and went through the fence where it's down and followed the ridge for quite a ways. I don't really know how far, say, an hour or so. Ended up overlooking the Buffalo Ranch. Angus and some other guy in a red shirt, who looked a lot like Eugene Hawk, were target shooting with arrows," she said, and then added, "at a bale of hay."

Lance put his fork down. "You've got to be kidding me. One of these days you're going to get into more trouble than I can get you out of."

"Oh, you sound like Uncle Eli. He followed me and then scolded me like I was a four-year-old child for being up there. You men think I can't take of myself."

"You've had your moments."

"Well, I'm just saying, Angus and whoever was with him are pretty handy with arrows, and isn't that what we're looking for?"

"*I*," he said. "That's what *I'm* looking for, not *we*. I think Eli is right. That's not a good place for you to be."

They finished eating and Sadie placed the dishes in the sink. "Don't worry," she said. "As soon as the fence is back up, I'll be relegated to my own property."

She placed a plate on the table and peeled the foil back, revealing a stack of brownies. She leaned down and gave Lance a kiss. "Let's call a truce, eat some dessert, and have a romantic evening."

"Deal," he said, as he crammed a brownie in his mouth.

Chapter 20

Sadie pulled into the grocery store parking lot and sat in her vehicle trying to remember what her Aunt Mary had asked her to get. She thought until it finally came to her. "Baking powder," she said aloud, happy with her recollection.

A car parked beside her and she recognized Becky, Grover Chuculate's daughter. "How's it going?" Sadie said as they fell into step together and walked toward the store.

"Great," Becky said. "I have a job and a place to stay already."

"So, you're going to stay a while. That's great news."

"Yes, I've decided it might be a good idea to get back to my roots." Becky said, laughing.

"You're not going to stay with your dad?"

"Oh, I would, but his place is so tiny. And, I found this job that provides room and board."

"Really?" Sadie said. "Where?"

"The Buffalo Ranch." Becky sounded proud.

"The Buffalo Ranch?" Sadie tried to hide her alarm by turning away from Becky and retrieving a grocery cart. "Doing what?" she asked.

They pushed their carts into the store and stopped in an open area next to the produce department to talk. "I'm going to cook meals for the hunters and clean up after each group leaves. It shouldn't be too hard, and the pay is pretty good. As soon as I can save up enough money and I can afford a place of my own, I'll look for a better job." She smiled. "But for now, it's not that bad."

"I hope it works out for you," Sadie said. "In the meantime, let's get together and visit some more. You know you have to pass my house every time you drive from the Buffalo Ranch to town."

"Really? Which one is it?"

"It's the white house that sits on the north side of the road about five miles from the Buffalo Ranch. I've got a small barn and corral, and you can usually see Joe and Sir William in the pasture."

Becky gave her a curious look.

"My horse and goat," Sadie clarified. "The mailbox says 'Walela' on it. My uncle and aunt live next door; their mailbox is red with no name or numbers on it. Stop by anytime. I'd love to have you. Do you still have my card?"

"Yes, I think so. Thanks." Becky looked at her watch. "I've got to get going. Nice talking to you."

As Sadie watched Becky push her cart toward the meat department, she couldn't help but think Becky had made a big mistake.

As Becky pushed her cart through the grocery store, she thought about what she planned to prepare. The first group of hunters wasn't scheduled to arrive for another week, but Angus said he wanted to test her skills in the kitchen. He'd asked her to prepare the meal on a smaller scale so he and his wife could judge her performance.

Angus had suggested chili, and she agreed that would be easy enough to fix. He planned to tell the hunters it was buffalo chili, but he told her to make it with regular ground beef. He didn't think the hunters were smart enough to know the difference, and he was quite certain neither was his wife.

If that's what he wanted, Becky wasn't going to argue. She quickly collected everything on her list, made a beeline for the checkout counter, and then drove to the Buffalo Ranch, anxious to show her new employer what she could do.

She pulled her car behind the bunkhouse and parked next to the back door. She carried the groceries into the large kitchen and put the meat in the refrigerator. The rest of the items—onions, garlic, tomato juice, chili powder, and her secret ingredient, green chiles—remained on the large island in the middle of the kitchen, which would serve as her work area.

As she gathered her personal items and headed for her small apartment, she smiled to herself. If there was one thing in this world she was good at, it was making chili. Her mother had taught her how to cook at a young age, a skill she hadn't used much during her years in Bakersfield. Her ex-husband, Levi, never appreciated her cooking; instead, he preferred to eat at a fast-food restaurant or pick up a pizza on the way home, but she'd never forgotten the lessons her mother taught her, and she thought Angus would be pleased. She couldn't wait for him to taste her first meal as the cook for the bunkhouse.

When she threw her purse on the bed, she noticed someone had left a short dress there. It had been placed on the end of the bed for her to wear, she assumed. She picked it up and frowned. It looked like it was the right size, but it didn't look like anything she was prepared to wear. It reminded her of a distasteful version of a maid's uniform. The black dress with the white frilly apron was too short and low-cut for her taste.

"I don't think so," she said aloud as she threw it back on the bed.

"Now, come on." Angus's voice caused her to jump. "I think you'll look right nice in that little outfit," he said. "I know the hunters are going to like it."

The tone of Angus's words scared her and fear crept up her spine. She'd seen that look of aggression before, and suddenly she became painfully aware that he stood in the middle of the only exit from her apartment. Adrenaline surged through her when she realized she had no way to escape. Her father's words echoed in the back of her mind—*crazy yonega . . . you do not want to work for him . . . he is evil.*

Becky forced a smile. "Well, we'll see how it fits later. I've got some things to do in the kitchen right now."

She moved forward with confidence, hoping he would withdraw from the doorway and allow her to pass, but he didn't move a muscle. She turned and looked out the window. There were no other vehicles in sight. Where was his wife? Who would hear her if she screamed?

"How about you try it on right now . . . while I wait."

"I've got another errand to run first," she lied. "I just realized I forgot something at the grocery store."

"It can wait," he said, as he closed the door behind him and flipped the deadbolt.

Becky began to retreat, knowing there was nowhere to go in the small apartment. Angus unbuckled his belt and began to unzip his pants. She looked around for a weapon, anything she could use to protect herself, but the bare apartment yielded nothing useful. Becky's knees almost buckled.

"No," she begged. "I'll do anything you want," she said. "But not this."

Suddenly he pushed her on the bed and pinned her arms above her head. His hairy chest and arms felt like oily rubber. He wiped his sweaty nose against her cheek, and she tried to pull away. His foul body odor and kerosene-smelling breath made her gag. "No!" She screamed as loud as she could. Kicking and clawing with all of her strength, she struck a blow to his crotch with her knee and bit hard on his forearm.

"Ouch," he yelled. "You bit me."

He picked her up and slammed her head against the headboard. Then everything faded to black.

When Becky came to, it took her a minute to remember where she was in the dark room. Her head hurt. She touched the back of her head and discovered a tender bump and then remembered being thrown against the headboard. Her body hurt all over and her mind raced. Then the sudden memory of what had happened and the realization that she'd been raped rushed over her like a tsunami, sucking the air out of her lungs and crashing down on her heart and soul.

She moved as quickly as she could, throwing the maid's outfit on the floor in disgust. She caught a glimpse of herself in a small mirror hanging on the wall, and turned away as silent tears blurred her vision and streamed down her face.

Angus. Where was he? How long had she been out? She could see the lights on in the main house, but it was too dark to see any vehicles. She quickly pulled on her jeans and torn tee shirt. She had to get away from this place as fast as she could before he came back.

Blindly, she grabbed her purse and fled the tiny apartment, unwilling to stop and think who might be nearby to stand in her way. She jumped into the safety of her car and locked the doors. Thankfully, the engine roared to life when she turned the key in the ignition. Gravel scattered against the side of the bunkhouse as the tires spun and she flew toward the main road. She glanced in her rearview mirror, and seeing no lights behind her, she breezed out the entrance to the Buffalo Ranch and into the night.

Her headlights illuminated the road, but her path blurred as tears continued to spill onto her face. What was it with her? How could she put herself in such a vulnerable situation again? Her father had warned her about Angus, but she'd ignored him. Her bullheadedness could have gotten her killed.

A deer standing next to the road caused Becky to slam on her brakes. Her car skidded sideways and came to a stop before sliding into the ditch. She burst into tears. Where was she going? She couldn't go home; she could never tell her father what had happened. He didn't even know about the horrible incident in California, how a drug-crazed criminal had violently raped her at knifepoint as revenge for the discovery of her husband's undercover job. Now it had happened again. How could she tell her father and bring dishonor to him and the Chuculate name? Her life was falling apart.

She sat in silence for several minutes, assessing her situation. Angus obviously wasn't pursuing her or he would have already overtaken her and her old jalopy. She involuntarily glanced in the rearview mirror. He was so arrogant he had probably already written her off. In fact, he most likely thought she was still there in the bunkhouse cooking up fake buffalo chili.

She lifted her foot from the brake pedal and coaxed the car forward. Before long, a red mailbox with no name appeared on the left side of the road. She punched the accelerator and drove a short distance to the next mailbox—S Walela.

Sadie's words from the grocery store came to her . . . *white house . . . north side of the road . . . stop by anytime.*

She stopped and stared at the well-lit farmhouse and barn that sat off the road to the left, with a paint horse and a goat standing in the pasture. Then she nosed her car onto the lane that led to Sadie's house.

As she approached the house, Becky's car slowed to a creep. She recognized Sadie's car, and assumed the old blue farm truck sitting in knee-high weeds probably belonged to Sadie, too. She let her car roll to a stop behind Sadie's Explorer and, as was the custom, sat and waited, exposed by the illumination of a strategically placed pole light.

The back door opened and the biggest dog she'd ever seen came near her car, sat on his haunches, and silently stared at her. She could see Sadie standing in the doorway.

Becky lowered her window. "Sadie, it's Becky Chuculate. Please help me."

The dog disappeared and Becky opened the car door. As she tried to stand, a pain as sharp as a knife buried itself inside her. She could see Sadie rushing toward her as once again blackness enveloped her.

Sadie saw pain cross Becky's face and watched her legs move restlessly under the white hospital sheets as if she were trying to escape a bad dream. When Becky finally opened her eyes, Sadie could see confusion on her face. She stood where Becky could see her more easily.

"It's okay," Sadie said.

When Becky raised her arm and saw the IV attached to the top of her hand, the confusion in her eyes transformed into fear. "Where am I?"

"Sycamore Springs General Hospital. They got your appendix just in time. It was about to burst."

"My appendix?" Becky looked around the room and blinked her eyes as if trying to bring everything into focus. "Thanks, Sadie. I don't even know how I found you," she said. "It's like your mailbox came out of the night and beckoned. I didn't know what to do."

Lance walked into the room. "How'd you get in here, Sadie?" he said.

Sadie smiled. "I lied and told them I was her sister."

Lance chuckled and stood beside Sadie.

"What happened to you, Becky?" Sadie said. "The doctors say you might've been roughed up. They have to report that kind of thing, you know."

Becky raised her eyes and stared at Lance, as if afraid to speak.

"It's okay," Sadie said. "This is Lance Smith. He's a good friend. He can help you. He's the deputy sheriff."

"No," Becky said, sounding alarmed. "I don't want the police involved."

"It's okay," Lance spoke up. "We just want to help you. Who did this to you?"

Becky fingered the plastic spoon in the Styrofoam cup of ice chips on her bedside stand. She raised her hand to her face and felt a bandage above her eye, and touched the bump on the back of her head again. She was afraid to think how bad she must look.

"I need to find someplace to stay," Becky said.

"Don't worry about that," Sadie said. "We'll either find you a place or you can stay with me until you've healed."

Lance spoke again. "Who did this to you?"

"I don't want to file any charges. I just want it to go away. I've been raped before."

"Raped?" Sadie exclaimed. "Is that why you told me not to call your father on the way to the hospital? Did your father rape you?"

"No, no, no. My father knows nothing about what happened. But I can't let him see me like this and I can't go back to California. My home there is gone. I have nowhere to go."

"I thought you were staying at the Buffalo—" Sadie stopped mid-sentence and let out a long breath. "Damn it," she said. "That buzzard Angus Clyborn did this to you, didn't he?"

Becky covered her face with her hands and sobbed.

A young woman doctor walked into the room with a clipboard in her hand. She acknowledged Sadie and Lance with a nod and approached Becky. "Are you in pain?" she asked as she felt Becky's wrist for her pulse.

"I'm okay," she said, wiping her face with the edge of the sheet. "When can I get out of here?"

"Probably tomorrow," she said, "if you promise to take it easy and not lift anything that weighs more than a couple of pounds." The doctor nodded toward Sadie with knowing eyes, "And your sister will promise to take care of you."

Sadie glanced down when she realized her lie had been found out.

Lance stepped forward. "Doctor, can you perform an examination to confirm if she's been raped or not?"

The doctor looked toward Becky with concern, as a tear fell off Becky's cheek. "Yes, but she will have to sign a consent form." The doctor looked sympathetically at Becky and rubbed her arm. "Do you want to do that, honey?"

Becky pulled her arm away. "What's the point?" she said. "It won't make any difference."

"Yes, it will." Lance spoke in a soft, comforting tone. "If you don't take the rape test, there will be no evidence in case you want to file charges later. Everything will be kept confidential. No one will know except the doctor and us."

"I was married to a cop," Becky blurted. "I know how word gets out."

"No, Becky, that won't happen here." Sadie stepped closer and touched her arm. "You can trust Lance. I promise."

"I don't know what happened before," Lance said. "But I can guarantee you one thing—nothing will be exposed about this incident until you decide what you want to do. However, we need this test to ensure that you're okay and that the person who did this to you didn't give you anything that could cause problems for you later. Let the doctor take care of you. You can trust her and her staff, and you can trust Sadie and me." Lance touched Sadie's elbow. "We'll leave you here with the doctor to make your decision. I hope you'll let her help you."

Becky cried and nodded at the doctor as Lance and Sadie left the room.

Chapter 21

Angus parked in front of the Party Barn Bar, grasped an unlit stogy with the corner of his mouth, and marched into the place like he owned it. The dimly lit bar looked like it had been standing at least a century; the smell of greasy food and stale cigarette smoke permeated the wooden walls and floor. Rosy, a robust woman mixing drinks behind the bar, let out a laugh that echoed around the room and out the front door.

"Love you, baby." She boomed her trademark answer to everything and everyone.

Angus straddled an empty stool right in front of her and gave her a wink. "How's my favorite barmaid today?"

"That's bar *owner* to you, baby face," she said, her low-cut knit blouse straining to cover her breasts as she wiped the counter. "Ain't been no maids around here in a long time." She exaggerated the word "long" and then belted out another laugh. "You come for your regular?"

"Yeah," he said. "And bring me some lemonade."

"Drinking heavy, I see." Rosy scooped ice into a glass and filled it with lemonade.

Angus pulled out his lighter, lit his half-smoked cigar, and waited for her to slide the drink to him. When she did, he grabbed her hand. "That's okay, Rosy. I don't need a barmaid, because I've got my own gen-u-ine Indian maid. She's a looker and says she can cook. We'll be finding out if that is true when the next round of hunters show up in a week or so."

"Find out what?" Rosy razzed him as she pulled her hand away. "Whether she's a looker or whether she can cook?" Her laugh echoed throughout the bar before she disappeared into the kitchen. The men in the bar let out a room full of belly laughs.

A voice rose above the laughter. "Angus, you're so old and stove up, you wouldn't know a looker if one strolled in here and sat on your lap."

Laughter erupted again as Rosy reappeared through the swinging kitchen doors, dropped a plate piled high with fried catfish, French fries, and coleslaw in front of Angus, and then moved on to wait on two elderly Indian men who had settled quietly at a corner table.

Angus rested his cigar in a nearby ashtray and popped a cornmeal hushpuppy into his mouth with his fingers. The bar had a regular group of lunch customers, and although Angus sat among them every Monday and Friday for the weekly catfish special, he didn't relate to any of them. Sure, they would give him a hard time and act like they were his best drinking buddies, but they were, in his opinion, nothing but a bunch of local drunks, and if he had to guess, they probably lived off welfare. His tax dollars at work, he thought. He liked to have a drink from time to time, even though he wasn't supposed to, but unlike him, these men were nothing but a drain on society.

The man sitting two seats down from Angus piped up. "Tell us more about that Indian maid you've got, Angus."

Angus grinned and talked with a full mouth. "Oh, she's nice. Real nice."

"That's all you've got," the man shot back at Angus. "She's real nice?"

Angus stood up, pulled his elbows back, and thrust out his pelvis twice. When he sat back down, he noticed the two Indian men in the corner and gave them a half-hearted smile before turning his attention to one of three television screens strategically mounted on the wall behind the bar. He resumed eating.

Rosy slapped a ticket on the bar in front of Angus. "I'll take care of that when you're ready, sweetie."

Angus grinned and gave a nod to Rosy. She shouldn't be calling everyone sweetie, Angus thought. She might end up with more than she could handle.

When he'd finished eating, he dropped several bills on his ticket, swung around, and slid off his stool. He stood, adjusted his pants, and strode out of the bar past the empty corner table.

"See you Friday, Angus Baby," Rosy called out behind him.

After spending the night at Sycamore Springs General Hospital, the doctor announced to Becky she could go home. Home? Where was that, Becky wondered. She didn't plan on returning to the Buffalo Ranch as long as she lived, even for the few belongings she'd left behind, and secretly, she wished the whole place would be struck by lightning and go up in flames. That, or maybe a tornado could come along and wipe the entire ranch off the face of the earth, leaving nothing but barren dirt, as if Angus Clyborn and anything he owned had never existed. She knew it wasn't right to wish anyone harm, but right now she hated that man with every inch of her mind, body, and soul.

The closest thing to "home" was her father's place, but she couldn't let him see her until the cut above her brow had healed. She had ignored his warning, thinking she knew more than he did. If he saw her, she was afraid he'd immediately know what had happened, and she couldn't allow that. She'd lied to him on the phone, told him she'd had a little episode with her appendix, but that everything was fine, and promised to come see him when she felt better. She hoped he wouldn't detect the deceit in her voice like he always had when she was a teenager. She had changed since she escaped Delaware County and fled to California, but she wasn't sure she could ever change enough to fool her father.

Sadie burst through the hospital room door. "I'm here to spring you," she said. Her cheerful voice lit up the room as she placed a brown paper sack on the end of Becky's bed. "I brought you some clothes, too," she said.

"I don't know how to thank you, Sadie." She could feel tears pooling in her eyes.

"I thought we might wear about the same size, so I took the liberty of bringing you some of my clothes. I hope you don't mind. If they're too big, we can stop and pick up something for you at the best department store we have in Sycamore Springs—Walmart."

The two women laughed, something Becky hadn't done too much of lately. She liked Sadie and thought their budding friendship was the only good thing that had happened to her in a very long time.

"I guess I've got some decisions to make." Becky said. "I don't know what I'm going to do . . . or where I'm going to go."

"Well, I've been thinking about that," Sadie said. "How about we start with my place? I've already fixed up the extra bedroom. It's nothing fancy, but you're welcome to stay until you can decide what you want to do."

Becky nodded and wiped at her eyes. "I don't know what I would have done if you hadn't come into my life right now, Sadie." She smiled and looked away. "Thank you."

Sadie helped Becky get dressed and a young nurse magically appeared at the door with a wheelchair. "Hi, I'm Todd," he said. "When you're ready, I'll take you downstairs."

"Oh, please," Becky said. "I don't need a wheelchair."

"Sorry," he said. "Hospital policy."

Becky made a face.

"We don't want you fainting or falling down and hurting yourself," he said, and winked at her. "You might sue us." Then he flashed a beautiful smile.

"Oh, okay."

Becky reluctantly sat in the wheelchair, and Todd wheeled her to the elevator with great pomp and circumstance, beginning with a modified wheelie.

"No one said we couldn't have fun, though." He giggled behind her.

She forced a smile. Would she ever be receptive to a man flirting with her again?

When the elevator doors opened on the first floor, Sadie turned to Becky. "Since you're in such good hands, I'll go get the car." Then she disappeared through the sliding front doors.

Todd wheeled Becky out into the morning sunshine and set the brake on her chair. Spring had given way to summer almost overnight, and the midday sun felt good on Becky's face. There was something about the air in Oklahoma that made Becky feel at home. And for a short moment, she forgot the injuries to her body and spirit and thought how good it was to be back in the land where she grew up.

In a few short minutes, Sadie's Ford Explorer rolled to a stop in the circular driveway in front of Becky. Todd opened the passenger-side door and helped Becky get in.

"Thank you, Todd," Sadie said.

Becky carefully adjusted herself on the seat. The young man made a limp salute with his right hand, spun the wheelchair around, and reentered the facility. Sadie pulled the car out of the hospital parking lot and together they headed toward Eucha.

"How are you feeling, Becky?"

"I'm still a little sore, especially where they removed my appendix, but the doctor said that was normal." Becky stared out the window for a moment. "The doctor told me the rape had nothing to do with my appendicitis. She said the appendix was infected and would have had to come out anyway."

Sadie turned her vehicle toward Eucha Road. "Do you want to talk about what happened, Becky?"

"Not really." Becky thought for a moment. "I took your friend's advice and let the doctor do the exam." She turned toward Sadie. "He seems like a real nice guy."

Sadie smiled. "He is."

"I hope he was right about keeping it confidential. I don't think I could handle the humiliation of a trial."

Sadie kept her eyes on the road and said nothing.

"I was married to a cop, Sadie. I know how it works. If I file charges and he refuses to give them DNA, then they get a court order to get a blood sample. Even when they match his DNA, we still have to go to court. I say he raped me and slapped me around, and he says he has no idea what I'm talking about. He'll say it was consensual, it was a fling, and that I asked for it. It'll come down to my word against his, and from what I can tell he's a big shot around here, so where does that leave me? I can't see that it's worth it." She looked at Sadie. "Can you?"

"I don't know, Becky, but it seems a shame that Angus will get away with beating and raping you without any consequences. If I had to guess, I'd say you're not the first. Maybe someone else would come forward."

"And in the meantime, I'm convicted in the court of public opinion, because I was raped before, in California. It will eventually come out, and my father will be devastated. He doesn't know about the first rape, and I don't know if I can keep both incidents from him, but I'm going to try." Tears began to fall. "I don't want to talk about it anymore."

"Fair enough," Sadie said. "But, remember. You can trust Lance to do everything he can to help you, and nothing will be said until you decide whether to file charges, or not. I think you need some rest, and that's what you're going to get at my house."

"Thanks, Sadie."

Chapter 22

On Friday morning Sadie and Becky stopped by the travel agency to see if Beanie needed any help before they drove out to visit Becky's father. Becky had been in contact with Grover by phone, vague and evasive conversations, but they both knew he would get suspicious if she didn't show up in person before long.

When they entered the travel office, Beanie jumped out of her chair as if she could hardly contain her excitement. "Sadie, guess what!"

"You won the lottery?"

"No, but it's almost as good." Beanie's face glowed. "Cory's boyfriend went to the Cherokee Casino in Tulsa and won $1,250 on the slot machines. Isn't that exciting?"

Sadie laughed. "Yes, I guess it is, for him."

"Oh, no. It's for the Three Sisters" she said. "All lottery ticket and casino winnings go into the Three Sisters' pot."

"Oh, I see. So there's actually Three Sisters plus one more." Sadie couldn't help but get caught up in Beanie's excitement.

Becky looked confused. "Who are the Three Sisters?"

"Go ahead and tell her, Beanie, while I check my e-mail."

Beanie launched into an explanation of the Three Sisters, who they were, and their mission to buy a piece of property for back taxes and then flip it.

"And who, again, are the other girls?" Becky asked.

"Cory Whitfield, she works in the trust department at the bank, and Lucy Clyborn, she works at the bank, too, in the customer service department downstairs."

"Clyborn?" Becky's face dropped.

Sadie spoke up. "She was married to Angus's son, but he was recently killed in Afghanistan." Sadie paused for a moment and then continued her explanation. "Lucy was a Walkingstick before she got married, and she doesn't appear to have much in common with her in-laws."

"Oh."

"She's real nice," Beanie interjected. "And her in-laws are mean to her."

"What do you mean by that, Beanie?" Sadie asked.

"Lucy just found out that the deed to the land that pompous blowhard supposedly gave to her and Jason was never filed at the courthouse."

Sadie looked up from her computer. "Are you sure?"

"Yes. She never got a bill for the property taxes, and she didn't think she could trust Angus to pay them. That's when she found out. She even got her copy of the deed out of the safe deposit box. There are no stamps on it from the county clerk. Lucy knew that, but she just assumed he made the copy before the deed was filed, but in reality, the deed was never filed." Beanie fingered some papers on her desk and looked away. "I feel so sorry for Lucy. She told me she hated Angus Clyborn so much she could kill him." A look of alarm crossed her face as if she suddenly realized what she'd said.

Sadie tried to comfort her. "We all say things we don't mean when we're angry, and heaven knows that poor girl deserves to be angry."

"I know Lucy would never do anything like that," Beanie quickly added. "She's a real nice girl, even when she's angry."

"I'm sure she is," Becky said. "Maybe I can meet her and your other friend before long."

"Great idea," Beanie said, and turned to Sadie as if trying to erase what she'd said a few minutes earlier about her friend Lucy. "I'm fine here, Sadie. Will you be back today?"

Sadie looked at her watch. "Yes, we're going to make a quick trip to see her dad and then we'll be back."

Sadie began to replay events in her head as she and Becky drove in silence toward the home of Becky's father, Grover Chuculate. It had been two weeks since the traumatic event at the Buffalo Ranch had landed Becky in the hospital with a bruised body and a broken spirit, but she'd rebounded nicely. She'd been Sadie's perfect houseguest, and for the last couple of days she'd been helping out at the travel agency, running errands and answering the phone when Beanie was busy. Becky got along well with everyone who came in the agency, and Beanie had accepted her as if she were a lifelong friend. Beanie had already arranged a job interview for Becky with First Merc State Bank.

Sadie broke the silence. "Becky, you know if things don't work out for you with the bank, you can stay with me as long as you want. I can't pay you much for helping at the travel agency, but it's better than nothing."

Becky smiled at Sadie. "I don't know how I can ever thank you for everything you've done for me," she said. "But we both know this has to be a temporary arrangement. I've got to find a job that pays enough so I can get my own place. You and Lance need to get back to normal." Becky sighed. "I have to admit, though, I'm a little nervous about the interview."

"You'll do fine. I've already put in a good word for you with Thelma in the personnel department."

Becky's eyes lit up. "Really? You know someone there?"

"Yes," Sadie said. "Let's just say I have a colorful past with that bank."

Becky raised her eyebrow.

"Don't ask," Sadie said as she slowed the vehicle at the Chuculate mailbox. She glanced toward the small trailer in the distance. "It looks like your dad is waiting for you."

Becky lowered the visor in front of her and checked her face in the mirror.

"Don't worry. You look fine."

"I hope so," she said.

Sadie parked next to an old truck, and Grover, who had been sitting in a lawn chair under the awning, rose to meet them. Sadie got out, reached down, and patted the head of a friendly dog that greeted her with both suspicion and a wag of the tail. Becky made introductions and then they joined the old man in the two extra lawn chairs he had obviously set up for them around a campfire pit.

There were no hugs of greeting between father and daughter, but Sadie wasn't surprised. Grover reminded her of her own father—an elderly Cherokee man who, even though he had experienced many things in his life, held his emotions in check. He may not have shown affection outwardly, but at his age, Grover probably held lots of wisdom close to his heart, waiting for someone to come along to share it with.

Grover had prepared three tall glasses of iced tea and handed a glass to each woman. "I thought you forgot where I live," Grover began.

Oh, no, Sadie thought. Not the guilt trip.

"Of course not, Daddy." Becky sipped tea. "I've been busy. That's all. But, I wanted to come by so you could meet Sadie. I've been staying with her."

"Oh?" Grover sounded surprised. "What happened to your job at the Buffalo Ranch? I thought you were staying there."

"I didn't like it," Becky said, and quickly moved on. "I've been working at Sadie's travel agency the last few days, and I have a job interview tomorrow at a bank in Sycamore Springs." Becky looked at Sadie for support. "Sadie thinks I have a good chance of getting a job."

Sadie sat forward in her chair. "We're keeping our fingers crossed," she said. "It's no guarantee, but I gave her a personal reference with some folks I know there."

Grover stuck out his lower lip and nodded.

Sadie decided to change the subject. "I believe your father used to have some land behind my place. Is that right?"

Grover nodded again. "Yes." He held onto the arm of his lawn chair and turned toward Sadie. "There was a young man out here asking about that not long ago. A lawman from the sheriff's office."

Sadie didn't want to reveal that she knew about their conversation. "Was it Lance Smith, the deputy sheriff?"

Grover nodded. "That's the one," he said. "Do you know him?"

Sadie smiled. "Yes. I know him."

Becky spoke up. "I think it's more than 'know him.' You two are pretty serious, aren't you?" she said in a playful tone.

Sadie looked at the ground. "Well, yes. He's a neat guy. I like him a lot." Quickly recovering, she changed the subject. "Did you sell that land recently, Mr. Chuculate?"

"Grover," he growled. "Call me Grover." He adjusted himself in his chair. "No. Like I told your friend, it belonged to my father, now it belongs to me, and when I die it will belong to my daughter." He patted Becky on her knee. "It would be hard to live on that land, but it could be done. You could carve out a spot among the trees for a small home. You might think about that, Becky. We could pull a small trailer in there and you'd have your own place to live. We'd have to dig a well and put in a septic tank. There's a nice spring on that property. You might be able to draw water directly from it. It'd take a little doing, but it could be done."

Sadie tried to hide her disbelief at what Grover said. He obviously had no idea that piece of land had changed ownership, and she wasn't going to be the one to tell him, at least not until she could do some more research.

"Well, if you ever want an easement for a road through my land, all you have to do is say so and we'll do it."

Grover nodded again.

Wanting to leave that part of the conversation behind, and sensing that Becky wanted some time alone with her father, Sadie rose. "Do you mind if I check out your horses?" she asked.

Grover shrugged his shoulders and Sadie headed toward the corral, where four beautiful paint horses stood switching flies away with their tails. She parked her right foot on the bottom railing and rested her forearms on the top, admiring them. A stallion, almost completely covered in black except for a few white splotches across his shoulders and a white mane and tail, stood taller that the others. Another black-and-white gelding had equal parts of each color across his entire body, with a black mane and tail. The other two geldings had almost identical brown-and-white markings except one had a brown mane, the other mostly white. They both had brown tails tipped with white.

Sadie loved horses, especially paint horses—horses she believed to be more beautiful than all the other horses combined. The paint horse, she believed, was God's gift to the Indian people.

All four horses migrated toward Sadie, nudging each other's nose away to get closer to her, as if sensing her love for them. She rubbed their foreheads and combed their manes with her fingers, each horse taking their turn at the rail. She patted their necks and spoke softly to them. If Grover loved horses, he was okay in Sadie's way of thinking.

Sadie turned and watched Becky and Grover interacting from a distance. They were deep in conversation, and Sadie wondered if Becky was going to tell her father about her ordeal.

When they stood, Sadie took that as her cue to return to the circle. When she approached them, she could see that Grover was leaning on a walking stick, and she wondered how he could get around and take care of his horses.

When she got close, Grover reached toward Becky's cheek and Sadie could see fear in her face. Could he see the new scar above her eye?

"You have your mother's face," he said.

Sadie let out a long breath.

"Don't wait so long to come back," he added. "Okay?"

Becky appeared to be holding back tears as she nodded. Sadie shook Grover's hand and thanked him for the tea. "You've got some nice horses there, Grover. Do you still ride?"

Grover grinned and his eyes came alive as he gazed at the corral. "Oh, every once in a while," he said.

Sadie and Becky climbed into Sadie's car and headed back toward the travel office.

"That wasn't so bad, was it?" Sadie asked.

"His health is failing, Sadie." Becky's voice broke. "I may have waited too long to come back home. I don't think he's going to last much longer."

They rode in silence, Sadie lost in her own thoughts as Becky stared aimlessly out the window.

Sadie parked her car in front of the travel office and turned to Becky. "Would you mind coming to the courthouse with me? There's something I want you to see."

"Sure."

Sadie checked on Beanie and, confident everything was okay, she and Becky walked down the block toward the county building. Once inside, Sadie directed Becky to the county clerk's office. Renny, the same young girl with the oversized glasses who had helped Sadie before, recognized her and walked to the counter.

"Oh, Renny, I'm so glad you're here," Sadie said. "I have more questions about the area I was looking at before. Can you help me?"

"Of course. Follow me."

Sadie and Becky followed Renny through the maze of shelves to the table with three computers clustered on it. On the wall behind the computers hung the large map Sadie had seen before.

"I'm sorry to be such a pest," Sadie said, "but can you show me again how to look up the ownership of the land that is adjacent to mine?"

"No problem. I'm glad to have something to do."

Renny sat in front of one of the computers and her fingers flew across the keyboard. "Walela, is that right?"

"Yes, ma'am," Sadie said. "Can you show me the property directly behind mine first?" She stepped to the map and pointed at the area.

"Oh, okay." In a few short minutes Renny had brought up the legal description of the property. "Same as I told you before. The owner is Anton Clyborn."

"That can't be," Becky said. "That's my father's land. It's in the name of Chuculate. Grover Chuculate."

Renny's large brown eyes shifted to Becky. "Are you sure he didn't sell it? I think it changed ownership a few months ago." She began to type again. "Just a minute, and I'll show you a copy of the deed that's on file."

A few seconds later a document appeared on the computer screen. "See? Grover Chuculate deeded it to Anton Clyborn on February twenty-fourth."

Becky looked stunned. "I don't believe it," she said. "That's wrong."

"Hold on and I'll print a copy for you." Then she stopped and looked at Becky. "It'll cost a dollar a page."

"That's okay," Sadie spoke up. "Print away." She pointed at the map again. "And, while you're at it, can you also print copies of the deeds to these surrounding properties?"

"No problem. Just give me a minute. If you want to wait up front, I'll bring them to you."

Sadie and Becky quietly filed into the waiting area and sat down, Becky staring into space as if she were in shock. In a few short minutes, Renny appeared with several printed pages and spread them across the counter.

"Here they are, in date order," she said. "It looks like most of them were notarized in the last six months or so. And, interestingly enough," she added, "they were all notarized by the same notary."

"Let's see." Sadie turned the pages toward her. "Do you happen to know this notary, Renny?"

"Virginia Blackburn. I'm pretty sure she works for Eugene Hawk. You know, the tribal councilor?"

Sadie blinked twice. "Some of this property changed ownership through the process of quiet title?"

Renny nodded her head. "It looks like it."

"What are these documents from the Bureau of Indian Affairs?" Becky asked.

"When Indian land, or land originally allotted to tribal citizens, is transferred to non-Indians," explained Renny, "the BIA has to sign off on it."

"Can we take these copies with us, Renny?" Sadie asked.

"They're all yours as soon as you give me sixteen dollars."

Sadie rummaged in her purse and pulled out a twenty-dollar bill. "Keep the change, Renny. You've been very helpful."

"Gee, thanks." Renny smiled. "Come back anytime."

As they walked out into the hall, Becky grabbed Sadie's arm. "Wait," she said, stopping Sadie in mid-stride.

They moved out of the way of several men in suits passing in the hallway. "Don't worry, Becky. We'll get to the bottom of this."

Anger flashed across Becky's face. "I've decided to file charges against Angus for raping me and for stealing my land. If that bastard thinks he can take whatever he wants from my family and me, and get away with it, well, he's wrong. Dead wrong."

Hawk ended the call, dropped his cell phone in his shirt pocket, and cursed. He was beginning to hate John Henry Greenleaf. It had been the chief's idea to steal a few buffalo from the free shipment being sent to the Cherokee Nation. They would hide the bison, he'd said, and then secretly sell them to a ranch in North Dakota and split the money.

But it had been up to Hawk to forge a relationship with Angus to hide the animals on the Buffalo Ranch. Now, he hated the day he'd first shook hands with Angus Clyborn. Angus had demanded to keep a few of the bison for the hunting ranch, along with a cut of the money for hiding the buffalo. Then he'd taken over the operation by hiring Kenny Sanders to facilitate the transfer of the bison from Yellowstone to Oklahoma through an outfit in Wyoming called Travers Bison Ranch. They were to deliver most of the herd to the Cherokee Nation and then drop off a few extra at the Buffalo Ranch for Angus, Greenleaf, and Hawk. No one would think anything about buffalo arriving at Clyborn's ranch, and then Hawk would doctor the original documentation so the animals couldn't be traced. Not even the employees at the tribe would know.

Now Chief Greenleaf was waffling, wanting to know how he could get some of the buffalo transferred back to the Cherokee Nation. Hawk didn't know if the chief was getting cold feet or was just stupid; at the moment, he thought the latter seemed more accurate.

He couldn't believe the Cherokee people had fallen for Greenleaf's lies and reelected him to a second term. Greenleaf was ruthless, and Hawk knew that if any of this came unraveled the chief would throw him to the wolves without a second thought, along with anyone else who got in the way.

He hadn't mentioned the white calf to Greenleaf. No telling what the money-grubbing chief would do with that information. He'd probably put the animal in a pen and sell tickets to his own Cherokee people to see it—even sadder, thought Hawk, they would probably go for it.

No, the white calf was a problem he had taken on his own shoulders and now he had no idea what to do about it. All he knew was he couldn't let Angus put it up for the highest bidder to be hunted down and stuffed. He could secretly move it back to the Cherokee Nation's herd and let them deal with it, but if he was going to do that, he was going to have to hurry. The calf was growing every day, and it wouldn't take a wizard to tell that it wasn't exactly a newborn anymore. How was he going to explain its magical appearance?

He guided Pepper into the trailer for another ride north to check on the buffalo cow and calf. He'd decided this time he would leave Pepper there. He was getting tired of transporting the horse back and forth, and Pepper could keep the cow and calf company. Then all he'd have to do is keep delivering food to the animals until he could come up with a solution to his mounting problems, and at the top of that list was the biggest problem of all—Angus Clyborn.

Chapter 23

Sadie folded the copies Renny had given her and shoved them into her purse. Her mind churned. She hated Angus Clyborn. He'd never been a part of the local community; he looked down at everyone and exuded such arrogance she wished he'd go back to wherever he'd come from. She had felt in her gut something was wrong with Angus's land grabbing from the beginning, and she was right.

"What are we going to do, Sadie?" Becky hurried to keep up with Sadie's quick steps. "He can't get away with this, can he?"

"We're going to expose the old goat for the criminal he is, that's what we're going to do."

Sadie pushed through the front door of Paradise Travel and strode to her desk. "Pull up a seat, Becky."

Beanie looked up from her computer screen. "Everything okay, Sadie?"

"It will be," Sadie said. "It will be."

Beanie answered the phone and Sadie began her computer search. Becky pulled her chair next to Sadie and watched.

"First, we're going to see if we can locate the other property owners listed on these deeds. Call them off to me."

One by one, the women searched for names. All but two, Becky's father and the man Sadie had recently seen on the courthouse steps, brought up obituaries.

"Damn, he's been forging dead people's names." Becky sounded exasperated.

"Every one of these obituaries list survivors," Sadie said, pushing her seat away from her desk. "And it looks like they all live out of state. They would have no idea what's going on with their ancestors' land."

Becky smoothed her hair behind her ears. "So, what do we do now?"

Sadie shuffled through the copies of documents again. "Look at this, Becky. Not only is the notary the same on all of these, but it looks like the signatures of the landowners have a striking resemblance."

"I think the same person forged all of these names, don't you?" Becky stared at the pages. "Why didn't somebody catch this?"

"I doubt either the county clerk or the BIA would question signatures that had been notarized, and unless the documents came across the same person's desk at the same time, no one would notice the similarities." Sadie turned to Beanie. "Beanie, do you know someone named Virginia Blackburn? I think she may work in Eugene Hawk's office."

"Yes, Virginia Blackburn was in my graduating class. I've heard of Eugene Hawk, but I don't know him personally."

"How well do you know Virginia?"

"Not very," Beanie said. "I remember she got in trouble for turning in a paper she got off the Internet. She got suspended and almost didn't graduate."

"Sounds like a fine, upstanding woman," Becky interjected.

"Would you know her handwriting?" Sadie asked.

"No." Beanie shook her head.

Sadie stood and began to pace, and then stopped mid-stride. "Beanie, does Lucy have access to signature cards at the bank?"

Beanie smiled. "She sure does. You want me to see if Virginia is a customer?"

"No, I don't want to get anyone in trouble."

"Not a problem." Beanie picked up her cell phone, but Sadie stopped her.

"Wait. I need to think this through," Sadie said.

Beanie placed her phone next to the computer and watched as Sadie paced in front of her desk.

"It's not Virginia's signature we need to see," Sadie said. "We need to figure out who forged the signatures that Virginia notarized." She dropped into one of the empty chairs facing Beanie and chewed on her lip before speaking again. "If Eugene Hawk is working the legal, or maybe I should say illegal, end to acquire these parcels of restricted land, then he's going to need someone he trusts to actually forge the signatures." Sadie looked at Becky and then back at Beanie. "Wonder who else works in Eugene Hawk's office?"

"I have no idea. I've never been in that office," Beanie said.

Sadie stood and walked to the front glass door of the travel agency and pointed with her head. "It's right there next to the drugstore, right?"

Beanie nodded, and Becky sat quietly staring into space.

"I've got an idea." Sadie walked to her desk, opened an empty manila folder, and began to fill it with travel brochures, business cards, and a yellow legal pad. Next, she pulled out her purse, applied some fresh lipstick, and ran a brush through her hair.

"What are you going to do, Sadie?" Beanie asked.

Sadie headed through the front door with the folder under her left arm. "Punt," she said.

Sadie strode up the sidewalk, crossed the street, and arrived in front of an antique-looking door with the words "Robert Eugene Hawk, Attorney at Law" emblazoned in ornate lettering on the glass. She took a deep breath and entered.

A young woman sat behind a metal desk talking on the phone. When she saw Sadie, she hung up. "May I help you?" she asked.

Sadie smiled. "Oh, I hope so. Ann, is it?" she said, nodding toward the nameplate sitting on the corner of the woman's desk.

The woman nodded. "Yes."

"I manage the Playin' in Paradise Travel office down the street." She extracted a business card from her folder and handed it to the young woman. "My company is giving away a trip to Maui, and I'm trying to get everyone signed up. Have you ever been to Hawai'i?"

Ann's face lit up. "Oh, I'd love to win a trip to Hawai'i," she said, and then she frowned. "What's the catch?"

"No catch," Sadie's heart began to pound. "All you have to do is write down your name, address, and phone number, then I'll enter your name in the contest—when you win we'll give you a call."

"Really? That's it?"

Sadie pushed the legal pad in front of her. "Just sign right there at the top of the page."

Ann began to write.

Sadie looked for other employees, but all she could see was an empty hallway. "Is there anyone else in the office you think might want to enter?" she asked.

"Ginny and Dot. Hold on." Ann picked up the phone. "Ginny, can you and Dot come up front for a moment?"

An Indian woman, her long black braid draped in front of her left shoulder, appeared and stood next to Ann's desk. "Dot's on the line with John Henry, uh, I mean, Chief Greenleaf," she said. "She'll be here in a minute." She turned to Sadie and offered her hand. "Hi, I'm Virginia."

Sadie immediately recognized Virginia, or Ginny as Ann had referred to her, as one of the women who had been with Chief Greenleaf at Jason Clyborn's funeral.

"Hello." Sadie introduced herself, gave her a business card, and explained the contest to win a trip to Maui.

An older Indian woman appeared and stood next to Virginia. "What's this I hear about a trip to Hawai'i?"

"You must be Dot," Sadie said.

"Dorothy," the woman said as they shook hands.

Sadie repeated her sales pitch, explaining how everyone should go to Maui at least once and how this was the opportunity of a lifetime. Each woman took their turn adding their name, address, and phone number to Sadie's makeshift prize entry form.

"Do you mind if I leave some brochures here for your customers?"

"I'll take them," Dorothy said, extending her hand. "I'll have to run it by Mr. Hawk first."

"Great." Sadie handed a stack of promotional material to her, concluding that, as the oldest of the three, Dorothy, or Dot as her coworkers addressed her, seemed to be in charge. "Thank you and good luck," Sadie said.

She left the law office and retraced her steps back to Playin' in Paradise. Beanie and Becky stood waiting at the front door.

"What happened?" Becky asked.

"Yeah, what did you do?" Beanie added.

Sadie produced her legal pad. "I have three women's handwriting, but there's a problem."

Becky took the pad from her. "What is it?"

"They printed instead of signing their names."

"I guess we're back to plan A, then," Beanie said. "Only this time, we're looking for signers for the Eugene Hawk Law office. Right?" She picked up the phone and dialed.

Sadie raised her eyebrow. "I don't want to get Lucy in trouble."

"No one has to know," Beanie said. In a few seconds, she was explaining to Lucy what she needed.

Becky and Sadie listened quietly to the conversation.

When Beanie hung up, she grinned. "Lucy said Cory will have it for you. All you have to do is go to her desk on the second floor and she'll have a copy of the signature card for you in an envelope. Lucy's got a line of customers this afternoon and she didn't want to fax it because the fax machine keeps everything in memory."

Sadie grabbed her purse and ran out the door. When she got to the bank, she slid through the door and waited for two men in matching khaki pants and navy blazers to exit the elevator before entering and riding to the second floor. When the elevator doors opened and her sandaled feet sunk into the thick carpet, she felt like she'd landed in a completely different place of business. She remembered from her earlier days of working at the bank how the trust department catered to the money crowd and, in doing so, worked at projecting an image of privilege.

The office looked empty except for Cory and a young college-aged receptionist. The receptionist smiled and started to speak, but Cory quickly rose and met Sadie.

"Sadie, it's so good to see you," she said.

Sadie took Cory's hands in hers. "Cory, how have you been? How's your mother?"

The receptionist dismissed the two women and went back to stuffing envelopes.

"We are all well," she said. "Thanks for asking, Sadie. Please have a seat." Cory guided Sadie to a chair next to her desk.

"Where is everybody?" Sadie asked as she scanned the empty office.

Cory looked at her watch. "Everyone leaves by four o'clock on Friday for happy hour at the Party Barn."

Sadie grimaced. "Isn't that bar a little grimy for the three-piece-suit crowd?"

"You'd think so." Cory rolled her eyes. "But, in my opinion, they're all a little grimy beneath those silk ties. I can't wait until I can get out of this place and find a real job."

"If I can ever help you, please let me know," Sadie said.

"Oh, I will. Beanie tells me all the time how great it is to work for you. Maybe someday I can sell Hawaiian vacations, too."

"Oh, I'd love that," Sadie said and then raised her voice for the benefit of the receptionist. "So, do you have any brochures?"

Cory smiled. "Of course." She slipped an envelope across the desk toward Sadie. "I think you'll find everything you need here."

Sadie took the envelope and slid it into her purse.

"Is there anything else I can do for you, Sadie?"

"No. I really appreciate this. Please stop by Playin' in Paradise anytime."

"I will. Have a good day."

Sadie left the plush trust department behind and didn't stop until she was safely inside the travel office again. She walked to her desk, pulled the envelope from her purse, ripped it open, and stared at it.

"Bingo," she said. "I believe we're on our way to proving who forged those documents."

"Yay!" Beanie sang.

Becky smiled and clapped.

"I've got a question, Sadie," Beanie said. "What if Virginia and the others find out you were lying about the trip to Maui?"

"I didn't lie," Sadie said. "Go to the main website and look. They always have a sweepstakes going to win a free trip. In fact, it will be your job to get these three ladies signed up." Sadie handed the legal pad to Beanie.

Beanie laughed. "Wouldn't it be hysterical if one of them actually won a free trip?"

The three women laughed together.

"Yes," Sadie said. "I guess it would."

Chapter 24

The static on Lance's radio disturbed his thoughts. He grabbed the transmitter and interrupted the white noise. "Go ahead," he said.

The voice of the dispatcher broke through. "We have a report of a man walking around at the sale barn carrying a rifle. No incident yet."

"On my way." Lance made a U-turn in the middle of the highway and headed north on Highway 59 toward the Delaware County sale barn, which was located halfway between the small towns of Jay and Grove. It was the only sale barn in the county and, on sale day, drew hundreds of ranchers and farmers wanting to either buy or sell livestock. While it wasn't unusual for country folks in northeastern Oklahoma to carry a firearm, brandishing one in a large crowd didn't seem like a good idea to Lance.

Lance pulled his truck off the highway and drove through the parking lot on two sides of the facility before parking near the front door. He got out, looked around, and entered the arena.

The smell of fresh dirt and manure hung in the air, and the coolness of the morning still clung to the inside of the concrete building. The sale always started early on Saturday morning so the livestock could be loaded and hauled away by early afternoon. By now, at nine thirty, most of the good buys had already been paraded through the arena while the auctioneer jabbered, trying to run up the price of each one. Lance could see young and old men alike anxiously making bids, all trying to appear nonchalant. He noticed one old man pull a roll of cash out of his bib overalls to make payment on the spot for his final bid for a red mare. No gun-toting going on that Lance could see.

Lance walked to the cashier's window, where an older woman with carrot-colored hair and unusually long nails flicked bills from one hand to the other before wrapping a rubber band around each stack and dropping it in a drawer. She looked at Lance and smiled big. "May I help you?"

"Yes, ma'am. I got a call that someone was walking around out here with a rifle. Do you know anything about it?"

"No, but I heard Raymond talking about it." She picked up another handful of bills and pointed with her head at a pudgy white man wearing a black cowboy shirt and a hat to match, standing near the edge of the arena. "Ask him," she said. "He runs the place."

Lance thanked her and headed toward the man she'd indicated. He stood by the man for a minute, watching the crowd before he spoke. "Are you Raymond?" he asked.

The auctioneer's voice boomed throughout the building. "Take a look at this nice buckskin gelding. Who'll start the bidding on this beautiful horse?"

Raymond nodded, pointed at his ear, and started for the door. Lance followed.

Once outside, Raymond spoke first. "If there's going to be trouble between Roy Carter and Angus Clyborn, I don't want it going on here at the sale barn."

"What kind of trouble?"

"Roy Carter's herd has been quarantined. They've got Bang's and he's blaming Angus for bringing it in with his buffalo. Angus likes to hang out here on sale day. I don't know why because he never buys anything, but Roy's been walking around carrying his rifle looking for Angus. I've never seen Roy so mad. I think he'd shoot anything that got in his way."

"What's going to happen to Carter's cattle?" Lance asked.

"They'll be sold for slaughter."

"I thought you said they were diseased."

"They are, but the meat can be processed because cooking kills the bacteria."

Lance made a face. "Remind me never to eat another rare steak." He looked away, scrutinizing the area. "He'd shoot a man over losing his cattle?"

"Yes, sir." Raymond pushed the brim of his hat up about an inch. "Roy's been building up that herd for a few years and they're damn near like pets to him. The look in his eyes scared me, and quite frankly, I don't scare that easily."

"How exactly does a man's entire herd come down with Bang's?" Lance asked.

"It's spread through the placenta when a cow has a calf. As I understand it, the other animals either aspirate or ingest it by sniffing at the afterbirth. It can spread through a herd like wildfire."

"I know, but aren't ranchers required to vaccinate their cattle for that disease?"

"Well, they're supposed to, but it's the rancher's choice to vaccinate. We document every animal that comes through this sale barn." Raymond walked over to one of the pens and pointed. "See that black cow over there? She's got an orange metal tag in her left ear. That means she's been vaccinated for brucellosis. That's Bang's disease, you know."

Lance nodded. "But you're saying cattle can come in from out of state and might not be vaccinated?"

"They're not supposed to, but you know how that goes. You can't catch them all, especially if they truck them in on back roads at night."

"So what's the chance Roy Carter's right?" Lance asked. "Could Angus have brought brucellosis in to his game ranch and it spread from there?"

"Oh, I suppose anything's possible, but I don't think so. Angus would have had to show proof that his animals had been tested before they crossed the state line."

Lance continued to scan the area. "Do you have any idea where Roy is now?"

Raymond walked into the parking lot and pointed at the corner of the building. "He parked his truck over there, but it's gone now. I'm hoping he cooled off and left."

"Ford Ranger?"

"Yeah, it's a white Ford."

Lance shook hands with Raymond. "Okay, I'll take it from here. Thanks."

Raymond returned to the sale barn, and Lance began to walk the perimeter of the parking lot, circling the arena and the livestock pens. He asked several ranch hands if they'd seen a man with a rifle. Two nodded and described Roy Carter. The other, a Hispanic man wearing worn leather chaps, shook his head and walked away.

Lance spent another thirty minutes searching the area, inside and out, then got in his truck and headed toward Roy Carter's ranch, hoping to find Roy and calm him down. He knew Roy assumed that brucellosis had spread to his ranch from Angus's Buffalo Ranch, but that didn't give Roy the right to be judge, jury, and executioner of Angus Clyborn. Lance thought if he could talk to Roy, explain the situation, it might save him some police work later on.

He drove across the cattle guard, parked near the Carter house, and visually searched the area surrounding the nearby barn. He couldn't see Roy's truck, which wasn't a good sign, but decided to see if anyone was at home anyway. Before he could exit the vehicle and approach the front porch, the door opened and a middle-aged woman appeared. She looked scared.

"Please tell me you're not delivering bad news," she said.

Lance stopped at the bottom of the steps. "No, ma'am. I'm looking for Roy. Is he around?"

The woman looked relieved. "No, I'm sorry, he's not here." She shoved her hands into the pockets of her jeans. "May I ask what this is about?"

"Are you Mrs. Carter?"

"Yes, forgive my manners." She seemed to relax, smiled, and took her hands out of her pockets. "I'm Marci Carter."

Lance acknowledged her with a nod. "I understand you lost your herd to Bang's," he said.

"I don't know exactly what happened. All I know is Roy had the vet out and then the next thing I knew he was loading up all the cattle and hauling them off. He was pretty mad when he left here this morning."

"Do you know where he might be?"

"Not really." She crossed her arms. "What did he do?"

"Nothing serious, yet," Lance said, and then added, "I hope." He took a business card from his shirt pocket and handed it to Marci. "When he comes home, would you mind asking him to call me?"

Marci took the card and nodded. "Will do," she said, turned, and disappeared into the house.

Lance drove away from the Carter's ranch and headed back toward town. He hoped the rifle-toting Roy Carter didn't end up creating yet another problem for him.

Chapter 25

The Monday morning sunshine disappeared and storm clouds began to gather, threatening to bring more showers to the Eucha area. Not wanting to wake Becky, Sadie quietly climbed out of bed and stumbled to the kitchen, where she hit the button on the coffee maker. She needed caffeine. While she waited for the first cup of energy to drip into the pot, she raised the aluminum foil on the pan of leftover brownies and helped herself to one. She didn't know what was better—coffee or chocolate.

After taking the last bite of the brownie, she licked her fingers and then moved to the sink to wash her hands. She gazed out the window that gave her a view of the upper pasture behind her house, the same place where Kenny Wayne Sanders had been found dead. A thin veil of fog clung to the treetops, giving the entire hillside an eerie look.

She turned her attention to the coffeepot, filled her favorite mug with freshly brewed coffee, added sugar and cream, and then returned to the window. As she sipped coffee, she contemplated the murdered man and recent events. She knew they had to be related, and not being able to figure it out frustrated her. She knew Sanders and Angus had known each other in the past, but she also realized that proved nothing. She wished she could be more like Lance. He took everything in stride. Part of being a lawman, she supposed.

The mysterious change in ownership and forged deeds of so much land and the empire Angus seemed hell-bent on amassing—all for killing animals for fun—made her stomach turn. Lance wasn't going to like the way she'd accumulated that information, but he'd get over it. She couldn't let Angus get away with stealing land.

Reflecting on a long conversation she'd had the night before with Becky, who now wanted to bring rape charges against Angus, Sadie couldn't help but think it would be an uphill battle. At least Becky had agreed to the rape test when she was in the hospital, meaning they had physical evidence. But, Angus was slicker than a mud-covered pig sliding his way through life, doing whatever he pleased, regardless of how it affected other people, and never paying for any of the wrongs he'd committed. The man had no conscience, and she hoped it wouldn't cause more pain for Becky.

Movement at the top of the hill caught her eye, and she strained to see through the fog. Probably a deer, she thought. Then she saw it again. She almost spilled her coffee when she realized it was a buffalo. Was it on her side of the fence? Or the other side of the fence? Had the workers already finished installing the new fence?

She put her coffee cup down and rummaged in the hall closet for her binoculars. By the time she returned to the window, the fog had thickened, obscuring her view even more. Through the strong lenses, she searched for the animal, and then she thought she saw a calf. The contrast between the brown mother buffalo and the cream color of the calf took her breath away.

Hurriedly, she dressed and left a note for Becky. She snatched her raincoat off a nail by the back door and ran to the barn. In only a few minutes, she had bridled Joe, climbed onto his bare back, and rode him out of the corral toward the upper pasture. As light rain began to fall, she whistled and Sonny appeared, obviously eager for an outing, raining or not.

The rain fell harder as they headed up the hill to the top of the ridge where she'd seen the buffalo. Joe trudged slowly and Sadie remained alert, suddenly aware of a feeling of being watched. Then she remembered her dream, and it gave her a chill.

Joe reared . . . Sonny growled and attacked . . . horse came running toward them at full speed . . . she ran to Sonny's lifeless body just as Joe began to fight with another horse . . . the stallions screamed and bit at each other . . . hoofs pounding . . .

It was just a dream, she told herself as she shook off the memory and called to Sonny.

"Stay close," she demanded, and he did.

When she reached the area where Kenny Wayne Sanders had died, she could see the completed fence—too high for her to climb over. She wondered why it took such a tall fence to secure buffalo, since she didn't think they could jump all that high. And quite frankly, she thought, given its size and strength, a full-grown bison could walk right through about any fence someone could erect.

She stayed on Joe's back, and with Sonny trotting alongside, she rode up and down her side of the fence. Where did the buffalo go? Was she hallucinating? Did she want there to be a white buffalo calf so bad, she had imagined seeing it? She could see a piece of silver metal on the other side of the fence. It looked out of place.

She jumped off of Joe and got as close to the fence as she could to see what it was. She thought it might be an ear tag, the kind used to identify animals. In this case, she assumed, to identify a buffalo. She could see a tuft of brown hair caught in the fence and assumed the animal had been scratching an itch and lost its ear tag in the process.

Sonny ran up beside her and pushed his nose under her arm. "I want that, Sonny," she said, as she searched for something to retrieve it with through the fence. She located a fallen tree branch and snapped off a slender portion, then returned to the fence and tried to reach the ear tag. It took several tries and a contorted body, but she was finally able to drag it toward the fence.

As she nudged the piece of metal closer, Sonny whimpered as if he wanted to help but didn't know how. Finally, she pulled it under the fence with her fingers. It was stained with what looked like dried blood and stamped with letters and numbers that made no sense to her. She shoved it in her pocket and looked around. A chill ran down her spine as, once again, she felt someone's presence. She quickly mounted Joe and reined him toward the house, encouraging Sonny to stay close.

Lightning cracked, and a tree limb split and fell in the distance. With adrenaline pumping and the images of her dream flying through her head, she yelled at Sonny. "Home!" She dug her heels into Joe's flanks and tore down the hillside. Sonny ran ahead, and when they reached the bottom of the hill, Sadie pulled Joe to a trot and then a walk. She called Sonny to her side as she turned and looked at the top of the hill where they had been moments before. For a moment she thought she saw the rear of a paint horse disappear like a ghost in the fog. With trembling hands, she guided Joe toward the barn.

After taking care of the horse, she reentered the kitchen and found Becky dressed and sitting at the kitchen table with a coffee mug in her hand.

"Good morning," Becky said.

"Good morning to you, too," Sadie replied, as she hung her raincoat on a peg by the back door and grabbed a towel to dry her face. "I see you found the coffee."

"I did." Becky eyed Sadie with a curious look. "Are you okay? It's kind of wet to be out riding, isn't it?"

Sadie relaxed. "Yes, and I just scared myself to death."

"What happened?"

"Oh, I think my imagination got out of hand, is all," she said, thankful for Becky's presence.

She always felt safe with Lance around, but he had a lot going on and hadn't been spending as much time there since Becky had become a guest.

"Say, Becky, when you were at the Buffalo Ranch, did you ever see a white buffalo calf?"

"A white calf?" A questioning look crossed Becky's face. "No, but I wasn't really paying much attention to the animals. Does that monster have a white buffalo calf?"

"I'm not sure," Sadie said. "I thought I saw one on his ranch not long ago, a newborn. Maybe I was mistaken."

"White buffalo are pretty rare, aren't they?"

"Extremely," she said, "but, like I said, I think I must be mistaken, so I'd appreciate it if you didn't mention it to anyone. If a rumor like that got started, it could cause all kinds of havoc." Sadie thought for a moment. "What about ear tags? Did you see any buffalo with ear tags?" She pulled the piece of metal out of her pocket. "Like this?"

Becky shook her head. "No."

Sadie turned the ear tag over in her hand. "What do you think these numbers and letters mean?"

Becky sipped coffee. "I have no idea."

"Do you know anyone who would?"

"Your computer?"

Sadie looked at the clock on the stove. "I've got to get to the office, and you've got an interview. Let's hurry."

The two women showered, dressed, and drove to Playin' in Paradise in record time. When they walked through the back door, Beanie greeted them with her usual bubbly smile.

"Good morning," she sang.

Sadie laughed. "Are you ever in a bad mood, Beanie?"

"Bad mood? Not today. I just won three dollars on a scratch-off ticket."

"I hate to be a spoilsport, but how much did it cost you to win three dollars?"

Beanie stuck out her lower lip. "You can't look at it like that. A win is a win."

"Oh, I see." Sadie lowered her chin and mustered her most motherly look. "Don't get in so far you can't get out, okay?"

"I won't." Beanie looked relieved when the phone rang.

Sadie grinned at Becky as she switched on her computer. "You've got a little while before your interview. Let's see what we can find out."

Becky pulled up a chair and together they began to search for information on animal ear tags. After several minutes of pulling up websites, Sadie finally thought she'd found something.

"It looks like the first two numbers identify the state the animal came from." Sadie fingered the metal tag. "This one starts with eighty-three."

"What state does eighty-three stand for?" Becky asked.

"I'm not sure," Sadie said. "Wait, here's a chart." Sadie studied the computer screen for a moment. "Wyoming. Eighty-three stands for Wyoming."

"I don't get it," Becky said. "We're in Oklahoma, not Wyoming."

"True," Sadie said. "It means the animal that lost this ear tag came from Wyoming."

"Oh. So what do the other letters and numbers mean?"

"I'm not sure, but I know who can help us." She picked up the local phone book. "Do you remember Brad Newsom?"

"I do." Becky tilted her head and stared into space. "He was in your high school class, wasn't he? Real good-looking guy with light-colored hair." Then she laughed and turned her attention back to Sadie. "And, he never gave me the time of day."

Sadie thumbed through the blue pages, and then picked up the phone and dialed. "Hello," she said. "I'm looking for Brad Newsom. Is he in?" After a few minutes of silence on her end of the conversation, Sadie continued. "You think I can catch him at the Waffle House, then?" Sadie smiled and nodded. "Great. Thanks so much." She hung up and beamed. "You can always catch a government man feeding himself."

"Why are you calling Brad Newsom?" Becky asked.

"He's the local livestock inspector," she said. "And, if I'm right, he can unravel the mystery of all the numbers and letters on this metal ear tag."

"Oh." Becky shrugged her shoulders.

Sadie picked up her purse. "I'm going to the Waffle House to find Brad. I'll meet you back here after your interview." She smiled at Becky. "I'll tell him you send your regards."

"Don't you dare." Becky jumped up. "I'd better go too so I can be a little early for the interview. See you later." Out the door she went.

"I'll bring us back some burgers from the Waffle House," Sadie said. "If that's okay with you, Beanie."

"Put some cheese on mine and hold the onions. I've got everything under control here, boss."

"Will do," she said, and followed Becky out the door.

The Waffle House, one of Sadie's favorite restaurants in Sycamore Springs, overflowed with an early lunch crowd. Sadie weaved through a group of local businessmen and scanned the room for Brad Newsom.

Sadie had known Brad for many years, having grown up not far from him. Being the same age, they had successfully traversed the halls of Jay High School together, taking many of the same classes. Sadie had a tendency to get in trouble, while Brad walked the straight and narrow, yet they had always been good friends. They'd both graduated with honors, but had gone their separate ways the following year. He'd gone to veterinary school while she, sadly, had become trapped in a short-lived, dead-end marriage. It would be good to see Brad again.

She quickly spotted him, sitting alone in a booth along the windows, eating a sandwich and staring at a small laptop. He hadn't changed much over the years. He still wore his blond hair cut short against his head, and his blue eyes complemented his tanned face. He'd gained weight, but not much.

"Hey, Brad. Long time, no see," she said, as she approached.

Surprised, he stood and gave her a light hug. "Sadie Walela. You look wonderful. How have you been?"

"I'm well. What about you?"

"Can't complain. Join me," he said, returning to his seat. "Can I buy your lunch?"

"Oh, no. I can't stay very long. Your secretary said I could find you here, and since I'm springing for lunch at my office today, I thought I'd kill two birds with one stone."

"It's hard to find a good secretary," he said. "She'd rat out my whereabouts to anyone and everyone and think nothing of it." Then he smiled. "But, today I'm glad she did."

The waitress came and Sadie ordered cheeseburgers, minus onions, for her and her cohorts. "Make that 'to go,'" she added.

"So, to what do I owe the pleasure of your visit?" Brad asked, finishing off the last of his sandwich.

"Can you trace an animal by its ear tag?" she asked.

"Yes, ma'am." He wiped his mouth with his napkin. "Why do you ask?"

Sadie stretched out her leg and pulled the metal ear tag out of her pocket and placed it on the table. "I'm looking for the animal that lost this," she said.

"Where'd you get this, Sadie?"

"Found it at the fence line of my property." She didn't think it was necessary to tell him she'd dragged it from the other side of the fence.

"Okay." He pushed his empty plate to the side and pulled his laptop closer, extracted a pair of skinny reading glasses from his shirt pocket, perched them on his nose, and began to peck at the keyboard with his two forefingers.

"Oh, yes." Sadie smiled. "Becky Chuculate said to tell you 'hello.'"

Brad looked up from his computer, peered over his glasses, and repeated her name slowly. "Becky? Oh, yes. I remember her. I always thought she had the prettiest eyes. A year younger than us, right?"

Sadie nodded.

"I never got up the nerve to ask her out," he said. "I thought she got married and moved to California."

"She did, but it didn't work out and she's back. And, I believe her exact words to me were something like, you 'wouldn't give her the time of day.'"

Brad frowned and briefly leaned back in the booth. "I can't believe she'd think that. However, I know how it goes—the not-working-out part, that is. Think she'd want to go out?" He pulled a business card out of his pocket. "If you see her, tell her to call me," he said, and returned his attention to the computer screen.

"I don't know." Sadie took the card and slipped it into her purse. "I'll let her know."

"Wyoming," he said. "It came off of an animal that was tagged in Buffalo, Wyoming."

"Buffalo, Wyoming? That's appropriate," Sadie said without thinking.

Brad looked over his reading glasses again. "A bison cow. Young cows are tagged with orange metal tags when they're vaccinated for brucellosis, but if they lose that tag, it's replaced with a silver tag. This was a replacement tag, so it looks like your bison cow has pulled off her tag before."

"So do those numbers and letters tell you where this bison cow was tagged? Like an owner, or a ranch, or something?"

Brad shoved his readers higher on his nose, tapped at the keyboard again, and looked at the computer screen. "Travers Bison Ranch," he said, and then looked questioningly at her. "What's this all about, Sadie?"

"I'm not sure," she said, as the waitress dropped a brown paper sack in front of her.

Brad took another business card from his shirt pocket, wrote the name of the ranch and a phone number on the back of it. "This doesn't have anything to do with Angus Clyborn, does it?"

Sadie had started to stand but sank back into her side of the booth. "What do you know about Angus, anyway?"

"I know he brought in some bison and other exotic animals with the intent of letting hunters hunt them. No, let me rephrase that—letting rich hoodlums kill them for fun. About everyone in this part of the state is pissed off at him."

"Is that legal, Brad? To kill animals like that? It seems pretty cruel to me."

"I know there are a lot of folks up in arms about Angus, but I don't think there's a thing anyone can do to stop him. Even if there were, he's friends with every judge in the county."

"So I've heard." Sadie stood again. "Listen, Brad, I can't tell you how much help you've been."

"Let me know if I can help you, okay?" Brad leaned back in the booth. "Oh, and don't forget to give my card to Becky."

"I won't."

"And don't be a stranger."

"Okay." She grabbed her sack of burgers and headed for the cashier.

When Sadie returned to Playin' in Paradise, Beanie was busy talking on the phone and Becky sat rocking in Sadie's desk chair. Becky didn't look happy.

Sadie dropped the sack on the corner of her desk and began to pull out burgers. "How did your interview go?"

"I'm not sure. There were three other women there interviewing for the same job. They had all worked at other banks, which I'm sure sounded better than my limited knowledge of managing a convenience store." Becky sounded depressed. "I don't think even you can pull this one off for me, Sadie."

"You never know. I'll call Thelma later and ask."

Beanie distributed cans of Dr Pepper from the small office refrigerator, and Sadie handed out multiple paper towels before placing a mound of catsup and mustard packets in the middle of the makeshift table. All three began eating what Sadie considered the perfect meal—juicy burgers and greasy French fries, both slathered in mustard and catsup. Eating dainty was not an option today, which seemed to comfort Becky somewhat.

Becky took a large bite and spoke with a full mouth. "Did you find Brad?" she asked.

"I did." Sadie wiped her fingers on a paper towel and pulled his business card from her purse. "And he asked me to tell you to call him if you'd like to go out."

Becky's eyes grew wide as she drank from her soda can. "What did you tell him?"

"He remembered you right off, said you had pretty eyes, and that he always wanted to ask you out."

Becky turned her head. "That's hard to believe."

They finished eating in silence. When Beanie got up to answer the phone, Sadie gathered the food wrappers and took them to the trash can near the back door, and Becky wiped off the desk.

Becky suddenly spoke. "What about the ear tag?"

"Brad proved I'm not crazy." Sadie plopped back into her chair. "There is, or was, a buffalo cow on the other side of that fence, and this ear tag came from her." She produced another card from her purse. "And, I'm going to call this place and see what information I can get from them."

Becky looked amused. "And, then what?"

"I'm not sure," Sadie said. She moved her phone to the middle of her desk, dialed, and hit the speaker button.

A woman answered on the second ring. "Travers. This is Kate, may I help you?"

Sadie used her most professional-sounding voice. "Yes, ma'am. I'm wondering, if I give you an animal identification number, if you can give me some information."

"On one of our bison? I'll see what I can find. What's the number?"

Sadie read the number on the ear tag to the woman.

"Hold on," she said. Music filled the air for several seconds before the woman returned to the phone and spoke in an excited voice. "Oh, praise the Lord, you have Sandy," she exclaimed.

"Sandy?" asked Sadie.

"She was the color of sand when she was born, before she grew up to be buffalo brown, that is, so we named her Sandy. Her mother died shortly after she was born and none of the other cows would take her, so the kids and me, we raised her as a pet. I thought we'd lost her forever. I am so glad you called. She disappeared, and I just knew she ended up on one of the trucks that went to the Cherokees. I'm so glad you found her. I've been trying to get in touch with that Mr. Sanders, but no one ever returns my calls. Is that where you're calling from? The Cherokee Nation? Do you work with him? I believe his name was Kenneth or Kenny Sanders."

157

Sadie's mind raced, trying to keep up with the woman's excited chatter. Becky and Beanie stood staring at the phone, mouths agape.

The woman continued. "He came up here to make arrangements to transfer the bison they bought, along with another man, Mr. Eagle, or something like that."

"You mean Mr. Hawk?" Sadie offered.

"Oh, yes. That's it. Mr. Hawk. He wasn't very friendly, at least not as much as Mr. Sanders. I don't think I want to talk to him. Do you work with Mr. Sanders?"

Sadie's heart skipped a beat. "Uh, he's not here anymore."

"I guess that's why he didn't return my calls. He was such a nice man." The woman continued without pausing. "We need to get Sandy back as soon as possible. I think she was the victim of a rogue Charolais bull. He's the prettiest big old white bull you've ever seen; I guess that's what Sandy must have thought too. Anyway, we need to take care of that calf. Oh, my. Are you calling because she already had her calf?"

"Oh, I don't know." Sadie's mind raced. "I just wanted to make sure we got a new ear tag back on the right animal." Did that make any sense? Sadie tried to think of what to say next.

"If you can get her to stand still, she's got an "S" tattooed on her upper lip. She won't hurt you. She's a big teddy bear, well, buffalo, I mean." Her laugh sounded genuine.

"Thank you so much for this information," Sadie blurted. "I'll see who took Mr. Sanders's place and have him give you a call. Thank you again so very much." Sadie quickly hung up before the woman could say another word. She drew a long breath and said, "Well, that was certainly enlightening."

Both Beanie and Becky looked shocked.

Beanie spoke first. "Sadie, our number is on her caller ID now, and when she calls back wanting her Sandy, she's going to know we are not the Cherokee Nation."

"I know." Sadie pushed the phone back to the corner of her desk. "I'll think of something. I've got to talk to Lance."

The phone rang and Sadie froze. The woman was already calling back, she thought. Beanie answered and nodded to Sadie. "It's Thelma."

Sadie picked up the phone and turned her back. After a few minutes, she hung up and turned to Becky. "I'm sorry. You were right. You were outgunned. She couldn't justify hiring you considering the experience of the others."

Becky looked dejected.

"But, she said she would keep your application on file and call you if anything else opens up."

"I'm going to have to move back to my dad's. Without a job I can't afford my own place, and I can't stay with you forever. Lance is going to get impatient."

"Don't worry," Sadie said. "We'll come up with something."

Becky nodded as tears welled in her eyes.

Chapter 26

Angus entered his house through the kitchen, plunked his briefcase on the island workspace that stood between the open kitchen and dining room, and bellowed for his wife.

"Camilla. Come down here, please." He knew his words sounded more like a command than a request, but at least he had added the word "please."

He pulled a stack of papers from his briefcase and dropped them on the dining room table and then retrieved a bottle of Budweiser from the giant refrigerator. He sat at the head of the table and propped his feet, boots and all, on the nearest chair, and admired his surroundings while he waited for his wife.

The bi-level house, built on the design of a mountain lodge, looked like it had been peeled from the pages of a slick magazine and planted in the middle of the Eucha countryside. Everything was oversized, from the kitchen filled with commercial-sized appliances and the dining area complete with a rustic table for twelve to the main living room filled with animal-skin rugs, overstuffed leather furniture, a pool table, and trophy heads hanging on high walls. A huge rock fireplace divided the living room and the dining area. Thick draperies hung on the windows, creating a cool darkness that carried throughout the house.

Camilla seemed to be in no hurry. Holding a highball glass and a cigarette in the same hand, she walked down the wide staircase from the second story of the house. It was where she spent most of her time, watching soap operas in the master bedroom when she wasn't off somewhere shopping. Her long robe trailed on the stairs behind her bare feet, and Angus caught himself hoping she'd trip and break her neck. They had stopped talking about anything meaningful a long time ago, and since Jason's funeral, she jerked away every time he tried to touch her.

She drank more and more, and he didn't much care for her disgusting behavior.

"Don't take all day," Angus fumed.

Camilla refreshed her drink before walking to the table and acknowledging him. "What is it now, Angus?" She pulled out a chair and sat down.

Angus pitched an ink pen toward her and then began to shuffle papers in her direction. "I need you to sign this trust agreement. The lines are marked with those little arrows." He pointed at her signature lines with his stubby finger. "There're two places—here and here."

He leaned back in his chair and pulled a fresh cigar and a lighter out of his shirt pocket. He ran his tongue up one side of the cigar and then down the other, stuck it in his mouth, and then sucked life into it from the flame of the lighter.

Camilla picked up the first sheet of paper, scanned it, and said, "What's this?"

"It's just some legal mumbo jumbo. Just sign it like I asked you to."

Camilla took a drink and let the paper drop on the table. "Give me the whole document," she said, "and when I get finished reading it, I'll decide if I want to sign it."

Angus took the cigar out of his mouth and spit a piece of tobacco onto the floor. Dredging up the nicest tone he could, he continued. "Now, honeybunch, don't you worry your pretty little head about the legal operations of this ranch. The way I've got everything set up, all you'll to have to do is sit back and watch the money roll in. Isn't that what you want?"

"Yes, of course, Angus." The corners of Camilla's mouth curled slightly and her eyes moved to the deer-antler chandelier hanging over the table. "I'll look at it in a bit," she said.

"No." Angus raised his voice. "I want to get this taken care of so I can take it back to the bank tomorrow. We've got hunters coming next week and I've got to go track down that cook I hired. I don't know where the hell she went."

Ignoring him, Camilla downed the rest of her drink, rose from the table, and returned to the staircase. "My bath water is getting cold. I'll be back shortly and we can talk about it some more."

Angus began to shake as Camilla disappeared at the top of the stairs. There wasn't enough beer in the house to quell his anger. "He was my son, too," he yelled. Then he pushed back from the table and tromped out the back door.

"Whoa." The rider spoke in a low tone and reined the horse to a stop, then bent forward and patted the horse on the neck. "Stand still," came the next command, and the horse stood like a statue, just as it had been trained to do. The rider noticed an apple core on the ground nearby and paused to study the surroundings. Confident of being alone, the rider balanced and adjusted on the back of the horse, and unslung a long gun.

From the high vantage point, the rider could see the house and all the other buildings situated on the Buffalo Ranch. Holding the rifle with steady hands, the rider peered through the Leupold scope, magnifying the entire area so much that the target appeared to be only a few feet away.

Angus Clyborn walked onto his back porch and out toward the barn. He entered the barn and reemerged a few minutes later. The powerful scope followed the short, stout man as he leaned against the side of the structure, pulled a lighter out of his pocket, and puffed life into the cigar that dangled from his mouth.

The rider dismissed all thoughts. There would be no thinking about the task at hand. It was simply something that had to be done, and the time had come to do it.

The rider gripped the horse tightly, signaling the steed to freeze, and zeroed in on the cigar, carefully lining up the crosshairs of the scope with the man's head. The fine lines of the sight came into focus and moved down Angus's body to the middle of his chest. The scope had already been adjusted for the distance the bullet would have to travel before hitting its target. The horse stood perfectly still as the rider slowly exhaled, took a breath and held it, and then pulled the trigger.

Angus didn't look like he knew what hit him as he slowly slid down the side of the barn and onto the ground. Mission accomplished.

The rider calmly lowered the rifle, balanced it on the neck of the horse, and then took the reins and spoke in a calm and quiet voice. "Good boy." The rider patted the horse on its neck and nudged it forward with gentle heels. Slowly, horse and rider retraced their original path down the other side of the ridge, the rider thinking about what had just taken place. For every action, a reaction. Now they were square.

Sadie turned off the paved road, stopping to retrieve her mail before continuing up the lane to her house. When she parked and got out, Sonny ran to meet her. She gave him a playful scratch on his head between his ears and bounced up the steps of the back porch with her mail under her arm. She turned around to look for Joe. He and Sir William stopped grazing in the pasture not far away and raised their heads in tandem, as if to acknowledge her presence, and then both went back to eating grass.

As she turned to go inside, something caught her eye. On the giant sycamore tree near the corral gate, she could see something that looked as if it floated in the air. She dropped her things onto the porch and walked toward the tree.

It was an arrow—an arrow with a white feather attached to it. She quickly turned in all directions, looking for whoever had left it. It didn't scare her. Her Cherokee father had always told her a white feather meant "peace" or "welcome," so she believed someone was trying to send her a message of peace. She started to pull it out of the tree and then decided to wait for Lance. He would want to lift fingerprints if he could.

Surveying her surroundings again as she walked back to the house, she gathered her purse and mail off the porch, went inside, and locked the door.

Upstairs in her bedroom, Camilla thought she heard the crack of a rifle firing and wondered if there were hunters around she didn't know about. She muted the sound on the television and listened. "He never tells me what's going on around here," she muttered. She rose from her chair and walked to the window. She could see the small herd of buffalo in the distance. They seemed content on the serene landscape. Turning from the window, she stepped out of her robe and pulled on a pair of jeans and a shirt, brushed her hair off her neck and secured it with a stretchy band. She sat back down and readjusted the volume on the television to its normal level. About an hour later, when the movie had ended, she put on a pair of sneakers, and returned to the kitchen.

Dusk had fallen when she glanced out the kitchen window looking for Angus. It wasn't like him to be so quiet. She flipped open his briefcase and pulled out the rest of the trust agreement, sat down, and began to read. The more she read, the angrier she became. "So you think I'm going to sign off on something that completely cuts me out of ownership of this place, do you?" she said aloud. "Only in your dreams, you son of a bitch."

She walked to the back door, opened it, and looked for Angus. Not able to see him anywhere, she called out his name. Nothing.

Her anger rose. She'd had enough. The only reason she'd stayed married to Angus all these years was because of their son. Now that he was dead and buried, she had little motivation left to hang around. The thought of fighting Angus for her half of their assets caused her stomach to knot. He was crooked and mean, and would put up a fight, but all she needed was enough to start over somewhere away from him.

She stepped off the porch and walked toward the barn, expecting to find him inside tinkering with something. When she didn't find him there, she came out of the barn and looked around. She started toward the bunkhouse, but her instincts guided her to the outer side of the barn. There he was, crumpled on the ground.

"Oh, Angus," she said, thinking he'd had a heart attack.

His lifestyle certainly made that a reasonable conclusion. But as she got closer, she saw blood on the front of his shirt.

"Angus!" She ran to his side, propped him up, and yelled at him. "Wake up, Angus!" In denial, she shook him and yelled again, but there was no breath, no movement. She felt his cold hand and looked at his gray face. It was too late.

Frightened, she stood and looked in all directions. Was the killer still here? Was she next? Was she going to die because of Angus and his meanness? She could see no vehicles, no lights, no one. And where was the new maid he said he'd hired? Nausea overcame her as her head began to spin, and she felt as if she might faint.

She'd been miserable since the day she'd said "I do" to Angus, had never loved him like a wife was supposed to. It'd been hard to turn her head from all his womanizing, but she did what she had to do to preserve a nice home for her and their son, Jason. She should have left him a long time ago, but with plenty of money to spend, it had worked out, she supposed. She'd been comfortable, hadn't she? Or maybe numb. She'd watched him build an empire of corruption, thinking if she ignored it, it wouldn't affect her. Now Jason was dead and Angus had gotten himself murdered. She felt her whole world crumbling around her.

Gathering her strength, she ran as fast as she could back into the house, picked up the phone, and dialed 911. When the dispatcher answered, Camilla's voice froze. She looked at the blood on her hands, Angus's blood, and panic struck. They would think she killed him. She could hear the dispatcher's voice increase in pitch on the other end of the line.

Finally, she blurted, "Please help me. Angus is dead."

Chapter 27

Lance parked, got out, and headed straight toward the arrow-struck tree. "Where'd this come from?" he asked, frowning.

Sadie jumped off the porch and followed him. "How in the world did you see that so quickly?"

He turned toward her and gave her a quick kiss. "That's what I'm paid to do," he said.

She smiled. "Aren't you going to give me a gold star for not touching it?"

Lance pulled out his handkerchief, used it to extract the arrow, and then scanned the surrounding area. "Did you see anyone?"

"No, but I think it's okay."

"What do you mean 'okay?'"

"It's a white feather, Lance. My dad and grandmother always told me that a white feather means 'peace.' I think whoever left the arrow is sending a message that they mean no harm."

Lance raised his right eyebrow. "Oh, yeah?"

"Well, what do you think it means?"

Lance walked with the arrow toward his truck. "I think it means we have a very unpredictable archer who has killed one person so far." He stored the arrow in the back seat of his vehicle and locked the door. "And he killed that person pretty close by. Don't be so naïve, Sadie."

"Okay, you win," she said, as they entered through the kitchen door. "Dinner's ready. Let's eat."

Lance slipped off his gun belt and sat down at Sadie's table in front of a plate heaped with meatloaf, mashed potatoes, and fresh green beans.

"I'm starved," he said, as he began to eat. "And it was nice of Becky to give us an evening alone for a change."

"I know. She's a nice girl, but I hope she figures out what she's going to do soon."

"I swear, Sadie, you'd take in a lost frog if you thought it needed a new pond." Lance took a bite of meatloaf. "This is really good, Sadie," he said, taking a long drink of Pepsi. "By the way, where is your froggy roommate?"

"She went to check on her dad."

"He's a nice man."

"She said she was going to call you. She wants to file rape charges against Angus."

"Oh?" Lance looked surprised. "Why'd she change her mind?"

"That's not all she wants to file charges for."

Lance laid his fork on his plate and looked questioningly at Sadie. "I'm waiting."

"He stole her grandfather's land."

A curious look crossed his face. "How'd he do that?"

"Angus is a jerk, and he can't get away with his criminal behavior forever. It's about to catch up to his arrogant white ass regardless of how many politicians he has in whatever pocket."

Lance took another bite of meatloaf. "And you're going to see to that, right?"

"Yes." Sadie reached for a pile of papers at the edge of the table. "I was going to wait until after dinner to talk to you about this, but we might as well start now. Angus has been acquiring land illegally, including the land adjacent to mine that belonged to Becky's grandfather. Look at this list. Angus has taken all of this land either by quiet title or forged deeds."

"What's quiet title?"

"It's a process used when someone wants to claim property, usually because it's next to theirs, the original owners are deceased, it's been unoccupied for a long time, and no one knows who or where the descendants are. An attorney draws up legal papers and runs an ad in the local paper, which will never be seen by the descendants if they live somewhere out of state, which is usually the case. If no one protests in a stated amount of time, about three weeks, the title is 'quieted' and ownership is transferred. The whole thing only takes about six weeks."

"And that's legal?"

"It is if you have a good lawyer doing it—like Eugene Hawk."

Lance leaned back in his chair. "That sounds kind of like stealing land to me."

Sadie nodded. "Yeah, it kind of is."

"But Grover Chuculate is alive and well," Lance said. "Wouldn't he find out when the property taxes came due and he didn't get a bill?"

"There is no tax bill on Indian land, remember?"

Lance nodded.

Sadie continued. "But that property was taken with a forged deed."

"How does someone forge a dead man's signature? George Washington Chuculate is dead and has been for a while."

"You backdate the deed to when he was still alive and then you wait to file it until a later date. It's called a 'dresser drawer' deed. People around here do it all the time. They think it saves them the cost of probating an estate. And, like I said, if you have a good lawyer . . . and Angus probably knows Grover is in bad health. We would have never known if we hadn't started snooping around at the county clerk's office."

"I really hate to ask what 'snooping' means."

Lance's cell phone rang. He looked at the number and dropped his fork. "Sorry, hon, I've got to take this. They know I'm off duty; it must be an emergency."

"Smith here," he said, and then listened for only a few moments before replying. "I'm on my way." He hung up and dropped the phone into his shirt pocket.

"I'm sorry, Sadie, I've got to run. There's an emergency at the Clyborn ranch."

"Oh, good grief," she said. "Angus Clyborn is always in crisis mode. Can't you at least finish your meal?"

Lance had already stood, buckled his gun belt in place, and attached his badge. "I'll be back as soon as I can," he said, as he shoveled one last big bite of food into his mouth. He pushed his hat down on his head and hurried out the door.

Lance sped the short distance from Sadie's house to the Buffalo Ranch and arrived to an emergency vehicle's flashing lights. Lance parked between the house and the barn next to the ambulance, got out, and flipped on his flashlight. He disliked working a homicide in the dark, if that's what it was, but with dusk falling rapidly he had no choice. Being the first one from the sheriff's office to arrive, he immediately took charge of the scene.

The anxious ambulance driver, a young Cherokee everyone called Big John, approached Lance. "Glad you're here," he said. "I think this guy's been dead for a while." Big John then led Lance to the body, still propped against the side of the barn. "Once we determined he was dead, I didn't think we should move the body until you checked it out."

Lance joined the other paramedic, who was standing several feet away from the body as if he didn't want to get too close. Shining his flashlight on the corpse, Lance barked into his handheld radio. "Dispatch. Call the medical examiner and get him to the Angus Clyborn ranch as soon as possible."

Big John backed away, looking relieved that Lance had taken over.

Lance surveyed the area carefully. Angus's cigar had fallen next to his body and thankfully burnt out. It could have easily caused a fire in the dry grass, taking Angus and the entire structure with it. Lance returned his attention to the body. The single bullet wound, at first glance, appeared to have entered Angus's chest from the front, and when Lance leaned the body forward, he could see no exit wound, indicating the bullet must still be inside the body. If they were lucky, they'd be able to retrieve it, which would give them more information about the murder weapon. Lance used his flashlight to search the siding of the barn but could see no evidence of any additional bullets. He would be able to tell more in the daylight.

Lance motioned for Big John, who was leaning against the front of the ambulance. "Did you see anyone else around?"

Big John nodded toward the house. "The wife called it in. She's inside."

"Let me know when the ME gets here."

Lance turned and headed for the back door as Big John waved an acknowledgment. The door behind the screen stood ajar, so Lance knocked on the doorjamb.

A woman's voice came from inside. "It's open," she said.

Lance entered and waited by the door, allowing his eyes to adjust to the darkness. "Ma'am," he said. "Do you mind if I turn on a light?"

"Suit yourself."

Lance found the light switch beside the door and flipped it on. A light above the kitchen work area radiated from the ceiling. Camilla sat at a table in the adjoining dining room, smoking a cigarette and sipping on what he imagined to be a strong drink.

"Are you alone, ma'am?"

"It's just me." Her voice sounded indifferent.

"May I come in?" he asked.

"Sure. Make yourself at home." She sat with her elbows on the table, holding her head with her left hand.

Lance joined her at the table. "Mrs. Clyborn?"

"The one and only," she said, taking a long drag from her cigarette and a gulp of her drink. Her smudged red lipstick had bled into the lines radiating from her lips, and her blonde hair fell like straw around her face.

"Do you know what happened to Angus?" he asked.

"It looks to me like someone got fed up with his bullshit and killed him." She stared straight ahead. "Serves him right," she added.

Lance tried to hide his surprise. "Do you know who might have wanted to kill him?"

Camilla grunted and turned her bloodshot eyes toward him. "Are you kidding me? I can't think of anyone who won't be delighted to hear the bastard's dead. He's been stealing land right and left, so any one of those landowners could have done it."

"Stealing land?" Sadie was always right, he thought.

"Yeah, he'd find a piece of land he wanted and then intimidate the people into selling it to him for next to nothing. If it was vacant, he'd have some papers drawn up and change the title, or if that didn't work, he'd just forge the deeds. A lot of land around here is just sitting there ripe for picking, and then no one seems to notice what's happened to it until it's over and he's taken title. I've been waiting for someone to strangle him barehanded."

Lance pulled a notebook out of his shirt pocket and began to make notes.

"Then there're the hunts." She returned her attention to her cigarette and took another drink. "One of those COWA people from Tulsa threatened to kill him to his face. I don't know what her name is. And then there's that damned white buffalo calf. I heard Eugene Hawk warn him about that, but Angus ignored him. Now the damned thing is missing. I think someone stole it. Maybe they came back and killed Angus. Anybody could've done it."

Lance made no comment, waiting for her to continue.

Camilla leaned back in her chair. "Quite frankly, I've thought about killing him myself. He's been trying to force me to sign over my interest in this place so he can put it into a trust. He wanted to make sure when he died that neither Lucy nor I would end up with ownership in any of it. He's already screwed Lucy out of her place. She thinks it's hers free and clear, but he never filed the deed. He's so stupid. He doesn't think I know any of this."

"But you wouldn't really consider killing your husband, would you?"

"After being married to that son of a bitch as long as I have? Yes, sir. Considered it many times."

Lance thought the liquor was talking, but he had to ask. "Did you?" he said, apologetically. "Did you murder Angus?"

"No, someone beat me to it," she said, looking down at her hands.

"Is there anyone else you can think of who might have wanted him dead?"

"His business-partner-in-crime, Hawk. I wouldn't trust that Indian as far as I could throw him."

"You mean the tribal councilor, Eugene Hawk?" Lance clarified.

"Yes. I've never met a more crooked man. I don't know how those Cherokees could be so stupid to elect such a corrupt man to run the tribe's business. He's not even a wolf in sheep's clothing. He's a snake."

"What did he do to make you come to that conclusion, ma'am?"

"He's the one who helped Angus find all this vacant Indian land and then drew up the paperwork and had it forged. It was all his idea."

"Why would he do that, ma'am?"

Camilla snorted and pushed her drink aside. "Why do you think? Greed. Money. Eugene Hawk is the greediest bastard I've ever met." She took another long drag from her cigarette. "Next to Angus, that is."

Lance exhaled slowly. "I'm going to need you to sign a statement. We'll send a car out for you tomorrow. Is there someone I can call for you? How about Lucy? Is she at home? You shouldn't be alone."

171

"No, leave her alone. I haven't seen her in days. She's probably gone home crying to her momma."

"What about another relative?"

"There's no one to call." She let out a puff of smoke and extinguished her cigarette in the ashtray. "It doesn't matter, anyway. I've been living alone ever since I married that man."

Lance left Camilla sitting alone and returned outside. The medical examiner arrived and Lance watched while he examined the body. In no time at all, he motioned for the paramedics to zip Angus up in a body bag. "I'll meet you at my office," the ME said. Then he turned his attention to Lance. "Getting a little carried away with murders on this road aren't you, Smith?" he said. "We've got an entry wound with no exit, so if we're lucky, we should be able to come up with a cartridge for you."

Lance nodded. "Call me when you have something."

"Will do."

As the ME followed the ambulance out of the Buffalo Ranch, Lance went to his truck and pulled out a roll of yellow crime-scene tape. Then he picked up the radio. "Sheriff, I'm going to need someone to secure this crime scene until daylight. I'll wait till they get here." Lance dropped the radio on the seat of his vehicle and began to mark off a large area around where they'd found Angus, including the barn. He would string some across the entry when he left, to keep people out. He returned to his truck and waited for whoever the sheriff was going to send to relieve him. While he waited, he made some more notes in his notebook.

A connection to the man killed earlier at the edge of Sadie's property seemed evident. If he had to guess, Angus had murdered him. But proving that was going to be hard, especially now that Angus was dead, too. Where did Eugene Hawk fit in? How was he making money off of Angus? Maybe Angus and Hawk got in an argument and Hawk killed him. That didn't make much sense if Angus was greasing Hawk's hand with money.

The sound of a garage door opening caught his attention. He got out of his truck and saw Camilla back a Cadillac out of the garage on the other side of the house and tear off into the night.

"Stop!" he shouted. "You're too drunk to be behind the wheel!" He stood next to his truck, hands on hips, watching the car speed away. "So much for the grieving wife," he said, reaching for his radio.

"Dispatch," Lance barked into the transmitter. "Notify Oklahoma Highway Patrol we've got a possible suspect fleeing the murder scene at the Buffalo Ranch, female, possibly intoxicated, in a dark Cadillac sedan, driving northeast on Eucha Road, most likely headed toward Highway 20."

"Ten-four," the dispatcher responded. "Is the suspect armed?"

"Unknown," Lance responded.

The sheriff's booming voice cut in. "Jennings left twenty minutes ago to relieve you at the crime scene."

"Ten-four." Lance said, as he dropped the mic on the seat and cursed into the still night air.

Chapter 28

When Lance left Camilla alone in the house, her mind had begun to race. She felt like a character in the *Twilight Zone*. Who killed Angus? If it was Eugene Hawk he could easily return after everyone left and do her in, too. Maybe he wanted the ranch. Maybe he'd fixed it up so he'd get some money if Angus died, being his business partner and all. No, that was crazy.

She ran her fingers through her hair, took another drag from a freshly lit cigarette, and gulped straight whiskey from her glass. Why did she tell that deputy she wanted to kill Angus? It was the truth, but not necessarily something she should have shared with law enforcement at a murder scene.

She could never kill anyone. Her vision blurred, then she gagged and placed her hand over her mouth to keep from throwing up.

Standing, she nearly tripped over her chair. The alcohol had impaired her muscle control, but not enough to quiet her mind. The room shrank around her and claustrophobia overtook her. She looked out the back door and could see the deputy nosing around the barn where Angus had died. With a little luck, she could get halfway to Tulsa before he even knew she was gone. Clutching her purse, she dug for her keys and ran into the attached garage. The garage door opener rumbled to life when she hit the control, and as soon as the car cleared the door, she slammed the accelerator to the floorboard as hard as she could.

She didn't even hit the brakes as she approached the entryway into the ranch and shot through it without hesitation. She needed to hurry. She'd have to get to the highway in order to elude anyone trying to intercept her. They probably didn't have enough cops in this insignificant county to catch her anyway. They were all busy trying to figure out what to do with her dead husband.

The Cadillac handled the deserted road well as she skidded around two curves. She laughed hysterically, caring nothing for her own safety or that of anyone else who might come along.

She rounded another curve and saw three deer standing in the road. "Get out of the road," she screamed, but the buck and two does stood frozen in her headlights. She slammed on the brakes and slid to the edge of the road. The guardrail crumpled but held as she twisted the steering wheel in the opposite direction, where she hit a concrete abutment and careened into the creek below. When the Cadillac rolled and landed on its roof, Camilla thought for a split second that she should have put on her seat belt. Then the absurdity of it all washed over her as cold water covered her face and took her breath away.

Sadie sat on her back porch watching the moon climb into the sky, waiting for Becky to return. Earlier in the day, Becky had said she had something to take care of and that Sadie should not hold up dinner for her; she'd get a bite to eat before she came home. It was Sadie's nature to worry anyway.

Becky's recovery from her appendix surgery had gone well, but Sadie knew it would take a long time to recover from being raped by Angus. Sadie also knew Becky had tried hard to hide her anger, but it didn't appear to be an easy task. Becky didn't want to talk about it, and Sadie reluctantly agreed to respect her new friend's request even though she knew Becky would eventually have to talk it out in order to deal with it. She made a mental note to check into finding a counselor who dealt with that sort of thing.

Her thoughts drifted to Lance. She thought she'd like to see him give up working for the sheriff. Maybe if he had a regular job and wasn't always running off to take care of some emergency, they could spend more time together. It seemed like the whole department would fold without him there to take care of every crisis.

The distant sound of metal scraping metal, followed by a thud, interrupted her thoughts. Someone had crashed into something. She ran into the house and grabbed her keys. In a few short minutes, she and Sonny were on their way to the bridge.

When they got there, she could see where a vehicle had left the road. It didn't look good. With flashlight in hand, she and Sonny jumped out of her car, ran to the bridge, and looked over the edge. The vehicle, a dark sedan, had landed upside down in the creek. Water rushed through an open window.

Thinking maybe someone had already climbed out of the vehicle and was hurt, she shouted. "Hello? Anyone there? Where are you?"

When no one answered, Sadie hurriedly climbed down the steep embankment and into the bone-chilling water. Sonny jumped in and followed. Holding the flashlight on the car, Sadie made her way to the driver's-side window. No one. She pushed her way around the vehicle and shined the flashlight through all the windows. The car was empty. Either someone had climbed out or they had been thrown clear. She hoped whoever the driver had been, that they had found a way to safety, but her gut told her it would have taken a miracle for that to happen. She could either keep looking for the driver or get help. She opted for help.

She and Sonny climbed out of the water, ran back to her car, and drove back home with Sonny dripping water all over the front seat. Once there, she quickly dialed 911 and reported the accident. The dispatcher took her information and told her she'd send someone out right away.

Lance, Sadie thought. She needed to let him know. She dialed his number and the call went immediately to voice mail. Wherever he was, probably still at the Buffalo Ranch, he was out of cell phone range. She left a message. He'd get it eventually.

As Sadie hung up, she saw headlights turning off the road toward her house. She walked back outside and watched as Becky parked next to Sadie's car and got out.

"What's wrong?" Becky asked. "Why are you all wet?"

"Someone just took a nosedive off the bridge into the creek," she said. "I tried to see if I could find the driver, but no one was in the car. I don't know what happened to them, so I came back here to call it in."

Panic crossed Becky's face. "You want to go back and look? They might be hurt."

Sadie nodded. "Yes, let's go."

Sadie got in the car with Becky and headed back toward the road, leaving Sonny behind this time. With emergency personnel on the way, a wolfdog would only be in the way.

When they got back to the bridge, Becky turned on her flashers so anyone driving along would see her car. They both got out and started shouting, hoping to get a response this time. Nothing.

"Sadie!" Becky screamed. "That looks like a car I saw at Angus's place!"

A truck sped toward the bridge and parked facing Becky's car.

"What happened?" Lance yelled, as he climbed out of his vehicle.

"Someone crashed," answered Sadie, who had already climbed back down to the edge of the creek, "but there's no one in the vehicle."

Lance swung his spotlight toward the vehicle and into the creek beyond, then retrieved his binoculars. By then, Sadie had climbed back up to the road and jogged over to him. Becky stood frozen on the bridge, staring at the creek below.

"Lance, Becky says it might be one of Angus's cars."

"Yeah, I know."

"Do you think it's Angus?"

"Nope, I think it is Angus's wife."

"How do you know that?" Sadie said, stunned.

Lance threw his binoculars back into his vehicle. "Because Angus is dead, and from the looks of that body floating against the edge of the creek down there," he pointed with his head, "I'd say, so is his wife."

Sadie gasped. "Oh, no."

"She got away before I could stop her. . . . I was hoping the highway patrol would intercept her before something like this happened," he added.

Becky began to retch. Sadie ran to her friend and put a hand on her shoulder.

"Are you okay, Becky?"

"No." She began to sob between gags. "I can't take this."

Sadie helped Becky into the passenger's side of her car, and then watched while Lance waded into the water and pulled the body onto the bank. When he returned to his vehicle, he grabbed the radio and barked orders at the dispatcher.

Sadie knew he was going to be busy for most of the night, so she walked over and kissed him on the cheek. "We're going back to the house. Call me when you can."

"I will," he said.

She climbed into Becky's car, made a U-turn, and headed home.

Chapter 29

"Sadie, I can't stay," Becky said after she and Sadie had returned from Camilla's accident scene. "I just came back to pick up my things. I need to go take care of Daddy. He fell and, somehow, I've got to convince him to go to the doctor in the morning to make sure he's okay."

"Oh, how awful," Sadie exclaimed. "Is he hurt?"

"I'm not sure. He fell in the corral, and then managed to drag himself into his trailer. He can hardly walk without pain. And, you know Sadie, he acts like he's well, but he's not. He was diagnosed with leukemia a while back. He refused treatment, won't have anything to do with doctors, said when it was his time to go, he'd do it on his own terms."

Sadie let out long sigh. "Is there anything I can do to help?"

"You've already done more than I can ever repay you for." She walked over and hugged Sadie. "He needed me and I didn't even know it. When I came home from California, I thought I was coming home for him to take care of me." She sniffed and a tear rolled down her cheek. "I've been gone too long."

Sadie helped Becky gather her things, put together a care package of cold meatloaf and brownies, and sent her on her way.

By the time the first responders had recovered Camilla Clyborn's body and Junior Casey had winched her water-soaked Cadillac onto the back of his tow truck, streaks of pale pink and blue had emerged in the eastern sky and exhaustion settled in Lance's limbs. The ambulance drove toward Sycamore Springs and the tow truck followed.

Lance realized he had hours of paperwork to do, a part of the job he detested. First, the murder of Angus, and now the death of Camilla.

He guessed no one would ever know whether her dive into the creek was a successful suicide, an accident caused by animals on the road, or the result of drunk driving. He didn't think her earlier demeanor exactly fit that of an overly distraught widow, but she had been drinking heavily.

He removed his Stetson, rubbed the sleepiness from his face and forehead, and replaced his hat. He was tired and hungry. He had his notes; the reports could wait until he got a couple hours of sleep. He climbed into his vehicle and headed up the road to Sadie's, hoping she had saved the rest of his uneaten dinner.

Sonny whimpered and touched his cold nose to Sadie's hand. She roused from an unsettling dream and heard the door of a vehicle close. She pulled on the jeans and tee shirt she had tossed on the floor the night before and walked into the kitchen. Sonny sat on his haunches in his normal sentry spot by the back door, and Sadie knew by his behavior it was a friendly visitor. She peeked through the curtains, saw Lance's truck, and released Sonny through the back door. The wolfdog ignored Lance and ran into the coolness of the early morning.

Lance stopped at the threshold, gave Sadie a kiss, and said, "Got any of that meatloaf left?"

"Yes, and I have so much to tell you," she said. "And, I want to know everything," she added, as she closed the door behind him and went to work in the kitchen. "I saved your plate. I knew you'd be back. What in the world happened to Angus?" She retrieved his plate from the refrigerator, shoved it into the microwave, and hit the reheat button.

"You know I can't discuss an ongoing investigation," he said and gave her a mischievous smile.

Sadie pulled the plate out of the microwave, waved it in front of his face, and then held it high in the air. "Oh, yeah? If you can't share your information, then I guess I can't share my meatloaf."

"Woman, you drive a hard bargain." Lance sounded tired. "I give."

"That's more like it." She slid the plate in front of him and took a seat. "Okay, what happened?"

"Someone pinned Angus up against the side of his barn with a high-powered rifle."

"Someone shot him?" Sadie couldn't hide her surprise. "With a rifle? From far away? What kind of rifle?"

"Yes, yes, yes, and, I have no idea. We'll have to wait for the medical examiner to report on the caliber of the round. There was no exit wound."

"Wow," Sadie said quietly as her mind raced.

"And so far I've got a list of suspects a mile long," he said as he continued to eat. "It appears everyone in Delaware County will be dancing on his grave."

"That's a terrible thing to say, Lance."

"Well, it's the truth," he said. He wiped some of the gravy on his plate with a piece of bread and placed it in his mouth.

"Who do you think did it?"

Lance leaned back in his chair. "Let's see, first off there's Roy Carter. He's convinced Angus infected his cattle with Bang's. He threatened to kill Angus at the sale barn on Saturday."

"Really?"

"Then, I'd like to see the list of people you think he stole property from. It could've been one of them. And after the incident with the mailbox, your Uncle Eli could make the short list, too."

"Lance, stop being silly."

"Could've been an irate woman. He raped Becky; I doubt she's the only one." Lance looked around. "Where is Becky, anyway?"

"Her dad fell. She went to take care of him."

"According to Angus's wife, a woman from the COWA group threatened to do whatever it took to stop his hunt-for-profit business. I guess you could call that a death threat." He poured some Pepsi into his glass and took a drink. "And then there's Camilla herself. She seemed to be more than happy Angus was dead. Plus, she had some pretty harsh words for Eugene Hawk." He rose from the table and headed toward the living room. "And now I've got to figure out what happened to her."

"I'll get my paperwork on the land deals and be there in a minute."

Sadie carried his dirty dishes to the sink, rinsed them off, and placed them in the dishwasher. A few minutes later, carrying a folder full of copied forged deeds and quiet titles, she walked into the living room where Lance had disappeared a few minutes before. She stopped short when she found him sound asleep on the couch. She placed the folder on the coffee table, covered him with a Pendleton blanket, and tiptoed back into the kitchen. There would be plenty of time to talk when he woke up. In the meantime, she had a lot of thinking to do, which included the white buffalo calf, now that she knew it was not a figment of her imagination.

An hour later, Sadie emerged from the shower and heard Lance talking. She quickly toweled off, and confident that what she heard was one side of a phone conversation, she slipped into the bedroom and dressed. By the time she'd poured him a cup of coffee, he had already strapped on his gun belt.

"Wait," she exclaimed. "You can't just take off before we've had time to talk. I need to tell you about the white buffalo calf."

Lance walked over to the kitchen sink, splashed water on his hands and face, and dried with a paper towel. "I'm sorry, Sadie. I've got to get going."

Sadie shoved a cup of coffee into his hand. "Here, at least drink this first."

Lance blew across the top of the steaming liquid and took a sip. "Oh, thank you, hon. This is what I needed. Can I take this with me?"

Sadie pulled an insulated travel mug from the top shelf, filled it to the top with black coffee, and snapped the lid in place. "Well, I just want you to know I'm not crazy. There really is a white calf, only it's likely half-French."

Lance took the travel mug from Sadie's hand and wrinkled his forehead. "French?"

"Charolais. I spoke to the owner yesterday. Charolais are white, you know, which could explain the white calf."

"Sounds interesting, but I don't have time to worry about the buffalo calf right now. I'm on my way to pick up a search warrant so I can get into the Clyborn house, not to mention I've got a ton of reports to fill out, and then I've got to see if I can run down Roy Carter and find out where he was yesterday. And, let's just hope he can convince me it wasn't shooting Angus Clyborn. I've still got to turn in the arrow you found, too."

"Go get 'em," she said, and kissed him on the cheek right before he disappeared out the door.

Chapter 30

When his cell phone rang, Eugene Hawk turned and looked past Ginny's head at the clock on the dresser. It read 5:15 a.m. He untangled his legs from hers, picked up the phone, and tried to focus enough to identify the caller. Ginny opened her eyes for a moment, rolled over, and began snoring again.

It was Dorothy. Why would she be calling at this hour of the morning? He waited for the voice mail icon to light up and then accessed the message. He listened for a moment and then sat straight up in bed. He cleared the sleep from his voice and quickly returned the call.

"You want to elaborate on that?" he said into the phone.

Ginny began to stir. She slid the sheets up over her naked body and pushed herself up on one elbow. "Who is it?"

"Are you sure?" Hawk held the phone to his ear, pushed the covers back, and started fishing for his clothes from a nearby chair. "Okay, thanks, Dot. No, don't call anyone else. I know, I know. I'll get back to you later."

"What's going on?" Ginny whined. "It's not even daylight yet."

By then Hawk had fumbled his way into his clothes and began searching for his shoes and socks. "Go back to sleep. I've got to go." He shoved both socks and cell phone into his pocket, pushed his feet into his shoes, and hurried out the door.

"You've got to see a doctor, Dad," Becky pleaded. "Look at you. Your arms are skinned up and you can hardly walk."

"Oh, stop mothering me. I've been taking care of myself since I was twelve years old." Grover sounded angry. "I'll be fine. I just don't have the balance I used to, that's all. What kind of a fool Indian falls off his own horse, anyway?"

"Horse?" Becky said, failing to hide the exasperation in her voice. "You were riding a horse?"

"Horses are good for what ails you," Grover said. "And, besides, Blackie is real gentle."

"Okay, Dad, you win. I'm going to stay with you for a while, until I know for sure you're all right."

"Good." Grover nodded his approval. "Now, can you help me back into bed? I'm a little tired."

Becky helped her dad into bed and then sat down on his worn couch to assess the situation. She got up, pulled one of his prescription bottles from the kitchen cabinet, and wrote down the doctor's name. She glanced into the bedroom where her dad had already fallen asleep. She needed some information and it was obvious she wasn't going to get it from him, so she left a note and headed toward the Indian Health Clinic in Sycamore Springs.

The landscape disappeared from her mind as she drove. She couldn't take care of herself, how could she be expected to take care of her dying father? They had never shared secrets with each other, and in her estimation, it seemed too late to start now. She doubted anyone at the clinic would talk to her, but she had to try.

She parked and walked into a crowded waiting room full of weary-looking elderly people, young pregnant women, and crying babies. Walking over to the receptionist's window, she mustered the most positive attitude she could.

"Hi," she said. "My name is Rebecca Silver. My dad is Grover Chuculate. I was wondering if I might be able to talk to his doctor."

The middle-aged Indian woman sitting on the other side of the glass enclosure looked past Becky into the waiting room. "Is your dad with you?"

"No, he isn't. He fell yesterday and he doesn't want to come in."

The woman smirked. "It's kind of hard to do anything for him if he ain't here."

Becky bit her tongue and remained silent.

"Sign in," the woman said, "and I'll put you on the list, but I wouldn't hold my breath about getting any information from anyone around here unless your dad has already signed the form to allow you to do that."

"Oh, could you check?" Becky asked.

"Have a seat. I'll get back with you." She slid the glass window shut.

Becky retreated from the window and noticed a man in a white coat appear behind the unfriendly woman. They spoke for a few moments and the woman, looking unhappy, disappeared through a door. The man smiled at Becky and followed. A minute later, a door opened and the man in the white coat called Becky's name. "Ms. Silver?"

Becky jumped to her feet and walked toward him. "Yes?"

"Come with me," he said.

Becky followed the white coat down a long hallway and through an open doorway into what appeared to be an employee break room.

"Have a seat," he said, nodding toward a small table in the corner. "Would you like some coffee or a soft drink?"

"Whatever you're having," she said.

He pulled two bottles of water out of a refrigerator, placed them on the table, and sat down. He looked too young to be a doctor. He had kind eyes, black hair and brown skin, and a confidence that filled the room.

"I'm Mickey Barehead," he said, and offered his hand. "I'm a physician's assistant here at the clinic."

Becky shook his hand and realized her hands were sweating. "Becky Silver," she said. "Grover Chuculate's daughter."

"You're just as beautiful as Grover said you were." His smile lit up his entire face.

"You know my dad?"

"Yes, ma'am. I've known your dad for a few years now. He gave me riding lessons two years ago, and he's been known to take me fishing on occasion. He even taught me where to find the best wild onions. He always talks about you."

Becky looked down at her hands, trying to will her eyes to absorb the tears that were trying to escape.

"You know, legally, I can't tell you anything about your dad's medical records. But I can tell you stories about a friend I have and you can draw from that."

Becky nodded. "He fell," she said. "He won't let me bring him to the clinic."

Mickey grinned. "I'm not surprised. He's pretty much done with doctors from what I can tell."

"Well, I can't just let him suffer."

"He's been suffering for quite a long time, Becky. Has he told you he has leukemia?"

"Yes."

"He has refused treatment to prolong his life. Once he reaches the point where the pain is too much to bear, he promised me he'd call so we could make arrangements for hospice. I'm not sure he will do that, though. Do you think we're at that point?"

Becky drew in a quick breath. "He didn't say anything about that to me."

"Your dad is tough, and he made me promise he could die on his own terms. I told him it was his call, and I plan to stand by my words."

Becky began to sob. "I waited too long to come home, didn't I?"

He spoke in a comforting voice. "You're here now. That's what counts."

Becky tried to collect herself.

"I tell you what," he said. "How about I make a friendly non-doctor visit before long?"

"Oh, would you?"

He handed her a box of tissue from another table and she dabbed at her eyes and blew her nose.

"I'd love to. Tell him I'm overdue for an update on his fishing tales and I'll try to get by and see him in the next few days. I've got to get back to work and see if I can help empty out that waiting room."

A nurse poked her head into the break room. "Break's over, Mickey. Get your ass back to work."

"See you later," he said, and disappeared into the hallway.

Chapter 31

Lance took the travel mug of hot coffee Sadie had given him and drove toward town to pick up the search warrant he'd already called about. The warrant was waiting for him when he got to his office, so after locking the arrow with the white feather in the evidence cabinet, he grabbed the warrant, refilled his travel mug with more coffee, and drove back toward the Buffalo Ranch in record time.

Besides searching the house, Lance wanted to scrutinize the crime scene again in daylight to see if he'd missed anything the night before. Then he'd turn it over to the lab team to collect evidence. The sun had made its grand entry earlier, as the pink and orange streaks in the sky faded to a solid powder blue. It promised to be a long day, and he was already tired.

Sheriff Long had assigned Deputy Jennings to secure the murder scene the night before. It would be interesting to see if Jennings had managed to stay awake on the job.

A trail of dust followed Lance's vehicle all the way to the Buffalo Ranch. When he got there, much to his chagrin, he could see yellow crime-scene tape flapping in the morning breeze. Someone had breached the perimeter of the crime scene. He let his vehicle roll to a stop as he scanned the area. Jennings had better be paying attention.

Behind the tall fence, the small buffalo herd grazed in the distance, and Lance wondered who was going to take on the task of caring for them. But that was for someone else to figure out. He just wanted to know who had killed the man who owned them—the man everyone hated.

As Lance approached the barn where Angus had died the day before, he saw Jennings' vehicle near the barn and a black Lexus in front of the house with the trunk popped wide open. Lance parked behind the

Lexus and got out as Eugene Hawk came out the front door carrying a long gun.

"Morning, Councilor. You're up early this morning." Lance placed his foot on the back bumper of the Lexus. "What do you think you're doing?"

Hawk stopped in mid-stride and straightened his spine. "I just stopped by to pick up some of my things."

"Your things?" Lance nodded toward the entrance to the Buffalo Ranch. "Do you see that yellow crime-scene tape blowing in the breeze down there?"

Hawk's eyes shifted toward the road and then back to Lance.

"I guess you must've skipped class the day they talked about tampering with evidence at a crime scene, so I'll refresh the information for you. Everything on this side of that yellow tape belongs to my criminal investigation, regardless of whether you think it is yours or not. And now your freaking fingerprints are all over it."

Jennings opened his car door and scrambled toward the house. "Something wrong, Lance? He said he was Clyborn's lawyer."

Lance shot a warning glance at the deputy. "Get some gloves on and take this rifle from Mr. Lawyer and take it back into the house. I'll deal with you later."

Jennings turned and ran back to his vehicle.

Lance, his foot still planted on the back of the Lexus, turned and scrutinized the items in the trunk—six bottles of water, an empty cardboard box, and a camouflage-colored high-velocity crossbow, complete with a pistol-type grip, a trigger pull, and an attached quiver of three arrows.

"This is a pretty fancy crossbow you've got," he said. Pulling his handkerchief from his pocket, he picked the crossbow up and raised it into the air. "I guess you know I'm going to have to confiscate the contents of your trunk, too."

Hawk spoke with urgency. "That crossbow is mine and has absolutely nothing to do with Angus. You can't take anything out of my vehicle. I know my rights."

Lance looked up at Hawk, who had moved closer to the edge of the porch.

"Really?" Lance said. "I guess I'm a little vague on those rights, so I can either take this crossbow, or you can come with me and explain those rights to the judge." Lance stared into the distance as if trying to remember something and then pinned his gaze back on Hawk. "However, best as I recall, the judge took a couple of days off, gone fishing I guess you'd say. But you can wait in jail until he comes back if you want. Probably be only a few days, maybe a week."

Jennings reappeared wearing a pair of blue rubber gloves and threw an identical pair to Lance. Jennings walked up to Hawk, took the rifle from him, verified it was unloaded, and then carried it back into the house.

Lance laid the crossbow back down, shoved the handkerchief into his pocket, and pulled on the rubber gloves. He carried the crossbow to his vehicle and put it in the back seat, and then walked over to the Lexus and glanced through the windows. "I'm going to have to ask you to leave my crime scene, but before you go, is there anything you'd like to share with me regarding your dead client? Like who might've killed him?"

Hawk walked to his car, slammed the trunk lid closed, then stopped and turned toward Lance. "I'll have your badge, Smith."

Lance grinned. "Give it your best shot, Esquire."

As Hawk drove away, Lance shook his head. His next task—figuring out what Hawk was hiding.

Lance bounded up the steps to the house and entered. A pool table, surrounded by leather furniture, sat in the middle of the dark living room. Exotic animal heads stared blankly from the high walls. The air reeked of stale cigars and cigarettes, and empty beer bottles covered the top of a corner bar. With no television or entertainment center anywhere in sight, Lance wondered where the Clyborns had spent their evenings. He couldn't imagine that playing pool and drinking beer captivated their entire lives.

A collection of rifles rested inside a glass display case. Lance opened it and surveyed the weapons. Still wearing his rubber gloves, he checked each firearm to make sure it was unloaded and then sniffed at the barrel of each one. He realized his method of investigation wasn't very scientific, but he was quite sure none of these rifles had been fired recently. Conversely, the odor of gun cleaner was not present. Nonetheless, he'd have the lab add this arsenal of weapons to Hawk's rifle.

Hoping to find a note, he continued working his way through the house and into the dining room and kitchen where he'd talked to Camilla the night before. Maybe she'd committed suicide by purposely careening into the creek.

Her empty glass remained on the table next to an ashtray full of cigarette butts. He moved to the counter and thumbed through a stack of junk mail. On the bottom of the stack an opened envelope from the Delaware County Treasurer with the words "Do not discard—Tax Bill Enclosed" in large red letters caught his eye. He pulled out a tax bill and couldn't believe what he saw. The Clyborns were about to lose the Buffalo Ranch for unpaid back taxes.

Lance returned the bill and the envelope to the counter. While the tax bill was a surprising revelation, it didn't help answer the question of who murdered Angus.

He walked out the back door and toward the barn to study the crime scene. The barn, the house, and the other buildings sat in a carved-out valley surrounded by hills and ridges covered with red oak, blackjack, sycamore, pine, and cedar trees, not to mention underbrush so thick a man could hide in it for weeks and never be found. To discover where the shooter had taken the fatal shot would be next to impossible. He would have to solve this murder some other way.

Eugene Hawk sped away, leaving the Buffalo Ranch behind him. He was past caring what happened to the ranch and its entire herd of bison, including the embezzled animals the chief had demanded he hide there. Angus Clyborn was dead, and even though he wasn't even buried yet, Hawk could feel the arrogant white man's hands tightening around his neck, choking off his last breath. He involuntarily coughed and stretched his neck as he drove toward Sycamore Springs.

Deputy Sheriff Smith had complicated his life even more this morning. If he'd gotten there a little sooner, he could have had his belongings and been long gone before Smith showed up. But this hiccup would go away soon enough. As soon as he could, he would pay a visit to the district attorney and see what he could do to complicate things for

Smith. In the meantime, he still had one large problem looming over his head—the white buffalo calf.

He'd tried to do the right thing by hiding the calf, but everything had changed now, and he was running out of time. He couldn't risk being found out. He'd already put his career in jeopardy by agreeing to embezzle buffalo for the chief, and hooking up with Angus had been the worst mistake of his life. Just being in the same room with Angus had made him feel like he needed to take a dip in the creek to wash off the stench of the *yonega*.

As a child, Hawk had lived with his grandparents, accompanying them to stomp dances, Green Corn Festivals, and other Cherokee gatherings. His grandfather taught him to respect his elders and to share with his neighbors. He taught him about the right path in life, tried to teach him the Cherokee language and the traditional ways of his ancestors.

But when Hawk got older, he rebelled. He decided he didn't want to be Cherokee; he wanted to be like his white friends. He found himself struggling, falling into the abyss between the worlds of Indian and white. He forgot about his grandfather and, in doing so, he lost his moral compass. He had sold out for status and money, turning his back not only on his grandparents, but all of his ancestors.

When the white buffalo calf appeared, he thought it was a sign. He'd tried to remember the lessons of his youth, rekindle his knowledge of his Cherokee heritage. But it was too late. He hated what he had become. The decision he was about to make to save himself would completely destroy the last shred of what he knew about being Cherokee. Sacred or not, the white buffalo calf was simply going to have to disappear. And, the quicker the better.

Hawk parked his Lexus in front of Ginny's house, got out, and let himself in through the side door with the key she'd given him six months earlier. He liked Ginny. She was always available for him, for whatever he wanted. A nice arrangement.

She slipped up beside him and ran her hand up his back. "I heard you drive up. Why did you have to leave in such a hurry like that?"

"Lots going on," he said and pushed her away. "Honey, I need to pick up that rifle I had you store for me. Is it still in the hall closet?"

"No, I moved it. It's in a box under the bed."

"Under the bed?" Hawk frowned. "I hope it's not getting dusty," he said. He headed down the hallway toward Ginny's bedroom.

"I taped it up," she said.

"What about the box of ammo I left?"

"It's all there," she said, sticking her lower lip out. "Aren't you going to stay?"

"I'd love to, hon, but I don't have time."

He got down on his knees and retrieved the long cardboard box, sliding it out from under the bed with his hand. Ginny helped him peel back the tape and open the box. Hawk carefully pulled the vintage Winchester 30.06 bolt-action rifle out of the box and instinctively moved the bolt back to verify the gun was still loaded. He stood and pointed the gun out the window and stared through the attached scope with his right eye. This rifle didn't have the power of the Remington 243 Model 700 he'd had to leave behind with the obstinate deputy, but he could lay down any animal at a hundred yards with this rifle—including a white buffalo calf.

He kissed Ginny's cheek. "I'll be back later. Okay?"

She gave him a pouty look as he walked out the door. He placed the rifle on the back seat, got in, and drove off.

Chapter 32

Sadie picked up the phone and dialed. Beanie answered on the second ring.

"Hi, Beanie. How's business going this morning?"

Sadie listened while Beanie responded on the other end of the line. "Quiet," she said. "Squirrel called a while ago. She's going to bring her lunch over around noon and we're going to eat here at the office. She won four dollars this morning."

Sadie could hear the excitement in Beanie's voice, and it was apparent the news about the Clyborns hadn't reached her yet. She decided to let the local gossip spread at its own pace. She didn't feel up to going into it on the phone.

"Oh, before I forget," Beanie said, "you got a call back from that woman about her pet buffalo this morning. She said to tell you one of her ranch hands is on his way to pick it up. He left yesterday and should be here this evening."

Sadie bit on her lower lip before she spoke. "Did she say anything when she found out she was calling a travel agency?"

"She did. But I figured out who she was right away and told her the Cherokee Nation had its own travel office."

"Oh, dear. What a tangled web . . . okay, I'll take care of it."

"Do you need me to do anything?" Beanie asked.

"No." Sadie balanced the phone on her shoulder while she washed her hands in the kitchen sink and stared out the window at the exact spot where she'd first found the metal ear tag. "I'm going to check on that buffalo," she said. "I'll be in later."

"Okay, boss. Later," she said and hung up.

Knowing that Lance would be busy most of the day, Sadie grabbed her hat, closed the door shut behind her, and whistled for horse and dog.

Joe walked around the corner of the barn and snuffled. Sonny and Sir William followed.

A few minutes later, Sadie, Joe, and Sonny left a bleating Sir William behind and ambled into the pasture. She could see her Uncle Eli working with one of his horses near his corral. He waved and she acknowledged by taking off her hat and holding it in the air for a moment before continuing on toward the newly installed fence where Kenny Wayne Sanders had been killed and the property where she hoped she would find Sandy and her white calf.

Having had her unsettling moments here in the last few days, she admonished Sonny to stay close and he complied. When she got to the fence she reined Joe to the right, since that appeared to her to be the direction the men had been working. Her intuition told her that with all that had gone on at the Buffalo Ranch in the last few days, the workers had probably left Angus's fence-building job and moved on.

She proceeded cautiously for about a mile when she found what she'd been looking for. The tall fence halted abruptly, and a short section of the old fence lay on the ground. Tools lay beside it as if the workers had instantly disappeared. "Look, Sonny. Scotty beamed them up." The visualization made her chuckle. "I don't think this is going to keep too many bison secure," she said aloud. "It's a good thing Sandy is a tame buffalo."

She slid off Joe's back and guided him through the opening, making sure there were no nails for the horse to step on. She noticed horse hoofprints in the soft soil, probably made when it had been raining. Bending down, she saw that one of the hooves had a unique print, with a chip missing on the outer edge. Dismissing the hoofprints, she climbed back onto Joe's saddle.

She tried to remember the map in the county clerk's office. She thought she was still on the Chuculate property that Angus had so artfully stolen. She pondered on Angus and all his shenanigans. It was no wonder someone had killed him. And with him dead, who would take care of his buffalo? She didn't exactly have the right to hand over the buffalo known as Sandy to anyone to haul off, and there was the question about the calf. Was it really a white buffalo, or a mixed-breed Charolais? What a mess.

She continued to think as she rode into a steep ravine, dodging thick brush and low-hanging tree limbs. Of course, if the woman had sent papers with her ranch hand showing she owned Sandy, they would have to give the buffalo to him, right? But the metal tag with the identifying number on it wasn't attached to Sandy anymore. Sadie had it. Of course, the ranch hand would probably know to look for the tattoo on the animal's lip. This was getting more and more complicated.

When she reached the bottom of the narrow valley, she found a small meadow. Suddenly, she realized Sonny had disappeared. She whistled and heard him bark. Maybe he'd found Sandy. She rounded a thicket of scrub oak and found Sonny lapping water from a clear water creek. She slipped off Joe's back to look around and let Joe have a drink, too.

She heard pounding hooves and looked up to see Sandy and her cream-colored calf. The sight mesmerized Sadie for a moment, but then she realized Sandy was not happy. The crack of a rifle caught Sadie off guard and a bullet whizzed by her ear. She fell to the ground when Joe reared. Another shot sounded and Sonny yelped. She tried to catch her breath, her heart beating so loudly she could hardly hear. It was her nightmare coming true. She twisted around and saw Sonny on the ground and Eugene Hawk aiming at the calf.

"No!" she screamed. Joe backed away as she ran toward Sonny, not caring whether she was in the line of fire or not. Sonny was already on his feet and hurling himself toward Hawk, teeth bared. She could see blood on his fur, and so much adrenaline ran through her veins that she screamed and ran headlong toward Hawk and Sonny. She heard another round go off, only this time it was a different, louder boom. She could see Hawk falling backward, the rifle in his hand falling away, and heard her uncle screaming in Cherokee.

She got to Sonny just as he clamped down on Hawk's arm and began to shake the man's upper body back and forth like a rag doll.

"*Alewisdodi*!" she yelled. "Stop, Sonny!"

Hawk screamed. "Get him off before he kills me!"

Sonny let go, stood over Hawk, and snarled.

Eli rode up, jumped off his horse, kicked the rifle out of Hawk's reach, and kicked Hawk in the side. Sonny yelped again.

"Are you hit, Sadie?" Eli yelled.

"No," she cried. "But Sonny's bleeding."

Eli retrieved a rope from his saddle. "Get up Hawk! You're not hurt."

"My hand is bleeding," Hawk cried. "You shot me in the hand!"

"If we're lucky, maybe you'll bleed to death," Eli said.

Sadie pulled Sonny back and stroked his head, trying to calm him as her uncle tied Hawk to a nearby oak tree.

With Hawk restrained, Eli knelt beside Sadie and the wolfdog. Sonny leaned hard against Sadie and began to pant wildly, but remained still while Eli ran his hands along the wolfdog's body from his head, down his legs, and to his tail.

"I don't think anything's broken, but he's losing a lot of blood." He pulled off his shirt and tied it around Sonny's hindquarter.

Sadie watched her uncle work carefully, but with purpose.

"What do we do?" she said. "Do you think we can get him on Joe's back so he doesn't have to walk all the way back to the house? He's too heavy to carry that far." Joe stood not far from the buffalo cow and calf.

Eli got up, walked over to Hawk, and backhanded him. "Where's your vehicle?"

Fear crossed Hawk's face as he pointed with his head. "Through the gate," he said. "It's parked on the forest road."

"Where's the key?" Eli said as he started emptying all of Hawk's pockets until he finally found what he was looking for. He returned to Sadie and threw a ring of keys to her. "Come on. You're going to take Sonny to the vet in Hawk's car. Can you hold Sonny's head? I don't want him to bite me when I pick him up."

Sadie talked to Sonny quietly and held his head, and together they carried him toward the road.

"Wait!" Hawk yelled. "You can't leave me here!"

Sadie and Eli ignored him as they made their way to the car. Once they got to Hawk's Lexus, Sadie opened the back door and urged Sonny to climb onto the back seat.

Sadie's shock turned to rage when she heard Hawk screaming. "You can't let that dog bleed all over my leather seats!"

She started toward Hawk, but Eli grabbed her arm and motioned her back toward the car. Then he walked back to the tree where Hawk was trying to wiggle his way free.

"*Jalulogv.*" Hawk spit out the Cherokee word and then repeated in English. "You're crazy."

"If that dog dies," Eli said, "I will show you crazy." He put his hands firmly around Hawk's throat. "I will kill you with my bare hands. You got that?" He picked up his rifle, then turned to Sadie, and spoke deliberately. "Send the law, but don't wait too long. I'm not sure if I can control myself."

Sadie jumped into the driver's seat, started the Lexus, and directed the air conditioning toward the back seat. Gravel flew as she and Sonny raced toward Doc Cody's.

Chapter 33

Two and a half hours after Lance caught Hawk trying to walk away from the Clyborn home with evidence, the team from the lab arrived. Lance handed over the crossbow and the Remington 243 Model 700 rifle that he'd confiscated from Hawk, explained the importance of each to the lead man, and pointed out that they would most likely be covered with Hawk's fingerprints. He explained that he had already gone through every room in the house, but he would appreciate their going through it again. He pulled out his notebook and made a note to remind the ME to send a copy of Angus's fingerprints to the lab, then he instructed Jennings to keep the crime scene sealed until the team had finished. He needed to get moving.

Lance sped away from the Buffalo Ranch and headed toward his office. He had taken notes all evening as well as this morning, but sooner or later he had to fill out the obligatory reports. He decided on later. First, he would pay a visit to Roy Carter.

As he drove past Sadie's house, he fought the urge to stop. He could use another cup of coffee, but knew it would cost him valuable time, so he continued to drive. He promised himself he would make it up to her later. Then he began to organize his thoughts.

If the medical examiner could retrieve a bullet from the body of Angus Clyborn, and he felt confident that he could, the ballistics report would throw the investigation into high gear. It would either convict or eliminate Roy Carter. Roy had made a lot of threats to kill Angus, and right now he appeared to be the prime suspect. Losing his herd of cattle to Bang's had done more than put Roy in a bad mood, but Lance found it disheartening to believe a man would murder someone in cold blood for something like that.

Then there was the question of why Hawk was trying to abscond with the Remington rifle. Hawk had presented himself to Lance as Angus's lawyer and business partner. From Hawk's reputation, if money was involved and he was benefitting from the arrangement, it didn't make sense for Hawk to cut the head off the golden goose, so to speak. However, if the bullet that killed Angus matched the Remington, Hawk would have a lot of explaining to do.

Lance remained puzzled about the conduct of Angus's wife, Camilla. Why did she flee like that? Did she know who killed Angus? Lance thought it unlikely she'd done it herself, but it would have been easy enough for her to hire it done. She certainly had the means, and his behavior with women could have sent her into a rage. Did she suddenly have buyer's remorse and run from fear of being found out? Most likely, she'd been driving too fast and simply lost control in the loose gravel. If she'd swerved to miss an animal, which was a good possibility, she could have overcorrected and easily hit the concrete bridge abutment, causing the Cadillac to flip into the water. Nevertheless, unless she'd left a note behind that he hadn't been able to find yet, she was no help to him now.

Then there was Eli. Eli could be an angry Indian with a bad temper or a stalwart member of the community. He would give you the shirt off his back if you needed it, but if you tried to take something without asking, he wouldn't think twice before breaking your arm. No one pushed him around, including Angus, and Eli had proven that by blasting out the taillight and back window of Angus's truck. Granted, Angus had provoked him, but in pure textbook theory, some would have considered that attempted murder. Eli had threatened to kill Angus, and most people took him at his word. If Eli had killed Angus, that was going to create more problems than Lance cared to think about at the moment. He would put Eli on the bottom of his list for now.

Lance wondered who else hated Angus enough to kill him. Becky flashed into his mind. She certainly had reason to kill Angus after he raped her. Then Lance wondered how many other women he had raped.

Lance had told Becky a trial could be rough, and he wondered if that comment had provoked her into taking things into her own hands. But then, he had a pretty good handle on people's character, and he didn't think Becky had it in her to kill Angus, or anyone else for that matter. Instead, she, like most rape victims, was more likely to simply suffer in silence.

Then there was the possibility it was an accident. He'd caught more than one poacher on this road. Someone could have taken aim at a deer, shot from the window of his truck, and missed. If the rifle and the ammo were high-powered enough, the bullet could have traveled past the intended target of a venison dinner and hit Angus instead. If that were the case, the shooter might not even know what had happened, and if it had gone down that way, there would be no weapon to compare to the ballistics report. Out of the realm of possibility? Not completely.

Lance's thoughts moved on to the crossbow. The arrows in the attached quiver looked suspiciously like the arrow that had killed Kenny Wayne Sanders, leading him to believe the two murders were clearly connected. If the lab team could lift viable fingerprints from the arrows, it might shed some light on the Sanders investigation. Soon enough, they would know who killed Sanders. Now all he had to do was figure out who killed Angus.

When Lance got to Highway 20, he turned east and took the second turnoff, toward Roy Carter's ranch. He parked in the same place he had before and slid out of his vehicle. Before he reached the porch, Roy Carter walked out the front door. He looked hungover, with tousled hair, disheveled clothes, and bare feet.

"Can I help you?" Roy said.

"Hard night, Roy?"

"What's it to you?"

"Did your wife tell you I came by?"

"Yeah. She said so. I've been busy."

"I bet."

"What do you want?"

"Where were you yesterday afternoon?"

"I can't see that that's any of your business."

"Make it easy on yourself, Roy. I'm not in the mood to play games with you. From what I understand, you threatened to shoot Angus Clyborn, and that's exactly what someone did yesterday. So, that makes you suspect number one in a murder case."

"What?" Roy looked shocked. "You mean someone beat me to it?"

"Did you kill Angus Clyborn, Roy?"

He laughed. "Sounds like someone saved me the trouble. Good for them."

"Just tell me where you were, I'll verify it, and move on in my investigation. If you don't have an alibi, well, then you're going to have to turn in your rifle for a ballistics test. It won't take long to get a search warrant."

"I was at the Party Barn, drinking." Roy looked defeated as he glanced back into the house. "Marci's not too happy with me."

"Who were you with?"

"Anyone and everyone. I don't even remember driving home."

"What about your son, Robert?"

"He left for south Texas last week." Roy looked off in the distance. "Said he was going to get a summer job hauling hay. It's not good money, but at least it's honest work."

"He didn't, by any chance, take a rifle with him, did he?"

"He keeps a rifle in his truck, just like I do." He looked past Lance again toward the barn. "You don't have to worry about Robert. He's just a kid, not a killer."

"Roy, you need to know that Angus didn't bring brucellosis into Delaware County. I don't know how your cattle got infected, but I checked with the livestock inspector, and he told me he'd already verified the bison at the Buffalo Ranch had been vaccinated for the disease before they left Wyoming."

Roy looked down at his feet.

Lance relaxed. His years in law enforcement had taught him to read people fairly well, and Roy's demeanor didn't exactly scream guilt. Instead, the rancher appeared tired and beaten down. Angus might be dead, but so were Roy's cattle, and as sad as it seemed, the herd was a bigger loss to Roy than the life of a boisterous game hunter.

"Okay, Roy, I'll talk to Rosy. I think you're telling the truth. But if you're not, you'll have to deal with me. Understand?"

Roy walked off the porch and to his truck. He opened the passenger's side door, reached in, and pulled out a rifle. He slid back the bolt to show it was unloaded, and offered it to Lance.

"Go ahead and take it," he said. "I have nothing to hide."

Lance took the rifle and then tensed when Roy's wife, Marci, walked out onto the porch carrying a shotgun.

"Here," she said. "Take this one, too. I'm tired of having all these guns around here."

"No, ma'am," Lance said. "That's not necessary. I'm only interested in the rifle."

Roy stepped back on the porch and pulled the shotgun from his wife's hands. Marci turned on her heel and reentered the house.

"Sorry about that," Roy said. "She's been under a lot of stress lately, losing the cows and all."

"That's okay, Roy. Don't be taking any trips, you hear?" Lance climbed into his vehicle and lowered the window. "And, Roy, you'd better get some sleep. You look like hell."

Roy turned and walked back into the house, allowing the screen door to slam shut behind him.

Lance left the Carter ranch and dove toward town. His first stop would be the Party Barn to see if Rosy would corroborate Roy's story, then he would go to his office and see if the ME had come up with the bullet that had killed Angus.

As he drove, he thought about Roy and Marci. They were good people who had worked hard for what they had. This setback had upset the balance in their lives. He hoped Roy's rifle could be cleared sooner than later. He hated to think either one of them were caught up in Angus's murder.

Lance parked in front of the Party Barn Bar and went in. The lunch crowd had come and gone, leaving only a few regulars at the bar.

"Lance, baby," Rosy boomed. "Where you been? Haven't seen you in a coon's age."

Her laughter filled the room and Lance took a seat on one of the round wooden stools at the end of the bar where he could see the entire room, including the entry door.

"Catching crooks, Rosy," Lance replied. "Catching crooks."

She stood on the other side of the bar and leaned in toward Lance. "Speaking of crooks," she said, "rumor has it Angus Clyborn bit the big one."

"You know I cannot confirm nor deny any rumors." Lance winked at her. "Let's just say I hope he didn't owe a very big bar bill."

"Is that right?" Rosy straightened her back and placed her hands on her hips. "I'll be damned. What happened?"

"We're still trying to figure that out." Lance's phone rang. He looked at the caller ID, saw it was Sadie's cell phone, and let the call go to voice mail. He put the phone back in his pocket. He'd call her back later. "But can you tell me if Roy Carter was in here yesterday?"

"Oh, yeah. He drank his limit and then some. Poor guy. He was not in a good mood."

"About what time did he get here and leave?"

Rosy thought for a minute. "Oh, I'd say he got here for happy hour around four and some of the guys put him in his truck and pointed him toward home around midnight. Why do you ask?"

"Just doing a little research is all. Say, I'll take a burger if you can make it quick."

"Are you kidding me? Quick is my middle name," she said and disappeared into the kitchen.

Lance pulled out his notebook and wrote down the information Rosy had given him. He considered Rosy a reliable source, so unless the rifle came back with a different result, Roy was off the hook. Lance would know more as soon as he talked to the ME.

Sadie drove as fast as she could back to the main road, thankful that the forestry road into the back of the Chuculate's property wasn't too bumpy. As soon as she got to the highway, she floored the gas pedal of the Lexus, glancing periodically at Sonny. He was holding his head up and panting, which she took as a good sign, but the shirt Eli had tied onto his leg was already soaked with blood.

"It's okay, boy," she said. "We'll have you at Doc Cody's in no time."

She pulled her cell phone out of her back pocket and hit the speed-dial button for Lance's cell. When the call went to his voice mail, she tried to keep her composure as she left him a message telling him she had an emergency situation, was on her way to Doc Cody's with Sonny, and to call her immediately. She put the phone on the seat beside her as she maneuvered curves at high speed. As soon as she slid into a space in front of the animal hospital, she laid on the horn. A few seconds later, Doc Cody appeared at the front door.

"Help me," she yelled. "Sonny's been shot!"

Doc ran to the car and opened the back door. Sonny rose up on his front legs and growled.

"Do you think he can walk, Sadie?"

"I'm not sure."

"Pull the car around to the side door. I'll meet you there with my assistant."

Sadie did as the veterinarian instructed and together they coaxed Sonny off the back seat and onto a gurney. Then the doctor wheeled him straight into an examination room and began to fill a syringe.

"Hold his head, Sadie. I'm going to need to knock him out so I can take an X-ray and work on him."

The next thing Sadie knew, she had been relegated to the waiting room, while Doc Cody, having assured her Sonny would be fine, performed surgery to stop the bleeding. Suddenly, the door swung open and Lance rushed inside. Unable to contain her emotions any longer, she fell into his arms and sobbed. Lance guided her back to a chair, where they sat for a few minutes until she regained her composure. Then he started peppering her with questions.

"Are you okay? What happened? Where's your car? Why is Hawk's Lexus in the parking lot with blood all over the back seat?"

"Oh, Lance. I took Sonny and went looking for that white buffalo calf, and when we found it, Hawk was getting ready to shoot it. Sonny either got in the way or he scared Hawk or something, I don't really know, but Hawk shot him. If it hadn't been for Uncle Eli . . . oh, Lance, you've got to get out there. Eli has Hawk tied to a tree and he's really pissed, Uncle Eli, that is." She stopped for a minute, wiped her nose, and then kept talking. "Uncle Eli made Hawk give me his car keys to bring Sonny to the vet. The forestry road off of Eucha Road, between Eucha and the highway, takes you into the back side of the property. You'd better hurry."

Lance pulled her head to his chest. "Is Sonny okay?"

"I think so."

"Is Joe okay?"

Sadie nodded.

"And Eli's not hurt?"

"No, but he's really mad. He threatened to kill Hawk."

"Is Hawk hurt?"

"His hand was bleeding. Eli shot the rifle out of his hand." Sadie felt a tear slide down her cheek. "You know he could have killed him if he'd wanted to."

"I know." He kissed her forehead. "Are you okay?" he asked again. Sadie nodded. "I'm okay."

"Stay here. I'll be back as soon as I can. Okay?"

Sadie sniffed and nodded again, but Lance was already dialing his cell phone as he disappeared out the door. A moment later Sadie could hear the siren wail as he peeled out of the animal hospital's parking lot.

A smiling Doc Cody appeared through the waiting room door and Sadie jumped to her feet.

"You've got a very lucky wolfdog, Sadie," the doctor said. "I was able to stop the bleeding. The bullet went clear through his leg. I have no idea how it did that without hitting something vital, but it did. Nothing is broken. You're going to need to keep him inactive for a few days, but he'll be fine."

"I need to be there when he wakes up."

"As soon as we get him cleaned up."

"He's not going to be happy if he wakes up in unfamiliar surroundings."

"I know. We'll put him in a room by himself and you can stay with him until he's okay to go home."

Sadie followed the doctor through the door that led to where her best friend and guardian slept. Today, she would be his protector.

Chapter 34

After the urgent care clinic had bandaged Hawk's hand and given him an ice pack for his bruised face, Lance delivered him to the county jail and locked him in a cell by himself. He picked up the phone and dialed Sadie's cell phone and learned she was still at the animal hospital.

The doc had wanted to keep Sonny overnight, she explained, but then reluctantly agreed to let her take him home. Probably, Lance surmised, because the veterinarian didn't want to have to care for an ill-disposed wolfdog that didn't usually listen to anyone but Sadie.

"Don't worry," Sadie said on the other end of the line. "Uncle Eli and Aunt Mary are on their way to pick us up with my car. We'll get him home. I talked to Beanie and told her to close the travel office when she needed to go. She's kind of freaked out about everything. We'll regroup tomorrow. Can you send someone to get Hawk's car?"

"I'll take care of the car," Lance said. "Tell Eli I'm going to need to get a statement from him. Okay?"

"Okay. And, Lance? Thanks for not yelling at me."

"I love you, Sadie. Please take care of yourself. I'll call you as soon as I can get loose from here."

Rowdy Canon downshifted his Ford F-250 truck as he approached a stoplight on Highway 10. He remained on the bypass so he wouldn't have to pull the cattle trailer through Tahlequah. Following the road signs, he turned south again after he'd cleared the traffic congestion. Checking his watch, he pulled off the highway in front of a large brick building with a sign that read, "Cherokee Nation Tribal Headquarters."

It was late in the afternoon, and he hoped everyone wasn't already gone for the day.

His body ached from the long drive as he slid out of the truck and made his way into the building. The first person he ran into pointed him toward his destination. Walking past an empty secretary's desk, he pushed the door open that read "Chief John Henry Greenleaf." The silver-haired man glanced away from his computer and peered over his reading glasses with a look of surprise. "May I help you?" he asked.

"I'm here for Sandy."

An exhausted Sadie was sitting in the animal hospital next to a sleeping Sonny, her hand resting on his chest so she could feel the rise and fall of his breathing, when her cell phone vibrated. She pulled it out of her pocket and saw that it was Beanie and answered quietly.

"Are you okay, Beanie?"

"Yes, I'm fine," Beanie replied. "I was getting ready to leave when that woman from Wyoming called again. She said her ranch hand is at the Cherokee Nation and no one knows anything about her pet buffalo. What do I tell her? She's on the other line."

"Can this day get any crazier?" Sadie let out a long sigh. "Get her number, tell her I had an emergency, and that I'll call her back shortly. I've got to talk to Lance, and I'd say the less she knows the better."

Sadie hung up and Sonny raised his head. "It's okay, boy, I'm here."

He closed his eyes and laid his head back down.

She dialed Lance's phone and he answered on the first ring.

"Lance, I haven't had a chance to tell you all this, and it's kind of a long story, but the owner of that buffalo cow with the white calf is here from Wyoming. Well, actually he's in Tahlequah, because they think she was accidentally taken with a shipment of buffalo to the Cherokee Nation. I don't know how Angus ended up with her, but she isn't supposed to be in Oklahoma at all. They want to pick up the cow and calf and take them home. She's a pet, for heaven's sake. I know this isn't what you want to hear, but can I just tell them where she is and let them go get her?"

"Hold on, Sadie. Is this buffalo stolen?"

"I don't know. I just know that when I found the ear tag, I took it to Brad . . . oh, none of that matters . . . but the woman verified the tag belonged to her pet buffalo, Sandy." Sadie searched for words to explain the situation without making it too complicated. "She told me the cow was due to deliver a calf that was half-Charolais, which would make it appear to be a white buffalo, but it's not, it's half-Charolais half-buffalo, and she and her kids were in a panic because they didn't know what had happened to her. There's a connection with Kenny Wayne Sanders and Hawk. According to this woman, they went there together to set up the delivery of the buffalo to the Cherokee Nation."

The line went silent, and Sadie knew Lance was trying to digest everything she'd just told him.

"Does anyone else know about this?" he asked.

"Beanie and Becky. They were both there when I first called the woman."

"Give me the woman's phone number, and I'll make arrangements to meet her man tomorrow. He can take the buffalo, providing he can prove it's his to take. Tell Beanie to keep this to herself."

Sadie hung up and called Beanie and relayed Lance's request. "Let me know if she calls again."

"I will, boss. I'm going home."

Doc Cody walked in and Sonny rose onto his front feet and growled. Sadie quickly put her arm around his neck. "It's okay, boy."

"Boy, that's a fine how-do-you-do for the doc that just fixed your leg." The veterinarian smiled. "Just for that, I'm sending you home."

Eli walked in and stood behind the doctor. Sonny relaxed.

"Let's go home, Sonny," Eli said.

"I'll second that," Sadie said.

Lead lab technician Robby Summerfield slumped into one of the chairs facing Lance's desk and dropped a manila envelope in front of him.

"I just came from the ME's office and he asked me to drop this off. Said you weren't going to be very happy."

Lance left the envelope where it landed. "You want to cut to the chase? I'm tired."

"Yeah, so am I." Robby ran his fingers through his thick black hair. "In a nutshell? Nothing. You got nothing."

Lance let out a long sigh. "Want to elaborate?"

"The bullet that killed Clyborn hit his backbone and fragmented. It was a six-millimeter jacketed, soft-nosed bullet, and they disintegrate every time. So, there is no way to know what specific kind of a bullet it was, or even run a ballistics test. And, it'll take a month of Sundays to piece that bullet back together well enough to do any kind of a test on it. It would probably take an expert from the FBI to do that, and if they could, then maybe, and I emphasize the word 'maybe,' we could match it to a weapon. The entry wound was made by a six-millimeter bullet, but that's all we can say with any certainty. The Remington 243 could have made that entry wound, but why would the murder weapon be in the dead man's house?"

Lance rubbed his face with both hands. "What about fingerprints on the Remington 243 and the crossbow?"

"Two sets of fingerprints—Clyborn's and Hawk's." Then he explained. "The ME took Clyborn's prints, and Hawk's prints were on file when he was bonded as an officer of the court. Of course, you said you took the bow from him anyway, didn't you? However, the prints on the arrow that killed Sanders—all Clyborn's."

"Get any prints off the arrow with the white feather?"

"Clean as a whistle. Purposely, I'd say. But you should know, even though that arrow looked similar to the one that killed Sanders, someone else made it. Making arrows is a fine art, and that arrow, the one with the white feather, was made by an excellent craftsman. The one that killed Sanders, not so much."

"Hm." Lance pushed out his lower lip. "That's interesting."

Lance's office phone rang and Robby rose.

"Okay. Thanks for the info," Lance said, as he picked up the receiver and answered. "Smith here," he said. After listening for a minute, he replied to the caller. "Yes, sir, Chief Greenleaf, I understand," he said into the phone. "Oh, really . . . yes, sir . . . I'll let you know."

Lance hung up and shook his head, retrieved Hawk from his cell, and led him into an interrogation room.

Hawk sat down and stared at Lance. "I'm a lawyer and I know my rights."

Lance pulled up a chair and sat across the table from Hawk. "Yes, I know. You said that this morning. You also said you'd have my badge, but so far it's still pinned to my chest and you've got some explaining to do."

"Bring me a phone. I have a right to make a call."

Lance nodded. "Yes, you do. But before you make that all-important phone call, I thought I'd give you a chance to come clean. You being a lawyer and all, I'm sure you recognize the fact that a little good will could go a long way in a court of law."

"I'm not only a lawyer; I'm a Cherokee Nation tribal councilor."

"Yes, I'm aware of that. I just spoke with Chief Greenleaf on the phone a few moments ago and he wanted to make sure I knew that the Cherokee Nation attorney general is filing charges against you for embezzling buffalo from the Cherokee Nation." Lance chuckled. "You know, I think the correct term is something more like 'buffalo rustling in plain sight.' What do you think, Esquire?"

Hawk narrowed his eyes. "That bastard."

"Now," Lance continued, "I've heard there's honor among thieves, but we all know that's not really the case. Is that what happened to Kenny Wayne Sanders? He knew too much? You killed Sanders, didn't you? It's just a matter of time until we match the arrow that killed Sanders to the crossbow you tried to escape with this morning. Isn't that right?"

Hawk's nostrils flared. "You cannot pin that murder on me. Angus was a hot-headed *yonega*. Sanders threatened to expose our plan to take extra bison from the tribe's shipments and sell them for profit. I told Angus not to involve Sanders, but he had to do everything his way. Angus killed Sanders."

"So, why were you trying to take the crossbow?"

"Because it belongs to me, jackass. I knew this whole thing was going to come back and bite me on the ass."

"Is that why you killed Angus?"

Hawk looked terrified. "I did not kill Angus. I don't know who did, but I'm not surprised."

"Perhaps someone you helped steal land from for Angus's empire? How much was he paying you to file forged deeds and quiet titles?"

Hawk looked at the bandage on his hand. "I need to make that call now."

Lance took Hawk back to his cell and locked the door. He started to walk away, and then turned and said, "Oh, yeah. There's a little matter of the attempted murder of a wolfdog. I talked to the owner and she agreed to settle out of court. Her representative will be Eli Walela, and he said he'd iron things out with you as soon as you're released."

Fear crossed Hawk's face. "That Indian is crazy, and I'm going to file charges against him for assault and battery."

"Oh, yeah? You let me know when you come up with some witnesses to that."

Lance walked away as Hawk screamed at him. "Bring me a phone!"

Chapter 35

Two weeks later, Sadie stood at her kitchen sink and sipped coffee while Sonny lay sleeping on the floor next to the back door. She stared at the hill behind her house where Kenny Wayne Sanders had been killed. His murder had put into motion the events that led to the eventual deaths of both Angus and Camilla Clyborn, and the indictment of tribal councilor Eugene Hawk for embezzlement from a federally recognized tribe.

Hawk was facing charges not only for stealing buffalo, but also for aiding in the unlawful taking of Indian land through forgeries and other unethical means. Whether he'd ever spend a day in jail was yet to be seen. The same held true for the women in his office who had helped create and forge the documents.

The day after her and Sonny's encounter with Hawk, Sadie had placed a call to Kate, the woman at Travers Bison Ranch in Buffalo, Wyoming, to assure her that Sandy and her calf, both healthy, were on their way back home. After Rowdy had showed the tattoo on Sandy's upper lip to Lance, he'd helped load the buffalo cow and calf in Rowdy's trailer and sent them on their way, happy to have the problem of the white buffalo calf resolved.

Sadie had painfully confessed to Kate that the Cherokee Nation travel office did not really exist, and then admitted she'd had absolutely nothing to do with the transfer of buffalo from Wyoming to Oklahoma. She'd lied, pure and simple, and apologized.

But when Sadie relayed the story of how she and Sonny, along with her Uncle Eli, had averted the death of Sandy and her calf, Kate thanked God for those lies because they had saved her precious Sandy, and then she broke down in tears. After promising to stay in touch, Sadie, too, closed the chapter on the white buffalo calf that wasn't a white buffalo at all.

Lance came into the kitchen from the bedroom, poured himself a cup of coffee, joined Sadie at the window, and put his arm around her.

"You know," he said. "You're still in trouble for taking off on your own and almost getting yourself killed. I'm going to owe Eli for years to come for watching out for you." He kissed her. "I don't know what I'd do if something happened to you, Sadie."

Sadie smiled. "Now you know how I feel while you're out chasing crazy crooks."

"Point made," he said.

She kissed him, and they sat at the table.

"What's going to happen now?" she said.

Lance cupped his coffee mug with his hands. "We're still waiting for the FBI to piece together the bullet they took out of Angus, but the agent told me yesterday not to hold my breath. It doesn't look promising."

"So, how are you ever going to prove who killed Angus if you can't find the murder weapon?"

Lance sipped and thought. Then he smiled. "Divine intervention, I guess."

"What about Roy Carter?"

"I think Roy was angry and wanted to take his pain out on somebody, namely Angus, but Roy doesn't have it in him to murder someone in cold blood. Besides that, he's got a solid alibi at the bar. Rosy has no reason to lie."

"Maybe his son did it for him."

"If he did he's quite a time traveler." Lance leaned back in his chair. "The entire crew he's working with swears he was slinging bales of hay onto the back of a truck in south Texas the day Angus was killed."

"What about Camilla? Maybe she killed him and then freaked out and ran?"

"I don't think so. None of the rifles we took from the house had her fingerprints on them, and we didn't find any weapons in the car she was driving when she died."

"You think her wreck was just an accident, then?"

"I think so. The skid marks on the road indicate she may have swerved to miss an animal. She just couldn't control the car before she hit the bridge."

"She must have lived a terrible existence with Angus. It's too bad she had to die. She could have had a new life without him." Sadie shrugged her shoulders. "Who else then?"

"I guess I'm still working on that. The group from COWA had a protest rally in Oklahoma City that day. Besides that, I don't really think they would go that far, do you?" Lance downed the rest of his coffee. "You don't think your Uncle Eli took out his frustrations on Angus, do you?"

"Lance!" Sadie pushed away from the table. "I can't believe you said that."

"I've got to check all the possibilities."

"I can tell you one thing. If Uncle Eli had wanted to do Angus in, he wouldn't have done it from afar. He would have marched up to him and strangled him with his own hands."

Lance grimaced. "Yeah, you're probably right."

The phone rang and Sadie answered. It was Becky.

"Oh, Becky, are you sure? I'm so sorry. Yes, of course, we're on our way."

Tears filled her eyes as she hung up and looked at Lance. "Grover's dying."

Together, Lance and Sadie drove straight to Grover Chuculate's small trailer, where Becky had been taking care of him for the last few weeks. Two Indian men and their wives sat in lawn chairs under Grover's shade tree, quietly singing Cherokee hymns.

Becky came to the door and hugged Sadie. "Thank you for coming. He said he wanted to talk to you and your lawman friend." She smiled through tears. "He described Lance as 'the one who ate wild onions with him.'"

Lance removed his hat as they entered the small trailer and stood at the foot of the bed, where Grover's brown skin stood out in stark contrast to the crisp white pillows propped under his head. Sadie thought he looked frailer than he had the last time she'd been there with Becky. It was hard to believe he was dying. She hated cancer and she hated the Agent Orange that caused it.

Sadie's eyes moved to a walking stick leaning in the corner near Grover's bed. It was adorned with several white feathers, and she immediately thought of the mysterious arrow that had struck her tree.

Grover's eyes followed Sadie's, and he grinned. Then he pointed a shaking finger at Lance, and Sadie quickly retreated, closing the bedroom door behind her, leaving the two men alone.

Grover motioned for Lance to come closer and pointed at an open Bible. "Do you read the Bible?" he asked.

Lance shook his head. "Not much, I'm afraid. Do you want me to read to you?"

"No." Grover rocked his head back and forth on the pillow. "There's a part in there where a woman was raped. Her brothers came in from the fields and took revenge, killed everyone."

Grover's remarks seemed confusing to Lance, but he immediately wondered if Grover had somehow found out about Becky's rape. He remained quiet and let Grover talk.

"God punished them for taking revenge. It's right there in the Old Testament."

Lance nodded, unsure of what to say.

Grover pointed toward the closet. "What you're looking for is there."

Lance walked to the closet and pulled out an old Savage 243 with an attached scope and held it up for Grover to see.

Grover raised his head and nodded. "That's the one." He showed no emotion. "He shouldn't have done it. I wasn't there to protect her," he said with sadness in his voice.

"How did you know?" Lance asked.

"He's a loudmouth. I heard him brag about it in Rosy's bar. He didn't say her name, but with Becky in the hospital, it didn't take me long to figure out what happened. And when I saw her, I could see the pain in her face." After a few minutes of silence, he continued. "Among Indians," he said, "there has always been blood law. You take from me, I take from you. You kill me, then you or someone from your clan dies. It restores balance. But, no one does that anymore. We have a different kind of law now, like you," he nodded at Lance again, "to make things right." Grover looked toward the window.

Lance remained quiet, allowing Grover to speak in his own time.

"I warned him about the land," he said. "He was sitting in his truck at Old Eucha one night. I stuck my rifle in his face and told him to stop stealing land," he said. "But he was so damned drunk, I doubt he even heard what I said. It was pitch dark. He never knew it was me." Grover frowned. "I'm sorry I didn't tell you all I knew about the dead man by the fence. I knew you would figure it out." He gazed toward Lance. "I was there; I watched Angus kill him with a crossbow. Angus was evil."

Lance remained quiet.

"He didn't know I was there," Grover said. "He got on his four-wheeler and took off. From a distance, I saw the wolfdog come and sit down by the body. I left when I saw Eli coming."

"How did you get on the ridge to kill him, Grover?"

"The way all good Indians get anywhere." He grinned. "On my horse." Then his tone changed. "I don't want Becky to know what I did."

Melodious voices filtered through the open window. The singers had switched to English and were singing "How Beautiful Heaven Must Be."

Lance stood quietly, still holding the rifle.

"God punished the men in the Bible," Grover said. "But it says God is a forgiving God. Do you think He will forgive me for killing a man?"

Lance searched for the right words. "I think so."

"*Osda.*" Grover nodded. "It's good now." Then he closed his eyes.

Lance took the rifle, left the room, and motioned for Becky. "He needs you," he said. Then he carried Grover's rifle to his truck and locked it inside.

When Sadie left Lance and Grover to talk, she walked straight to the horses that were lined up against the fence staring toward the trailer. They knew he was dying, and the thought shook her to the core.

As she moved toward them, she noticed the black-and-white paint stallion favoring one foot. She climbed over the fence and approached the lame horse. She talked to him in soft tones, stroked his forehead, and then slid her hand down his neck and shoulder to his front leg. Careful not to frighten the horse, she gently raised his foot. The hoof, chipped and splitting on the outer edge, needed attention. Sadie put the hoof back down and continued to stroke the horse's back.

She'd seen this horse's hoofprint before, near the fence that divided her land from the Chuculate land. Grover had been there to check on his property, she guessed. Did he know Angus had stolen title to it? Her mind raced. Did Grover kill Angus? Tears welled in her eyes as she quickly dismissed the thought, then she promised herself to help Becky restore her rightful title to the land.

She gathered herself and glanced at the other three horses. They all needed their hooves trimmed. Knowing that Becky had a lot to handle right now, she would call a farrier for her. When Grover passed, Becky was going to have a lot of decisions to make, and one would involve the future of his horses.

She climbed back over the fence and walked toward Lance. One of the singers looked at her and said, "He's with his ancestors now." She turned and watched as the horses walked away together.

Three days later, Sadie and Lance stood in the Eucha cemetery at Grover's graveside, listening to a Cherokee preacher read from the Bible and then pray in both Cherokee and English. There was no American flag, no taps, and no twenty-one-gun salute—all at Grover's request.

To Sadie's surprise, Brad Newsom stood quietly behind Becky. Once the small crowd had streamed by and offered condolences, the people slowly dispersed. After the plain pine casket had been lowered into the ground, Sadie walked with Becky toward Brad's car while two Indian men, the same men who had sung for him in his final hours, began to shovel dirt into the grave.

"I'm going to help close the grave," Lance whispered to Sadie.

Sadie turned and watched as he broke away from the sparse crowd, walked to his truck, and retrieved Grover's rifle. She left Becky with Brad and joined him as he carried the rifle to the grave and let it fall on top of the casket.

"There are a few things a man takes to the grave with him," Lance said. "He wanted to be buried with his rifle."

The two men nodded their approval.

"*Osda*," one man said. "Good."

Lance nodded.

Sadie wiped a tear from her eye as the men began to shovel the rest of the dirt into the grave.

Chapter 36

Sadie straightened files on her desk while Lance sat across from her, reading travel brochures.

"Maui," Lance said. "I think we should go to Maui."

"Yes!" Sadie couldn't contain her excitement. "I've been trying to get you to myself for a long time." Then she laughed. "I love it. Once we get there, you'll have no choice but to lavish all your attention on me and ignore every call from the sheriff's department. They'll have to learn to survive on their own for a change."

Lance grinned. "But the question is, can you handle *me* for a solid two weeks?"

"Why, yes." Sadie beamed. "I believe I can."

Beanie burst through the door with a newspaper tucked under her arm. "Wait until you read this," she said.

"What is it?" Sadie said.

Lance glanced at Beanie, and then returned his attention to the travel brochure.

"The Cherokee Nation is purchasing the Buffalo Ranch to expand their buffalo herd there."

"Really?" Sadie said.

"I'm not surprised," Lance offered.

Beanie flopped down in her chair. "I'm afraid so," she said, and stuck out her lower lip.

"Come on, Beanie," Sadie said, turning her attention to the young girl. "You knew it was a long shot for the Three Sisters to get the Buffalo Ranch for back taxes." Sadie started handing more Maui brochures to Lance.

"I know," Beanie whined. "But with the Buffalo Ranch being sold, Lucy loses her house and that little piece of land that Angus promised to her and Jason. That just breaks my heart. After all, she was married to their son. Shouldn't they have given it to her?"

Lance spoke up. "You know, the court had to sell everything, Beanie, including the animals, to pay off Angus's debts."

"So why did Angus kill that Sanders guy, anyway?" Beanie asked.

"I'm not sure we'll ever know for sure, but I'd say it was because he knew too much about Angus's illegal operations," Sadie explained. "He probably wanted money to keep his mouth shut, and Angus thought it was easier to kill him."

"Do you think we'll ever know who killed Angus?" Beanie continued.

"God only knows," Lance said, his head still buried in a travel pamphlet.

Sadie carefully glanced at Lance and then continued sorting brochures.

Beanie looked up from the newspaper. "It says here the Cherokee Nation is going to tear down all the buildings except one barn, and that the buffalo that's there will remain where they are." Beanie turned to Sadie. "Didn't that attorney, Eugene Hawk, steal them from the Cherokee Nation to begin with?"

"Yes," said Lance, "that, along with a lot of land from unsuspecting people."

"What's going on with that?" Beanie asked.

"The court has contacted all of the heirs," Lance said, "and the land is being restored to the rightful owners. When that happens, the Buffalo Ranch won't be as big as it once was." Lance dropped the brochures on Sadie's desk. "Did you know that the Cherokee Nation attorney general dropped the embezzlement charges against Hawk?"

"You're kidding," Beanie said, with surprise in her voice.

"No," Lance said, "and from what I hear, Chief Greenleaf and Councilman Hawk are best buddies again, just like nothing ever happened. They swept everything under the rug and kept right on going." He shook his head. "It's amazing."

The door opened and Becky walked in. "Hello, Beanie. Hi, Sadie, Lance. Wanted to drop by and tell you that I'm not going back to California."

Sadie smiled. "That's good news, Becky. How have you been?"

Becky pointed at the newspaper on Beanie's desk. "I can't tell you how glad I am that the Cherokee Nation is restoring that land to its original state. I'm ashamed to say, I hoped the whole ranch would be wiped off the earth. I guess this is close enough."

"You know if you need anything," Sadie said, "all you have to do is call."

"I know. But you've done enough already. It's time for me to spend some time alone and get my head straight."

"Alone? I saw you with Brad in the grocery store. Remember?"

Becky's face brightened. "Brad has been wonderful, but it's going to take me a while before I can think about getting into a serious relationship again."

Sadie nodded.

"He's been helping me deal with Dad's estate." Becky looked at the floor. "I had no idea there was so much paperwork to do when someone dies." Then she smiled. "I discovered that Dad had a life insurance policy. It will give me enough money to start over, and even share with others. I'm going to rebuild on Dad's place, where the house burned, and Brad's going to help me."

"It seems like Brad is good for you," Lance said.

"I hope it works out," Sadie said, "and when it does, I'm giving you two a free trip to Maui."

Becky blushed. "You've done so much for me. I don't know what to say."

Sadie got up and hugged Becky. "Just say you won't be a stranger around here."

"That goes without saying, Sadie." Becky wiped a tear from her eye. "Anyway, Brad and I are off to lunch. Thank you for everything, Sadie. I'll be in touch."

Becky left and the three sat in silence, as if digesting all that Becky had told them. A few minutes later Beanie's cell phone rang.

"What?!" Beanie yelled into the phone. "She did what?" Beanie put the phone to her chest as tears spilled onto her cheeks. "Oh, Sadie. Becky is buying that little corner of the Buffalo Ranch and giving Lucy her house and land, free and clear. Can you believe it?"

"Yes," Sadie said. "I can." She began to laugh and cry all at the same time.

Lance smiled and nodded. "*Osda,*" he said. "As Grover would say, 'It's good.'"

About the Author

Sara Sue Hoklotubbe, a Cherokee tribal citizen, is the author of the award-winning Sadie Walela Mystery series, which also includes *Deception on All Accounts*, *The American Café*, and *Sinking Suspicions*. She is the winner of the WILLA Literary Award, the New Mexico-Arizona Mystery Book of the Year Award, and the Wordcraft Circle of Native Writers and Storytellers Mystery of the Year Award. She and her husband live in Colorado.